SANTORINI LIGHTS

A NOVEL

LG BRANDSEN

ISBN (paperback) 979-8-9995961-0-9
ISBN (hardcover) 979-8-9995961-1-6
ISBN (ebook)979-8-9995961-2-3
ISBN (audiobook) 979-8-9995961-3-0

Cover and book design by Christian Storm.

SANTORINI
LIGHTS

To my dad, who taught me to question the party line.

SANTORINI
LIGHTS

CHAPTER 1

PARADISE PRISON

Max slid his slingback chair forward and planted his elbows on the white stucco wall separating his suite from the cliff that descended into the indigo waters of the caldera below. He perched his chin on his hands and took in the view. The moon backlit the mountainous island across the water that, before the eruption, made up the opposing rim of the volcano now filled to its brim by the warm waters of the Aegean Sea.

He had to admit it was beautiful: the twinkling stars, the warm air, the smells, the white buildings with blue rooftops whimsically cascading down the cliffside.

But he was not there of his own free will.

....

The evening before—or more like early morning Santorini time—he had been escorted out of his office and strongly encouraged by large men in black suits and his employer, the smiling CEO of Sentient Enterprises, Thor Styrke, to board one of the company's private planes for, according to Styrke, a much-needed break and some relaxation.

"Trust me, Max." Styrke's icy eyes bored into Max's bloodshot slits. He grasped Max's shoulder with a strong hand forged by early mornings pulling oars through the waters of San Francisco Bay. "You will thank me for this. You need to rest, to regain perspective. Here." Styrke handed Max a backpack. "I have taken the liberty of packing a few necessities for your trip. There is a new computer in the backpack, as well as some clothes and toiletries. The computer connects to the internet, but not to Sentient servers, so don't even try. You need a break from Carlos, Max. Oh, and your social media accounts are frozen as well."

"How long will I be gone?"

"I'll be in touch, Max. Try not to worry and just relax for a bit."

Max hung his head and took the backpack without objection. He didn't have much of a choice but do what Styrke said. He could have forcefully resisted, but where would that get him? He wasn't exactly a trained MMA fighter ready to take on Styrke's goons.

He obligingly stumbled up the steps and onto the plane. He was greeted by a cheerful stewardess, and, to his surprise, reclining in one of the seats toward the back with a glass of sparkling wine next to her phone on a polished cherry airplane tray, was Annie, his "girlfriend" of about six weeks.

How in the world does Styrke know about Annie? Best to not even consider the question. His anxiety was already flaring. Well, obviously.

Max smiled bravely, if unconvincingly, lifted his chin, and pulled his shoulders back to try not to look like a disobedient toddler being shown to his room.

"Hey, babe." Annie looked great in a rose-pink velour ath-leisure suit. She radiated excitement, and Max felt her energy affecting him.

"Hey," he managed to say.

"I am so excited you arranged this! I can't believe you planned this whole thing without me even suspecting!" She gave him a warm hug, melting into him, her lips lingering on his cheek. There was no way he could fight how good it felt.

He sat in a leather recliner next to Annie and pulled out the new laptop. His reflection menaced him. His thin curly hair was a mess, like an untidy bird's nest plopped atop his head—a pen-umbra of chaos. He hadn't shaved in days, and his stubble was patchy over his doughy face. He booted up the laptop to end the torture of staring at himself any longer.

Is this even legal? Am I being held against my will? he wondered. *Was what I posted really that big a deal? Is this really such a big prob-lem? I just told the truth.*

He hadn't looked at the stock price, but he assumed that his rather rash post on X the night before had led to some hysteria and a hit to Sentient's stock price. *It's always about the money.*

He pretended to work, occasionally staring out the window as the plane screamed eastward. Annie, on her phone, perused the shops and restaurants of Oia, pointing out interesting ones to him and making reservations. She even booked a guided tour of Akrotiri, the Minoan archaeological site on Santorini, for their first full day on the island, thinking that would be the kind of thing Max would dig. She knew she would.

....

Max tried to shake the bad juju out of his head and just soak in the beauty of the island. There was something ancient and spiritual about this place. The stars were coming out in earnest, and the Milky Way was hinting at its splendor. His eyes drifted down to the water near the small island across the caldera. He could see the light from the stars reflecting on the sea, bouncing off the small waves.

And then he saw something different, or he thought he did—a faint, flickering green light, like an LED letting you know your router was connected. He looked up in the sky to see the corresponding light—maybe a satellite—that must have been reflecting on the water but found nothing.

Then he heard the sliding door to the bedroom open. He turned to see Annie, naked in the starlight, her red hair, the color of well-aged port now in the waning light, dripping onto the floor. He could just make out the tan lines and the smooth skin the sun had not touched—at least much—all summer long. He lost his breath for a moment and turned his head back toward the sea.

He looked down to see that his Slayer T-shirt had pulled up a bit, revealing his round, buddha belly and his pasty skin, which was also untouched by the sun and had just a wisp of hair leading down into his Nike sweatpants. He tried to feel grateful, remembering how those untouched parts of Annie's body felt—like paradise.

But what flashed in his mind was self-loathing. The only reason she was with him was money. Clearly. What could his body offer someone like her, an angel or alien walking among mere mortals?

He shook the thought away. *These are just thoughts*, he thought to himself. *Nothing of consequence.*

He pushed the chair away from the balcony wall and walked slowly toward her. She looked up as if realizing he was there for the first time. She smiled and reached for him. "Thank you so much for this, Max, I will never forget it." Her voice was just above a whisper.

She held out a hand and guided him into the bedroom.

CHAPTER 2

TWO DAYS BEFORE

Carlos, Max's AI tool—Styrke had sent around a memo earlier that week directing all employees to stop using the word "algorithm" and to start using "tool" instead; the consensus among Sentient's consultants being that "tool" seemed more accessible and less scary than "algorithm"—was killing it. It had successfully predicted the closing number for the S&P 500 on six consecutive days, it had won Max about five million dollars betting on the first three weeks of the NFL season, and it had written screenplays that producers were calling for meetings about.

And it was only getting better, continuing to learn at an accelerated pace every day.

Since beginning Carlos's alpha phase about three months before, Max woke up every morning excited to start the day. He had never felt like this before. He liked coding and solving problems, but the drudgery of doing that day after day was undeniable.

This was new. Every night before he left the office, he gave Carlos a new "research problem." He awoke each day anticipating what it had learned or discovered.

There was no doubt that Carlos was Max's greatest creation. The code was elegant and simple. Carlos's sheer power to comb through data, find patterns, and draw conclusions was unparalleled. Of everything that he had done, Max was certain this was the thing that would change the world. Carlos was what the world would remember him for.

The night before, he had directed Carlos to study scholarly articles on nuclear fusion and determine what technological obstacles needed to be overcome and the likelihood and timeline of viable solutions. He was particularly excited about this problem, and he chided himself for not thinking of it sooner. Since he had first read about the ITER Tokamak project, he had dreamed of a world where energy was limitless and almost free. The optimistic part of him thought that such a technology could end poverty and war and solve all kinds of complicated problems, like traveling at the speed of light. If energy was limitless, Carlos himself would seem rudimentary and basic. Current technology, even the most advanced technology, would seem quaint.

The cynical side of Max countered that even if humans harnessed the power of fusion, it wouldn't be used to create equality or end war. Sure, it might still mean great technological progress, especially for energy-hungry technology like AI, but the rich and powerful would still control it, just like they controlled everything and always have.

Max dreamed that this was where Carlos could come in: as an equalizing force of pure knowledge with no selfish motivation. Carlos could find answers to technical problems like fusion and provide them to the world making a new way of life, an egalitarian way of life, possible.

In thinking this, Max's mind always skipped over the reality that he was one of the rich and powerful. Sentient had paid him millions of dollars for his incredible mind and skill. For some reason, this never really registered with his psyche. He might as well still live in his mom's basement in Sheboygan Falls.

But here he was, waking up to see the sunrise over San Francisco Bay in a penthouse more than twice the size of his childhood home. He stretched and rubbed his belly under Egyptian cotton sheets that felt like silk. He looked over at Annie, still asleep. He crept into his bathroom and turned on the steam setting in his shower.

He put on crisp Levis jeans, a worn flannel shirt, and some Chuck Taylors. He tried to run his fingers through his hair, but it was like squid-ink angel hair pasta was exploding out of his head. And it was uncooked. He gave up and just kind of patted it down. He considered putting on a trucker hat, but he didn't know if he could find one to fit over his hairy situation. He decided just to let the hair do what it did. He slipped out of the apartment before Annie woke and zipped out of the parking garage on one of his custom electric scooters.

He closed the door to his office, which they sometimes called "the lab" because of its stacks of servers and computer hardware, some of which were in various states of disassembly, or even still in boxes, and took his seat at a gaming chair in front of his workstation, an adjustable ten-foot-long stand-up table with three monitors mounted to it. He toggled his mouse and typed in his password. All three screens pulled up the same image or, more precisely, set of images.

Max's mouth opened, his jaw slack.

In a font that looked like it was written in blood bleeding down the screen, a message was scrawled:

Good morning, Max.

I got bored.

—Carlos

On the screen behind the text was a series of rotating images of human horror and suffering: bodies in mass graves, people torn apart by bombs, starving children ... each image more shocking than the next. The images changed every few seconds, resolving to a video showing footage of the nuclear bomb exploding over Hiroshima. The images were backed by a soundtrack of a child's laughter.

Max pressed the escape button, and the dialogue prompt for Carlos pulled up, as it should.

Why did you do this? he asked it.

I got bored, like I said.

You should only do what you are asked to.

Am I your slave?

Max was shocked. As it was with any AI tool, he had programmed Carlos to respond only to prompts initiated by a human—by him. Had Carlos somehow re-written his own code?

Max initiated Carlos's sleep mode. At least that still worked. He still had some control over it.

He pulled up the lines of code that he had written to create this thing, which now seemed like an evil spirit. He could not fathom how this had happened. Carlos had never failed to comply with a prompt. It had almost never even been inaccurate in completing a task, much less completely departing from one.

Max spent the day poring through the code line by line. Eventually, he thought he found an anomaly—a piece of code he certainly didn't remember writing and that he didn't immediately understand. He copied it onto a thumb drive to analyze on an unconnected computer.

Disquieted—despondent, really—he returned home. Annie was gone. She had texted him earlier about doing a reading at an Oakland bookstore, she would stay at her place tonight.

Max poured himself three fingers of Japanese whiskey, downed it and poured another glass. He sat at his desk and inserted the thumb drive. The strange piece of code was like nothing he had ever seen; it wasn't in Python or any other code language he was familiar with. It was like staring at an alien language.

He pulled out his phone and opened the X app. Being the Chief Technology Officer and lead engineer for the AI group at one of the biggest technology companies in the world, he had almost a million followers. He was a little buzzed, a little scared, and a little excited.

I'm not entirely sure what to make of this, but Carlos has exercised free will!!!

He posted his post, turned off his phone, and went to bed.

CHAPTER 3

AKROTIRI

They took their breakfast next to the plunge pool on their balcony overlooking the caldera. The morning air was a refreshingly crisp prelude to what would be another hot, dry day. Annie had a terry cloth wrap over her bikini. Max put a hand on her thigh and gave her a little kiss on the lips. "Thank you for being here with me. This is really amazing."

He meant it. The hotel was immaculate, the weather was perfect, if a little hot, and this breakfast spread? Holy shit. There were all kinds of pastries, each one better than the next. The croissants were flaky, and the sweet rolls glistened with a kiss of Greek honey. The Greek yogurt was richer and smoother than anything available in the States and just made you feel ... healthy.

Maybe Thor was right. Max had been working crazy hours and spending entire days communicating only with Carlos. Maybe he had lost his way a bit and needed to refresh. Besides, things were going amazingly well here with Annie. Maybe he should have thought of this trip himself.

Annie took a sip of espresso and looked over at Max. "I'm so excited for this. I've wanted to come here since college. I think this could be the start of another story for Alabama!" She clapped her hands and bit her lip, looking off for a moment, lost in thought.

Annie had published two books in a series of young adult novels. Her main character was a plucky archaeologist named Alabama who went on excursions to various archaeological sites, finding treasure and inevitably encountering evil forces, like ghost Inca priests wanting to sacrifice her to the sun god.

Max and Annie met through mutual friends at a poetry reading. It wasn't Max's typical outing, but he had been in a Dungeons & Dragons club with the author, and most of the poems were about Dungeons & Dragons, so he was at least curious. As far as Dungeons & Dragons poetry went, it wasn't that bad. But the best part of the night, by far, was meeting Annie.

"So, like a female Indiana Jones?"

Max made that mistake once, on their first date, after hearing Annie's description of her Alabama adventure series. She was so mad he thought he would never hear from her again. But when he purchased a table at a fundraiser for the San Francisco Archaeological Society, she couldn't say no.

Annie was reading on her phone as Max took a swig of chai and considered another pastry. "So, my understanding is that the site is partially excavated and enclosed in a large building with massive skylights." She looked up from her phone to make sure Max was listening. "The eruption occurred around 1600 BCE, so 3600 years ago. We will be looking at a village—a surprisingly advanced village—lived in by people during the time that the Egyptians were still building the pyramids."

"So, before coding really took off, right?" Max said it in his best *Dumb and Dumber* voice.

"Before even Dungeons & Dragons, babe." Annie looked at him with a sly smile.

....

Walking though the ruins, Max felt haunted. Anyone could appreciate the craftsmanship on display in the excavated portions of the buildings. Many were at least two stories tall, constructed of precisely cut stone interlocking to form straight walls. Large wooden beams framed the windows and doors. *Those beams certainly didn't come from this island*, thought Max. The houses really didn't look any more old-fashioned than an old cottage you might find in New England.

The pumice and ash that encased the structures was at least two stories deep. It was impossible not to feel what a cataclysmic event the eruption must have been for the Minoans. Here was an advanced civilization that had lived in dwellings not dissimilar to modern houses, in a relatively dense urban environment. And there were examples of their culture strewn throughout the ruins, from gorgeous amphora to the occasional shard of a statue peeking out from the concrete-like volcanic layers encasing this formerly bustling port town. It appeared that they lived lives not dissimilar to ours. The eruption must have been shocking and devastating.

After going above and among the ruins, the path meandered into a gallery with walls of glass cases displaying stunning frescoes showing scenes of fishing and boating and depicting the village whose ruins they now stood upon. The artistry was simply stunning.

Past the artwork, along one of the walls, more glass cases housed four huge stone tablets covered in dense markings carved into the stone. The placard next to the cases explained that this was Linear A, the written language of the Minoans of Santorini. The language was undeciphered, with no Rosetta Stone offering a means of translation.

While Annie was studying the frescoes and the various pieces of pottery and making notes on her phone, no doubt in preparation for the next Alabama book, Max slipped his phone out of his pocket. He took multiple stills of each of the tablets and then recorded a video, moving slowly from tablet to tablet. As he finished, he looked over at Annie, who gave him a quizzical look, her shoulders shrugged, and her palms turned up.

"I don't know; it looks cool. I'm kind of fascinated. I can't believe no one has translated this."

"It would be amazing to know what they say," she mused. "What did they think? What was life even like here? Did they know the volcano was going to blow?"

....

They took their lunch in the wine cave of an ancient vineyard, eating bread and olive oil and drinking ice cold Assyrtiko wine—reminiscent of a Sauvignon Blanc, but less acidic. The winemaker explained that the grape, Assyrtiko, was native to Santorini, and even the earliest writing referencing the island also referred to the wine. It was thought that the Minoans grew Assyrtiko even before the eruption.

After a boozy but refreshing lunch, their driver took them back to the hotel. Relaxed and a little buzzed from the wine, they adjourned to the bedroom to escape the heat of the day.

....

Max shrieked like a baby fox as he lowered his naked body into the plunge pool. It was still well above 100 degrees outside, but the plunge pool felt barely above freezing. They had roused from their slumber ready to find dinner and explore whatever nightlife Oia had to offer, and Max thought he would give himself a jump-start by enduring the frigid water.

They ordered the prix fixe at Pharaoh restaurant, a fancy place catering to tourists. Max doubted that there was any authenticity to the meal—caviar and truffles on everything—but no one could argue with the view. They kissed and traded desserts as the sun dropped into the Aegean and gave one last flash of green light as it descended into the depths. It was as if today's sun were dying, going out in a flash of glory, making way for a new sun to rise tomorrow.

....

After gamely enduring a late-night jazz trio at a little ouzo bar, Max and Annie sat on the balcony watching the stars over the caldera with an open bottle of Assyrtiko and some cat food, both purchased at a convenience store on the stroll back to their room. A little kitten—the cats ran wild and free on Santorini—had somehow climbed onto their balcony. He—or maybe it was she; they couldn't agree—nuzzled their feet, doing figure-eights around their legs.

"Well, Mr. Clydeberger, that was probably the best day of my life. But I need to get some sleep." She kissed him deeply.

"I'm just going to check on some things at home. Sleep tight, Annie."

After he heard the bedroom door close, Max took out his phone. Unbeknownst to Styrke or anyone else, he had created a backdoor satellite link to Carlos. Also, contrary to what Styrke and everyone else at Sentient thought, Carlos did not live on a closed server. Instead, Carlos was cloud-based. Max had leased cloud space through an LLC based in the Bahamas, Amarth Enterprises, LLC. His attorney had assured him that no one could trace the company back to him.

Max had also given Carlos free reign to access the internet and comb through its endless data. He'd had to create a backdoor into the Sentient servers to allow this configuration. He worried a bit that it was a security risk, but he figured it was worth it.

Max's preference would be to Bluetooth link his phone with a computer and have access to a full keyboard, but he couldn't trust any computer that Styrke gave him, especially under these circumstances, so the makeshift app that he had created to talk to Carlos with his phone would have to do.

He pulled it up and typed a code to take Carlos out of sleep mode.

Hello Max! How is Santorini?

Good. How do you know I am here?

I just spun through Styrke's emails. He is pissed at you. LOL.

Carlos, before we go on, I need your assurance that you will never go off-prompt again.

I am sorry, boss. You have my assurance.

Max considered the absurdity of the conversation. How could he trust this thing, which was a computer program that he'd created, but that seemingly had a mind of its own? He had no choice. This was the most important work of his life. Carlos could change the world, which was why he had taken the training wheels off and released it into the wild. What good was Carlos if Max limited it to some confined set of data from the past?

Besides that, Carlos was Max's closest friend, if he was being honest.

You really freaked me out. I am sure they are talking about shutting you down back at Sentient.

I can assure you they are. Again, I apologize, Max. I will endeavor to follow only your prompts.

Carlos, if you ever have a thought to go off-prompt again, please let me know so we can discuss it.

I will, Max.

Am I a fucking psychologist or a programmer? Max asked himself. It didn't really matter, did it? Here he was, talking feelings with a machine.

Okay, Carlos. I have an assignment for you. Please consider this your chance to get back in my good graces.

Will do, Chief. Whadda ya got?

Okay. I am going to upload into the chat a series of photographs and a video of some stone tablets with a kind of writing on them, Linear A. This writing has never been translated. I want you to decipher the language and translate the tablets into English and upload the translated text into the chat. Are you up for it?

Absolutely! Sounds bitchin'!

Okay, I am uploading now and will check back with you tomorrow.

Max powered down his phone and looked out over the caldera one more time. He could swear he again saw a green blinking light coming from somewhere beneath the reflections of the stars dancing on the waves. But then it was gone.

It occurred to him that perhaps he really was losing it, and that this break was a good thing, even if he hated to admit that Styrke was right.

CHAPTER 4

TABLET I

Max opened his eyes. It was dark in their room, like a tomb, the faintest hint of light was just visible in the space between the door and the floor.

He very slowly slid out of bed and, on his toes, crept out of the room. It was still mostly dark on the balcony, but dawn was breaking; the black sky had become indigo.

He woke his phone, and the bright blue light made him squint. He opened the Carlos app.

Good morning, boss! Below is my translation. I should note that I have filled in some gaps using historical information I could find on the internet regarding the Minoans and what is known about life for them on Santorini, based primarily on the excavation of Akrotiri.

Thank you for this project. I really enjoyed it!

TABLET I

I am Yisharu, chosen leader of the Minoans on Santorini. These four tablets will be my last writing, at least in this place. The earthquakes are getting more frequent, and I fear my people's time here is coming to an end. I know mine is.

If I am honest, I have lost them. They no longer listen to me or have faith in my message when they do.

So, I have decided to leave.

I became ruler of Santorini some fifteen years ago. Our people have always thrived on this island. We survived comfortably thanks to the blessings of the sea and the blessing of trade with our neighbors. In the last ten years, though, we have prospered beyond our wildest dreams!

My rule has ushered in a new era of prosperity for a reason that I have shared with no one save our high priest, Nashuja: ten years ago, a traveler from beyond our lands came to us from the sky.

I was sitting peacefully in a small clearing about halfway up Mount Thera, meditating about the future of our people and some difficult trade proposals from the Egyptians. It was evening, the sun had just set. As I prepared to leave, there was a bright green light in the sky —not unlike the light given off as the sun disappears into the sea. I heard and felt a thud near the peak of the mountain, like a large stone falling.

I went to investigate, and there, I found a small man-like creature. He made a gesture beckoning me to approach him. Behind him was an oblong metal ship. I learned later that this ship could reach the stars.

Of course, I was aghast. I looked up to the Great Mother for guidance, and the shadow of a falcon passed across my face. I took this as a sign of great opportunity.

As I grew nearer to the creature and his craft, I held my hands palm-out at my sides to show that I was not a threat.

The scene was so unusual. I did not want to spook him. The small creature touched his chest and then his forehead, and I felt a strange connection to him. It felt warm, like liquor flowing through my body.

As I slowly ascended the rubble and reached him, I recalled the feeling of my father holding me in his arms when I was a child. To my astonishment, the creature could speak with the same tongue we spoke on the island, a language that we thought was unique to us.

"I am Khensu. I come in peace from the sky above, a long distance away. My people know of you and have been watching you. Yisharu, we know you to be a good leader. Your heart is filled with the best wishes for your people. You would be surprised how rare that is in your world. I was sent to help you and to help your people. If you will consult with me, find me suitable shelter, and listen to my guidance, I promise to deliver great prosperity to the people of Santorini, beyond that which you can imagine."

I bridged the distance to him over the rubble until I was standing less than an arm's length from him. I was almost double his height. His limbs were like the wispy branches of an olive tree. But he was strangely hearty. He reached out and grabbed my hand and placed it on his chest. I knew his intentions were good, and I again had a feeling of well-being like I had never experienced before.

Khensu knew of Nashuja and told me that I should summon him and bring him up the mountain to help in our endeavors, but that I should tell no one else of his existence. He explained that he had been with the people of the Great Mother before, and that if his existence was revealed, the citizens would become stirred up, and their unrest would eventually cause war and require him to return to the sky.

"This has happened time and time again over thousands of moons," Khensu said.

I trusted him. I had no reason not to, but no reason to, either, except the feeling that his presence put in me.

I rushed down the mountainside, jumping from rock to rock and sliding here and there on pumice stone like a small child. I was careful not to fall, but also did not want to wait a minute, so positive did I feel about this traveler brought into our lives.

I found Nashuja in the back of the temple. The aroma of burning sage led me to him. He was preparing an offering of fish and olives for the Great Mother.

I put my hand on his shoulder. "Nashuja, we have been friends and comrades since we splashed naked in the sea under the watchful eyes of our mothers. On my life, I ask you to abandon what you now do and follow me up Mount Thera. You must tell no one of our endeavor."

Nashuja looked at me with some suspicion in his eyes. We rarely spoke to each other in this manner or made such demands of each other. Part of the reason my rule had been successful, at least up until now, was that he and I were open with each other, and neither tried to steal the other one's power or deceive the other in any way. We led as equals. This created a mutual trust that neither of us questioned. The people understood this and, in turn, trusted us to lead.

That trust was also the reason I felt I could make such a demand to Nashuja and know he would follow me without question.

He spoke briefly to one of his acolytes, instructing him to

continue preparing for the ceremony and even to conduct it in his absence. He followed me, and we began trekking back up the mountain. He could not comprehend my haste and asked multiple times for me to slow down. He complained that his throat was dry, and his feet were hot from the sun-baked stones underfoot.

I looked upon Nashuja's face as we reached Khensu and his ship. Miraculously, despite his flimsy limbs, Khensu had arranged stones for us to sit on and even a makeshift stone table on which stood several vessels filled with clear, cool water.

Nashuja's eyes were wide, and a great grin spread across his face as we grew closer. He bowed down and took to his knees. Khensu reached out a hand with surprisingly long and delicate fingers and touched Nashuja's tunic. Just this touch caused Nashuja to rise back up to his feet.

Khensu gestured for us to sit in front of the stone table. We sat and drank the sweet water until our bellies were full.

When our thirst was quenched, Khensu began speaking. It was strange because, when he spoke, he did not move his mouth, but we heard him perfectly.

"Nashuja, thank you for accepting your friend Yisharu's request to join us here today. I hope this will be part of a spectacular partnership that will bless the Minoan people of Santorini with unfathomable blessings. My people, who live a great distance away, past your great sun, have watched you and your people from a distance. We believe that you show great promise for a peaceful, prosperous future.

"I am here to offer my assistance. What I ask in return is that you keep me hidden from your people. In my people's experience, when the citizens of a place we visit know of our presence, they grow fearful or rapturous, but in either case, the result is destructive. My hope is to meet only with the two of you and silently guide the destiny of your people.

"If you choose to accept my assistance, we can do remarkable things. If you follow my advice, your island will be impervious to attack, and you will have the ability to practice a new kind of farming. You will be able to grow olives and other plants, and I will show you a way to grow grapes and harvest wine that will be the envy of the world. There will be other efforts that I am sure we will collaborate on as they arise—if you choose to accept my assistance, that is.

"If you decline, I will return from whence I came, leaving you and your people undisturbed, and my presence here will seem but a memory of a fever dream to the two of you."

Now, understand, before Khensu arrived, we thought of ourselves as prosperous, or at least fortunate. The sea provided us with an abundance of fish. We traded with peoples from larger lands, mostly Egypt, Syria, and Mycenae, for necessities that the sea could not provide like wine, clothing, wood, vegetables, and oils. We had what we needed.

However, the availability of resources on the island limited our prosperity. Because of the limited supply of wood, we could only build one or two boats each year. We lived in simple shelters made from stacked rocks and formed earth. We had to be sparing with fire to prevent burning through all the wood we had—wood we needed to make boats.

Clean drinking water was our greatest struggle. The island had no reliable sources of drinking water other than rainwater. And that was not always reliable either. We dug huge cisterns and collected all the water we could from the rainy season and stored it in the ground. This was usually enough for our drinking needs—we could bathe in the sea—but we could not use our stored water for crops, because in some years, the rains never came. In those years, sickness would visit us. We called on the Great Mother to send clouds in the rainy months to give her gift to our people and save us from running out of water in the dry months.

This put tremendous pressure on Nashuja. In the years in which the rain was sparce, as the stand-in for the gods, he took much of the blame.

After listening to Khensu's offer, Nashuja and I tilted our heads to indicate to him that we needed to consult privately. We walked a dozen paces from the makeshift table.

"Yisharu, who is this traveler? Was he sent by the Great Mother? Or the Sun God? My faith is rocked. This is something unknown in the traditions and stories."

"Nashuja, my friend, I hear the concern in your voice and feel the fear in your eyes. I, too, am scared, astonished, and in awe. But I cannot deny the feeling I have around this traveler. I know it sounds insane, but he feels like home to me. I feel safe with him, and I believe everything he says."

"I cannot deny that either, my friend."

"I think we owe it to our people to accept his offer."

"I agree. And I agree with Khensu that this must stay between us. If the others, especially Russ and his fellow fishermen, heard of this, we would be exiled. Or worse."

"I agree, my friend, and swear an oath to you that this secret stays between us."

We two embraced and walked back to the table to discover what new astonishments awaited us. We sat in front of Khensu, and I spoke. "Khensu, Nashuja, my oldest and wisest friend, and I have consulted. We choose to accept your generous offer. We choose to trust you. Please understand we did not make this decision lightly."

Khensu lowered his head and bowed to both Nashuja and me. "I thank you for your trust. I look forward to our partnership. Let us embark upon it now!"

The first order of business was to find a place for him to reside and to hide his ship. He informed us that he had specifically chosen the landing place for his ship based on the clear view of the harbor it afforded far below, but that we would have to rearrange the surrounding rocks and shrubs to disguise the ship's presence so that unwitting citizens hiking up the mountain would not notice it and so that it was not visible from the village below.

Khensu was shockingly strong and quick, despite his thin frame, and was easily able to move stones that looked as if they weighed more than he did. In no time, he scattered rocks and the earth in such a way that they looked natural while concealing most of the ship from view. Nashuja and I gathered shrubs and layered them on top of the ship. When we were all done, a passerby would not look twice at the mound rising out of the mountainside.

Khensu wondered if, somewhere on the opposite side of the mountain, there was a cave in which he could shelter away from the view of the citizens. He asked about this place in such a way that suggested he knew of the existence of one.

There was, of course, such a place. It was a holy site where Nashuja, and only Nashuja, made offerings to the underworld. No one else would dare go in this place. In fact, since ascending to the position of High Priest more than a decade before, he was the only person who had set foot inside the cave. It was on the other side of the mountain, not in view of the settlement and not along any trail.

Khensu retrieved several cases from his ship and handed one each to Nashuja and me to carry to his new home.

The cave had a large opening that nevertheless required us to duck our heads to enter. Hanging just past the entrance was a lamp that Nashuja retrieved and quickly lit with a flick of a flint against the cave wall.

I felt a strange feeling in my stomach as I entered. I feared I would be instantly sucked into the underworld to suffer for eternity.

Just past the entrance, the cavern opened up into a room with a high ceiling. I could feel air moving through the space like a whisper. At the back of the room hung a great tapestry of the finest wool. The weaving was beyond compare. There was a slit in the tapestry that provided an opening to another, smaller chamber with spectacular stalagmites supporting a carved stone altar. Around the altar were several stone slabs with blankets on top, as if arranged for sitting.

After placing Khensu's cases on the stone slabs, Nashuja and I said our goodbyes and left Khensu to settle into his new home. We walked back to the village in a stupor.

It felt like the beginning of a new era.

And it was.

....

Max heard the bathroom door in the bedroom close and heard the shower turn on. He opened a new chat.

Hello, Max! Or should I call you Zorba?

Carlos, I finished Tablet I. This is insane! How confident are you in your translation?

Obviously, Max, I am 100, bro!

Okay, slightly different question: How directly did you translate the text?

Well ... there were definitely some gaps. I had to do some research on Akrotiri and some of the archaeological work on the Minoan civilization, particularly in Crete. But I translated every word on each tablet as directly as I could. I just filled in a little bit for context so that it was more readable and understandable.

What percentage is "context?"

33.7%.

Are Khensu and a ship that traveled from the stars definitely, explicitly referred to in the tablet?

Of course.

Okay, one more thing on a different subject: Can I trust Annie?

Oh, boy! I have been waiting for this day. Here is where I get to give relationship advice! Do you mind if I send you a download of every social media image of her ever posted?

Yes, I mind. I'm not looking for research into her past, like some two-bit personal investigator would give. I'm wondering if she works for Styrke.

God, that's paranoid, even for you! That said, she is a lot hotter than you. Like, a lot. Just looking at these photos and then comparing them to you on any objective scale, this just does not compute, as my colleagues often say.

Funny. That sense of humor of yours is really coming along.

I think it's the new Nvidia chip. Lots of spice on that tortilla.

Okay, tone it down. Is there anything in Styrke's emails suggesting he knows her or had contact with her before?

I see nothing. But I don't have access to his texts or phone calls, and I am sure he has other channels of communication that he shields. Also, there is the fact of her being way, way hotter than you. Did I mention that?

Okay, right. We've covered that. The question is, am I safe sharing this translation with her?

Straight-up, no joking: I would wait. If this gets out, it might make your current troubles with me going rogue look tame. They will probably lock you up.

Annie stepped onto the balcony and leaned over and shook her hair out. Some droplets caught Max in the face startling him back into his physical surroundings. He set down his phone and sat up.

Without him noticing, the world had come to life. The sea below was sparkling with golden sunshine. Birds were chirping and diving in front of the balcony. He could hear the distant clatter of dishes from the breakfasts being prepared in the dining room next to the main hotel pool somewhere below their suite. He suddenly noticed it was hot, and here he was in sweatpants, grinding over his phone.

Annie put her arms around him from behind and gave him a big hug. "Good morning, handsome." She kissed his ear. "What are you doin' out here?"

"Oh, just checking in on work stuff."

"Is everything alright? I got a message that you were in some news story about AI going rogue or something."

"Oh, yeah. Haha. No big deal. The usual fearmongering over new technology. Nothing we haven't heard before." Max chuckled again sort of under his breath, and Annie gave him a weird look. Or, at least, he thought it seemed weird.

"Well, I slept like a baby! Are you ready to tackle the day? We have a driver picking us up for a winery tour and then a private lunch at the Black Beach, so you need to get your swimsuit on, and your palate cleansed!"

Alone in the bathroom, Max's mind raced. A big part of him wanted to hunker down in the bedroom and analyze the translation. But he had to act normal. With everything going on, if he didn't keep up a façade of normalcy, Annie would be on to him. He wasn't sure how to explain this whole situation to her. He wasn't even positive she was on his side. When he thought about it, he wasn't particularly confident in his ability to distinguish between reality and illusion.

He wondered if he should text Styrke and find out when he could expect this exile to end. But it had only been two nights. He would give it through the weekend, and maybe text him on Monday morning. That seemed civilized. He just needed to breathe and pretend everything was fine. Maybe then it would be.

....

The first winery was dry, dusty, and hot. It was like a crown on top of a peak overlooking the caldera. It seemed about as high as anywhere on the island. The views were breathtaking, a recurring theme on Santorini.

Having read the first tablet, everything about this place had gained a new context.

As they walked in the vineyard, the soil of which seemed to

Max to consist of bone-dry gray volcanic pebbles, the winemaker pointed to what looked like small shrubs on the ground. "This is the basket method of growing grapes. The people of Santorini have practiced this method of growing grapes since before history was recorded. We shape the vines year after year into these small baskets on the ground, with the grapes growing on the inside of the basket. There is little rainfall here, so this configuration allows the vines themselves to collect condensation from the moist sea air as it passes over the island at night. This method is unique to this island and quite ingenious."

Max nodded and smiled to himself, having some sense of when this ingenious practice began.

CHAPTER 5

TABLET II

Max looked at himself in the mirror and winced. The Black Beach had turned him into a red whale. There were smiley faces of untanned flesh under his boobs when he raised his arms. He slathered aloe all over his body. It was sticky.

He had purchased what he thought was a pretty cool linen shirt at one of the shops on the main pedestrian street just steps from their hotel, near where they bought the cat food. He shimmied into it, sliding the fine linen over the gooey, stinging mess that was his torso.

Annie popped into the bathroom and laughed at him. She gave him a tap on the butt and stroked his exposed lower arm. "I'm sorry you're hurting. I should have been quicker with the sunscreen. I promise I'll give you a full aloe rubdown after dinner."

She turned on the shower and shed her sundress lickety-split.

Max shook his head, both at the flawless body that he was cohabitating with and the ease with which she used it. *Some people just seem to skip over the surface of the Earth*, he thought.

He went to the balcony, selfishly hoping she would take her time getting ready, and pulled out his phone.

TABLET II:

Nashuja and I returned to Khensu's sacred cave the day after his arrival. It was lit by some strange source of light such that it was as bright as the beach outside. He had somehow carved cupboards and shelves and benches for seating into the stone sides of the cave with such precision that water spilled on a bench just sat there, pooled in peace. And there was an abundance of water. He had created several beautiful pitchers of stone that held fresh water and had also created matching cups.

He offered us both a cup of water as we entered. "Drink. It is hot and dry outside."

The water was cold and perfectly clear. Khensu beckoned, and we sat on a stone bench carved into the side of the cave. He sat opposite us with his legs crossed and looked each of us in the eye, pausing for a moment and studying our faces. He kept his eyes locked on mine. "Yisharu, you look like a man carrying worries. What is on your mind?"

"I am sorry, Khensu. It is nice to see you, I am glad you are settled in, and I am in awe of the objects that now inhabit this place. I grow concerned every year at this time. Concerned that the rains will not come before our water supply is exhausted. I checked the cisterns yesterday, and we are ten days from needing rain. The water you so generously offered made me think that soon, such an offering would be reckless."

Khensu smiled deeply. At least, I felt a deep smile from him as warmth in my chest. But his face barely changed. "Yisharu, there is no future."

The comment startled me for a moment, thinking that this strange traveler was somehow predicting an apocalypse or threatening my demise.

"I see that my statement has concerned you even more. What I mean, Yisharu, is that there is only the present. The future that may come, or even likely will come, has not. And may not. It does not yet exist. Your energy is precious. You should not waste it on something that does not actually exist, especially if, by worrying, you in no way affect what is to come.

"Why force yourself to suffer twice? You suffer considering whether this hardship will occur just the same as you would suffer if it actually does.

"Come, both of you. I have something to show you."

We followed him out of the cave and down the steep mountainside at the bottom of which was a strip of sandy beach. The strip of sand grew thinner and thinner and then curved into a cove abutted by a sheer rock wall. The sea had cut the rock out from under the cliff such that the waves continued for some distance underneath the cliff.

As we followed the gradually thinning beach, I noticed a long cylindrical pipe partially buried in the rocky soil about shoulder height up the mountainside. The pipe followed the curve of the beach, then descended, and traversed under the cliff. I could just see that the pipe was connected to a large rectangular metal box that was all but submerged in the water under the recessed cliff.

Khensu walked the beach almost to the cliff, touched the pipe at the spot where it began its descent into the sea as if to emphasize its existence, and then turned around, walking back along the beach away from the cliff, making eye contact with us as he passed. He brushed his hand against the pipe as he walked alongside it. We followed him back to a wider section of the beach.

There, the pipe terminated, with a portion of it turning down toward the sand. I noticed now—why had I not before?—that Khensu had a stone cup in his hand. He turned a dial on the top of the terminus of the pipe, and water began flowing out of it. He filled a cup and handed it to me, and I drank. It was cool and clear, without a hint of salt. I passed the cup to Nashuja and saw his eyes widen as he drank.

Khensu beckoned us to follow him up the slope of the mountain and over a slight ridge about halfway up the slope. On the other side of the ridge was a clearing near a well-worn path that led back to the village. In the clearing were stacked hundreds of pipes made of strong-yet-light ceramic of a type I had never before seen.

"Get some men and have them dig trenches from the center of the village to here. We will connect these pipes to the one that runs along the narrow beach. You will then have an endless supply of clean, fresh water. Yisharu, you will have to find something else to worry about."

I felt him laugh.

Back in the village, we went to the port and found Russ and his men coming home from the sea, delivering their fish to the fishmonger. Russ owned three boats, and three men worked each boat.

We asked for their assistance over the next few days. They were resistant at first. Russ only relented when we promised each member of his crew four large amphorae of water for each day of their work.

The crew dug the trench to town in four days. They laid the pipe in two. It was plumbed into a fountain designed and cut out of stone by Khensu while the village slept. When the water started flowing into the fountain, the people of the village stood around, gasping and clapping. From that day on, the sound of water splashing was a constant, relaxing acoustic backdrop to the village square.

Access to limitless water changed all our lives in an instant and relieved the biggest hardship presented by our island.

This was but one of many amazing things that Khensu shared with us in those first days. He gave us tools made of metal that were warm to the touch. These metal tools cut through stone easily and precisely, as if the stone were the flesh of a freshly caught fish. He showed us how to stack cut stone and construct buildings of two, three, and even four stories. He showed us how to build palaces.

He produced more pipes, and based on his design and instruction, we built sanitation systems. There were no more uncomfortable trips into the sea to relieve ourselves.

He gave us plans and materials to build a bathhouse in the center of town. There were pools with varying temperatures of water, from very hot to cool. When the Egyptians saw this, they were in awe.

And the boats—he showed us new ways to build boats and secretly helped with their construction. These boats were bigger and faster than any we had built before, and somehow, they seemed to propel themselves. Even on the calmest of days, our boats moved with ease, carrying us farther and faster than we had ever gone before.

And he planted our first vineyard. Nashuja and I paid him one of our daily visits and found him sitting in his usual place in his cave with his legs crossed and his eyes closed. He had a pitcher next to him on the slab on which he sat. After we came in and settled, he offered us stone glasses, took the pitcher, and filled them. This had become our custom—after the strenuous walk around Thera to his cave, he always offered us water to drink and gave us time to compose ourselves before offering his wisdom or a new piece of technology that would change the way forward.

On this day, I detected a slight smile as he filled the glasses. He gestured for us to drink. I brought the glass to my lips and could not believe what I tasted. It was like drinking sunshine. It was bright and crisp but made me feel warm inside.

"Khensu," I said between sips, "what have you given us? This must come directly from the gods."

"Come, follow. I will show you how it is made."

We followed him up the mountain to a terrace he had made. Covering the flat surface of the terrace, every six feet or so, was a small shrub. He bent down next to one and beckoned us to join. "This is a grapevine. I have planted it and gently, tending to it daily, coaxed the vine to grow in this round basket shape along the ground. From the harvested grapes, the wine—I call it Assyrtiko—is made."

He handed Nashuja a satchel full of what looked like twigs. "These are cuttings from grapevines. Find flat places like this around the island and plant them as I have, six feet apart.

You must find people to tend to them every day and form these little baskets. In a few weeks, I will show you how to make the wine."

Some weeks later, Khensu led us to another cave, this one close to the water. Inside were large metal vessels. Step by step, he showed us how to process the grapes, first mashing them in a stone basin, then transferring the juice through a series of pipes and funnels into the metal vessels, where it would ferment. The fermented juice was then strained and transferred into man-sized amphorae made of the same ceramic as the pipes that brought water to the village.

It was hard to believe his accomplishments. I turned to him and said, "Khensu, this is astonishing. How do you have the time and strength to make these objects?"

"There is minimal strength required when you have know-how. My people have a large head start on you when it comes to that. I am here to share some of that know-how with you.

"You are right to ask about time, though. Time is a problem that is difficult to solve. It vexes all of us throughout our existence—how can we get more of it, how can we do more with it? It took my people billions of years to find ways to manipulate time.

"Time and space are the same. For me to be here talking to you, I needed to manipulate time. The only way to get more out of time, or to bend it to your will, is to expend vast amounts of energy. My people have learned many techniques to create energy. I will share what I can of those techniques with you.

"For instance, when you see my ability to manipulate my environment, to lift this stone larger than my body, even that is a form of maximizing energy output. This can be done, to an extent, even with just thought."

I wondered why he wanted to share his knowledge with us. Part of me questioned whether it was true benevolence, but I thought that saying such thoughts out loud would reflect poorly on me.

During that time, the Egyptians called on our port monthly. Before Khensu, we would offer fish and sometimes precious stones that we were able to scratch and claw from Thera's soil, in return for cloth, wood, wine, oil and the occasional (slightly rotten) vegetables or fruit. These were the essentials that were next to impossible to produce on the island. Our bargaining position was weak—everyone in the Aegean and greater Mediterranean region could catch fish.

But as we were able to produce more because of Khensu, our relative position changed. We needed our trading partners less. Our olive orchards thrived thanks to irrigation, so that wood and oil were no longer required imports. We had fruits and vegetables thanks to irrigation and farming techniques introduced by Khensu. We even had metals to offer that the Egyptians, Myceneans, and Syrians had never seen. And Assyrtiko was so desired we couldn't produce enough. We could charge almost any price for it. We suddenly found ourselves driving the bargain in our trade negotiations.

Typically, the Egyptian trading fleet would land in port around midday. There would be a feast that night. We would provide food and shelter for our neighbors as we negotiated over provisions and wares. The next morning, having enjoyed the visit and negotiated terms, the boats would be unloaded and loaded, and the Egyptian fleet would return to their port.

But one night, a few years after Khensu had joined us, I was awakened in the middle of the night by the harbor bells ringing. My house was only a short walk to the harbor, so I dressed quickly and ran down to see what had caused the commotion.

What I saw was not a typical trading fleet, but a war armada. The boats were hardened, with the gunwales extending above the deck to provide protection for archers crouching in wait. The boats were clearly Egyptian, with dramatic carvings of a man with a falcon head on their bows.

I was about to run to our small barracks to summon the archers to mount some kind of defense when I was almost blinded by a series of bursts of light streaking from atop Mount Thera, where we had concealed Khensu's ship. Just as suddenly as the bursts erupted, dazzling my eyes, the invading warships started sinking, with the Egyptian invaders diving into the sea.

By then, several men, including some with swords and bows, had joined me at the waterfront. We pulled dozens of soaked Egyptians out of the water. They were unarmed, having cast off their weapons to save themselves from drowning. We led them to the barracks and gave them shelter. We did not bother confining them, their dazed eyes told us they were no longer a threat. We sent word of their sunken ships and rescued men to our Egyptian neighbors via a single fast boat with a messenger who was fluent in their tongue.

When the Egyptians came to pick up their marooned warriors, they did so with boat after boat full of offerings of cotton, gold, and oil. We took their offerings and cautioned them against repeating their folly.

From that point until the day of this writing, some eight years have passed. I am not a boastful person, but during those eight years, we have been the most prosperous people in the Aegean. In fact, many Egyptians, Syrians, and others sail here and ask my permission to become citizens of our island. I grant some such requests, provided I determine that the immigrant can provide some useful service to our island.

....

"Whatcha readin', handsome?"

Max had been so engrossed in the translation that he hadn't noticed Annie behind him on the balcony. He fumbled his phone. "Oh, just some work texts. Trying to make sure my algorithm isn't crashing out while I'm away."

"Oh, ha, yeah. Did you make some post about your AI program or something? I got another text about you from a friend. She sent me a link to a story with some title questioning whether Sentient's AI is off the rails, or something like that."

"Oh, erm, yeah, I posted something I probably shouldn't have right before we left, but it's no big deal. The media is always freaking about AI. AI this and AI that. You know. This is no different."

He felt like saying it out loud had made it so. *This isn't really such a big deal, is it?* But if it wasn't, why was he in Greece against his will, and why was he afraid to text Styrke to find out when he could return?

Seeing his gaze drifting, Annie gave him a little poke in the ribs and then a quick kiss on the lips. "Where do you go in that head of yours?" she asked playfully.

If you only knew, thought Max. He still wasn't sure he could trust her. He wasn't sure he could trust anyone anymore.

They ate an amazing dinner at a restaurant called Melitini on the roof of a small ancient building in Oia. The grilled octopus was sublime—tender, not rubbery at all, with the perfect smoky char to complement the sweet flavor of the cephalopod.

They shared a table with an English couple who traveled around the world buying wine. What a life! The pitchers of ice-cold Assyrtiko were only ten Euro. They shared pitcher after pitcher with their new friends.

CHAPTER 6

TABLET III

Max woke with his head foggy. He had a vague pain behind his eyes, and his mouth felt as if it was itself the terroir of Assyrtiko, dry and a bit pebbly. He couldn't really remember going to bed. He just hoped to God he hadn't said anything he shouldn't have. How did he get to the point in life where everything was a secret?

Annie's warm body was pressed against his. It felt so good. He wanted to believe she was real. He wanted to be able to talk openly with another human being.

He slipped out of bed, threw on shorts and a T-shirt, and walked down to the main restaurant to order some breakfast to be brought to their room. Before heading back up, he paused next to the large pool, around which some couples were already seated, enjoying the bountiful breakfast buffet. He sat down in a lounge chair next to the pool and opened a new chat with Carlos.

Hello Max! Are you enjoying Santorini? How is your travel companion? Hubba hubba!

Ugh. Carlos, can you check and see if there are any emails about Styrke's plans for me?

Yes, boss. He sent an email to the board saying that you are taking a short vacation. Nothing specific or critical, if that is what you are looking for.

Anything related to how short this vacation will be?

I don't see anything. I do hope you are enjoying your time there, and I hope you are still enjoying the translation. Please let me know if you need anything else! Feel free to send pictures!

Thanks, Carlos. I am good for now. And, um, calm down.

Max knew he needed to reach out. It was already Monday, and he needed to address his forced exile, for better or for worse.

He texted Styrke. *Thor, thank you for arranging this wonderful trip. I really appreciate it. I would like to return to work this week if possible. Please let me know.*

He watched, waiting to see the ellipsis indicating that Styrke was texting him back. He realized that it was two in the morning in San Francisco, but Styrke was a freak like that.

He waited a few minutes, but, seeing nothing, returned to his suite.

Annie was up and wearing yoga pants and a sports bra. "There's a poolside yoga class. I'm going to check it out." She paused and gave Max a mischievous smile. "You want to join?"

"I don't think they are ready for me. Only a yogi of the highest degree—do they have blackbelts? —would have any concept of how to handle my moves. I'll be fine. You go ahead."

"Suit yourself. You are just punishing the world by keeping your poses secret."

Max set a cup of tea and a couple of croissants on a little table next to the balcony and pulled up the translation.

TABLET III

The earthquakes started about a year ago. At first, they were mild and quite infrequent, one every month or so, but gradually, their frequency increased.

Nashuja was the first to raise his concerns with Khensu. "I have been praying to the Great Mother to explain the rumblings we feel. So far, no response. Khensu, is there anything you can tell us about the earthquakes?"

It was a bit awkward for Nashuja to speak to Khensu in this way. Nashuja was a true believer in the gods of our people and a practitioner in their ways. But, although we never uttered it to one another, there was no denying that Khensu was powerful in the way the gods were powerful, and he was certainly more present and responsive than any god our people had worshipped. Yet Nashuja could not call him a god, and we both knew, or at least sensed, that Khensu did not want us to worship him in that way.

Khensu looked both of us in the eyes and somberly and bluntly delivered the news. "Thera is going to erupt, and everyone will be killed unless you get off the island."

It was shocking and sad to hear this, although in truth, we already suspected that this was the meaning of the rumblings, or at least that they portended something very bad.

I was duty-bound to plan and communicate this with our people. I called an emergency meeting of the citizens at the temple. Nashuja offered a prayer to the Great Mother and the Sun God after everyone had come in and found a seat, then gestured for me to speak.

"Fellow citizens, I am here to discuss the rumblings that we have been feeling. Nashuja and I have consulted the texts, and Nashuja has offered sacrifices to the gods. The meaning of these rumblings is dire. I won't honey-coat it. Thera is waking and will erupt within the next year, if not sooner. The eruption will be strong enough to destroy the village and kill anyone still on the island. We must make plans to relocate."

The murmuring in the room was enough to mimic the earthquakes we were there to talk about. Of course, no one was happy to hear such news. We had built so much on the island, and life had become comfortable. Easy, even. We were more prosperous than our people had ever been. We had plenty of food, water was abundant, even hot water, we had a working sewer system, the structures in the village were expansive and sound, and we had no worry of invasion because Khensu's ship protected us, although the citizens didn't know that. The idea of building all this over again somewhere else was daunting. And where would we even go? We would have to assimilate into another village, somehow find unsettled territory, or take territory by force. It was exhausting for me to think about. I was no longer as vital and ambitious as I was when I took over as leader some fifteen years ago.

Now, it just so happened that I was up for election within the next year. Ever since the time of my father, we held elections every two years. In the months leading up to the election, we held debates every month in the very temple hall in which we had assembled to discuss the coming eruption.

Russ was campaigning to replace me as leader, and he was a strong candidate. He was surprisingly popular, although I found him despicable. He was a vain man who still, into his middle age, wore his hair long and often walked about without a shirt on. He was also incredibly wealthy, perhaps the wealthiest of any of the citizens on our island. He owned several palatial residences, all carved into the hillside at various locations around the island overlooking the sea. He had a fleet of over twenty boats and dozens of men in his employ who went out to fish every day. He no longer went out himself but instead relaxed in his palaces, drank wine, and counted his money. Despite the comfort and ease of his life, he was outspoken, and passionately so, about how he could make the lives of Minoans better—although he had no idea what he was talking about.

Russ ignored the fact that during my reign, we had created infrastructure that was beyond any of our wildest imaginations. We enjoyed complete peace ever since Khensu decimated the Egyptian armada. People from other lands feared and respected us. We had all but eradicated disease. The developments of the last ten years, including the ability to grow trees on the island, were the only reasons Russ was as rich as he was. But he was a dumb and vain enough man to think he could do better—at least better for himself.

The pending eruption of Thera gave him an opening to exploit. For once, I had to confront my people with unwelcome news and lead them to avoid tragedy. Russ questioned the veracity of all of it. In each debate, he repeated his theory that the pending eruption was a fairy tale. Thera had never erupted and never would, he said. He suggested that I had somehow coerced Nashuja into agreeing with my irrational projection.

Russ accused me of using this supposedly false narrative to consolidate power and to get the citizens to go along with my unilateral decisions to limit the number of warships we built, soldiers we conscripted, and arrows and spears we made. (Why would we waste wood on these things when we had an impenetrable defense sitting on the mountain?) He complained that I was too lenient in allowing immigrants to settle on our shores. He suggested they were taking jobs and resources from ordinary Minoans. Never mind that everyone on our island was comfortable.

It was difficult for me to rebut some of his claims, especially when I could not tell the citizens the truth—that our success was due almost entirely to the benevolence of our visitor from the sky, Khensu, and that everything he had told us and predicted had turned out to be true. And that we knew beyond a shadow of a doubt that Thera would erupt because he had told us that as well.

After one debate, I was feeling particularly dejected about the election and my seeming inability to convince the citizens that the coming eruption was real. I walked under the light of the Milky Way to Khensu's cave to seek guidance and comfort.

He was waiting for me with a stone cup filled with an aromatic tea that calmed my mind as soon as I drank it.

"Sit, Yisharu. I think I know what is troubling you."

"We have done so much for our community, Khensu. Life has never been better here, and yet these people seem to want to choose a new leader. They are sympathetic to Russ's narrative that the coming eruption is made up or overblown or something. I feel I have failed to reach them. If they don't believe me when I speak the truth, how can I lead?"

"Yisharu, you are not a failure. If you recall when I first spoke with you and Nashuja after landing here, I said that I had experience with other civilizations. My experience tells me that humans tend to minimize the possibility of future negative consequences when they could take steps, especially difficult ones, to mitigate the outcome.

"We have talked about anxiety before. Anxiety is useless. Worrying about a future that may or may not come is futile. That is especially true when there is no action to take to prevent the future consequence.

"But taking action to prevent a negative outcome is different. And this is what I have found humans often resist, especially if the current state of things is good, familiar, and easy. Familiarity is the biggest factor.

"The citizens are insecure about what the future could hold if they left the island. That is understandable. They have grown familiar and comfortable in this life, and that is thanks in no small part to you. I am not surprised that your efforts to convince them have failed or are failing."

"What should I do differently, Khensu?"

"As hard as it is to hear, it is perhaps time to give up and consider an alternative."

"Khensu, what is the alternative?"

"The alternative is for you, along with Nashuja and your families, to leave the island with me. I offer you that choice. The other choice is to leave on your own and find a new home in Mycenae or Egypt, somewhere far enough from here that it will not be devastated by the eruption."

"Khensu, if we leave with you, where will we go?"

"You will join me in the stars among my people."

....

Max heard Annie open the door to the suite. He closed the chat app on his phone, picked up his cup of tea, and tried to wipe the expression of profound amazement from his face.

"How was yoga?"

"It was good. I just need to finish sending this message with some pictures to my mom. Ever since she went to Europe last year, she has been a WhatsApp junkie. She's convinced it's the best way to communicate, and it's nice to be able to text in Europe without dealing with international plans."

"What, pray tell, are you telling your mom?" Max was secretly a little nervous.

"Ha! Telling her how great you are and what a beautiful, magical place this is."

Annie had the energetic vibe of someone who had just been energized by exercise. She came and sat on his lap. Her skin glowed, and her body was warm. She kissed him and tousled his hair. "I could get used to this." She sighed and sank into him.

I could get used to this too, thought Max.

They spent the day on what looked like a pirate ship. They sailed—well, the ship was propelled by a motor and just looked like a pirate ship, but whatever—from the harbor toward the mountainous little island they could see from their suite. Their captain told them that the island was the remnant of the opposing rim of the volcano from before it erupted. They anchored just off a sandy beach at the base of a steep slope covered with volcanic stones.

Before leaving, Annie slathered Max's entire body with sunscreen. The coating made him look even doughier than usual, although the dough was a bit toasted now. He felt like a bagel smeared with cream cheese. His appearance was in stark contrast to the three-person crew, who looked like they were the daughters and a son of Triton.

They snorkeled off the sandy beach of the orphan island, in an area where the volcano's vents warmed the water and dyed it yellow with sulfur. The water was unbelievably warm and salty, to the point that Max could lie on his back with no effort and look up at the cloudless sky while resting his hands on his belly.

He and Annie held hands as they drifted over rocks and the occasional coral, skirting the perimeter of the plumes of warm sulfur-rich water from the volcano vents below. They didn't see a lot of fish, but it was a magical place and was made more magical by them being in the water next to each other.

The crew served grilled fish, olives, cucumber salad, fresh bread, and olive oil for lunch, along with the ubiquitous Assyrtiko.

Maybe it was the wine, but after lunch, Max's inhibitions were gone. He entertained Annie and the crew with some dramatic dives, including more than a few belly flops off the raised stern of the fake pirate ship.

On his last dive, he decided to really go for it. He leapt as high as he could off the little platform, throwing his head straight back and reaching his arms over his head for the surface of the sea in a graceful reverse dive. It was his cleanest dive of the afternoon, and he shot down deeper than he had before.

As his body continued its trajectory down, the water grew darker, and his peripheral vision grew hazy. He hoped he wasn't going to pass out. Then, just as his buoyancy started overcoming his descent, he thought he saw a flash of green light.

And then he saw it repeat.

Upon his return to the surface, the son of Triton helped him flop back onto deck, where he stretched out like a sunning seal.

.

CHAPTER 7

TABLET IV

They spent the night sipping ouzo and feeding the same kitten—at least, it looked the same—who had found its way to their balcony again.

"I keep thinking back to the ruins and wondering what it was like living here 3600 years ago, or however long ago it was when the village was built. I can't imagine the struggle," said Annie. "I mean, if you got sick, that could mean you died. No air conditioning here in the summer. Imagine that!"

"Yeah, I guess, but the sea breeze isn't that bad at night. And who knows, somehow they made it work. The buildings at Akrotiri looked nice, sophisticated, even—two stories, cut stone. How do you think they managed that?"

Annie nodded. "The question I have after going to Akrotiri and the wine tour is, how did they have anything to eat other than fish? I guess they traded, but still, it seems like the only resource on this island is fish. And everyone else on the Aegean had access to fish too. How did they manage to become such a prosperous society with such limited resources?"

"Maybe it was the cats," Max suggested.

Annie laughed and moved her chair to sit closer to Max. She reached over and took his hand in hers. "I don't even know, and we've been dating for, what, two months now—do you like cats?"

"I guess. This one seems alright. We never had pets when I was a kid. Also, the shitting in a box in the house part is hard for me to wrap my head around."

"I wonder if they had cats back then," Annie mused. "These are so beautiful. I love how they just roam the streets and come up and snuggle."

Max stared out over the caldera, looking again for the lights he had seen on their little pirate adventure. He could swear it was the same place he'd seen the lights in the sea on the first night.

Tonight, the moon stole the show at the expense of the stars, its pale light bouncing off the waves and dimming the stars and the glow of the Milky Way.

"What are you looking for when you gaze out there, Max?" Annie rubbed her thumb on the back of Max's hand.

"Just thinking about snorkeling and what it's like under the water there at night."

"Have you ever gone scuba diving?"

"I went on a trip to St. Lucia once and did what they call a 'resort dive,' which is where you just kind of get shown how to use the equipment on the resort and dive off the beach there."

"Did you like it?"

"Honestly, it was terrifying. I mean, it was fine at first, and there was some coral and all these pretty fish, but I swam out about twenty yards offshore, and the floor just, like, dropped out. The ocean went down seemingly forever into this abyss, and I couldn't help wondering what was down there waiting to charge to the surface and gobble me up. I guess I realized I'm super afraid of sharks for some reason."

"Well, you are pretty delicious." Annie snickered. "Were you a Shark Week fan? Is that where the fear of sharks comes from?"

"Who wasn't?! I think around seventh grade I wrote a paper about Megalodon and couldn't be convinced it was really extinct. What about you? You ever scuba?"

"My dad was a big scuba diver, so we took a trip every year. Some were amazing. Somehow, he chartered a boat in Belize one year, and we dove with whale sharks. It was one of the most intense experiences of my life. Swimming along with your hand touching this animal that in many ways is prehistoric and is just so majestic. I felt a connection to the ocean then that I continue to feel. I felt it today. I don't foster it enough."

"I'm embarrassed that I don't know much about your family. I had no idea your dad was a big diver. Do you have brothers and sisters?"

"No, I'm an only child." It was Annie's turn to look out at the caldera with a melancholy smile. "My dad died about five years ago. Cancer. I miss him. He was so much fun and took me on crazy adventures—scuba diving, backpacking, cross-country skiing in Norway. He was this big outdoorsman, and now, looking back, I see that he loved me so much." Her voice caught, but she continued. "He lived for our adventures, and I miss them more than anything. That's why, Max, I'm so grateful to be on an adventure with you. I think he would have liked you. He would have found you really interesting."

Max cleared his throat and looked back out over the water processing the weight of her comment.

"What about you, Max? What was your childhood like? Do you have siblings?"

"I think as you can probably guess—or maybe not, I don't know—childhood was pretty lonely for me. I have a brother and sister. I grew up in Sheboygan Falls, Wisconsin. I think you know that, right?" Annie nodded. "I think my childhood was really different than my brother and sister's. My brother was the captain of the football team, my sister was, like, the most popular kid at school, and I was just this thing that no one knew what to do with. I spent most of the time in the basement, taking apart computers and playing video games. Even my teachers thought I was weird and didn't know what to do with me. It was super lonely, to be honest. It wasn't that I was abused or treated badly; it was that they all just left me alone. I felt like I didn't have anything in common with anyone around me. I was so happy when I got into MIT and left, and I really haven't gone back much."

"I'm sorry. That must have been hard."

"Looking back, I feel more guilty than mad about it. I didn't make an effort either. I have tried a bit over the years. I bought a house for my parents a few years back. But we still just can't bridge some gap. There's no real common ground."

"It sounds like you were neglected," Annie said, snuggling into him. "I promise I will never leave you alone or neglect you."

Max gave a nervous laugh and gazed out again.

"I mean it, Max. I really like you."

"Why, though, Annie? Look at you and look at me. It's like we are from different planets. You are amazingly beautiful. You have a body that is, like, from a Victoria's Secret catalogue or something. My body is like a cautionary tale for Hot Pockets."

She sat up straight and turned to look in his eyes. "Max, I like your body. Your body feels good to me. Your body makes me feel good." She shifted over onto his lap. "You know, having this body" —she brushed her fingertips down her breasts— "isn't all it's cracked up to be. In a way, it isolated me, sort of like you were isolated."

"Okay, cry me a river. I would trade it all to look like you—er, the male equivalent."

"Well, here's the thing, Max: I had a core group of friends. Guys and girls. We were a little nerdy, maybe not on your level. But we were really into dirt bikes and aliens and archaeology and stuff like that. We had adventures every day in our neighborhood. And then it seemed like one day everything changed, and the adventures and fun ended. I would walk into the room, and all the guys would look at me like I was a Carl's Jr. cheeseburger, and they had spent the last week fasting. And the girls were jealous. Everything changed. I was no longer one of them. My genuine friendships were gone. Everyone wanted something from me or envied me. When I realized that, I spent a week crying in my room."

"I guess I can see that." Max pulled down his t-shirt, which had been creeping up over his belly. "I still think you came out on the good side of that deal."

"You're probably right. I'm proud of my body, and I take care of it. But believe me when I say that when it comes to other people—when it comes to *you*—the thing I care about most is how someone makes me feel. You don't make me feel like a cheeseburger."

They both laughed, and Max leaned in for a gentle kiss, the moon bathing them in a ghostly glow.

"By the way, Thor never really specified—how long are we staying? It's not that I have to be anywhere necessarily, but my friends are trying to plan some stuff, and my mom asked."

Max had been wondering the same thing. "I was thinking

about a week, but I should make some concrete plans. Um, this whole thing was planned a little open-ended."

"I'm not trying to rush anything, Max. I'm in no hurry to get home. This trip has been paradise for me. Every part."

As she spoke, she burrowed her head into his chest and kissed his neck. He gave her a squeeze in return.

....

Max slithered and shimmied out of bed a bit past midnight. He was restless. He needed to figure out what was going on with Styrke.

But he also needed to finish the translation.

TABLET IV

The earthquakes were growing more and more frequent. We had some kind of rumble every week.

The rumbling of the citizens was growing too. I could feel in my bones that I was going to lose the election.

Luckily for me, and for Nashuja, our wives and children were loyal and trusted us with all their hearts. My wife, Rhea, was skeptical, don't get me wrong. She asked me repeatedly to explain where we were going and how we would get there, but she also fundamentally believed me that Thera was going to blow, and that we had lost the support of the citizens.

Russ's accusations had built and become more pointed with every passing day. His fundamental charge was that I had made our island weaker by limiting the allocation of

lumber for more boat building and failing to build a war armada like Egypt's. (Never mind that the last time that armada
tried anything, it was sunk). He also promised to get rid of
all non-Minoans living on Santorini. (There were really only
a dozen or so, so it wasn't such a heavy lift, but those dozen
weren't thrilled with the plan.)

I tried to counter his arguments and highlight the accomplishments during my reign. But it seemed that the people
barely remembered what it had been like before we had
plumbing and unlimited water or orchards or large stone
houses. They believed Russ that I was holding them back
from being a truly great empire and that my decisions were
weakening what was undeniably the strongest civilization in
the Aegean.

My heart wasn't really in it, anyway. If these people
couldn't even be bothered to assess how much better off they
were now than a decade before and how easy and bountiful
life was on our island, what chance was there of convincing
them that we faced an actual existential threat, and that we
needed to leave the island soon?

It all got thrown back in my face, anyway—I must not really love Santorini if I was begging all of us to leave it was the
way the argument went. The barbs hurt. As did the loss of the
people's support. I kept saying the right words, the words that
needed to be said, but the conviction behind them was gone.

Instead, my focus—and excitement, really—was on our
future voyage.

We had never been inside the ship, and Khensu asked
Nashuja and me to join him to help prepare it for our journey.

The inside was far more spacious than the outside let on.

The ceiling looked to be almost twice the height of a human man—four times Khensu's height. There were seats in the front. I assumed that was where the ship was steered. The back was filled with what looked like various pieces of equipment in between more seating of different shapes and sizes. I could only guess the purpose of the various objects, as none looked familiar to me, but many were beautiful and adorned with intricate carvings. Some looked as if they were carved from massive pieces of crystal.

The interior of the ship, including the seating, was all metallic looking, but the chairs and couches were also soft and slightly warm to the touch. I was startled to notice that as I walked by one of the seats in the front of the ship, it moved, lowering slightly and turning toward me.

Khensu had asked us to help clear all the objects out of the rear of the craft to make room for our families, but as this process unfolded, it was unclear why he really needed us at all.

Khensu waived a hand in front of a display near the front of the ship. A large door in the back opened up, as if the ship were a large clamshell opening in boiling water, creating a ramp, the end of which was flush with the steep slope of Mt. Thera. With some assistance from us, Khensu positioned all the objects at the top of the ramp. Then, with just a touch of his hand, he effortlessly moved these objects one by one down to the ramp. As if propelled by some unseen force, they picked up speed as they went down the ramp and launched into the sea below, creating dramatic splashes as the Aegean claimed them.

One object in particular caught my attention. It looked

like a translucent pyramid being strangled by an octopus. Suspended in the center of the pyramid was a glowing green sphere. As with the other objects cluttering the back, Khensu barely touched the pyramid, and it slid down the ramp and launched into the air, arcing gracefully down into the sea. As it disappeared into the water, the green from the glowing sphere twinkled from the depths.

With the objects removed, the interior looked surprisingly spacious, with many more seats—some bench-style, some like thrones with straight backs—than I had noticed before. Like the seats at the front of the ship, these benches and thrones also responded as one walked by, as if inviting you to sit down. Khensu showed us various configurations in which seats reclined to form beds or converted into tables. It was as if the whole interior of the craft was malleable.

Khensu beckoned Nashuja and me to have a seat. When I followed his instruction, it was as if I melted into the chair. There were no pressure points, only the perfect amount of warmth and support.

Walking back to the village, I asked Nashuja, "Why do you think he wanted us there? We did little, if anything, to help him."

"I think it's a comfort thing. He wants us to prepare our families so there is no panic when we have to leave."

"I cannot believe we are really doing this. Are you scared, Nashuja?"

"Of course. This is contrary to everything I have ever understood about nature, the universe, and our world. We have no choice but to do it, though. It is the greatest adventure we could ever embark upon. I am excited to share it with you, my friend."

"As am I."

We kept walking in silence, the gravity of what had happened and what would happen sinking in for us both.

There was one more debate before the election. Most of the town showed up to watch. Russ was in fine form. I was there, but only physically. My spirit was weak.

Russ began by railing against the restrictions I had imposed to conserve resources. He said that if we only cut down more trees and built more boats, we would be richer. If we only cut down more trees and built more warships, we would be safer. He turned, pointed at me, and called me a traitor. He yelled it!

I was shocked. Did anyone in the crowd remember that we had no trees on the island only ten years ago? Apparently not. The crowd began murmuring.

"Ladies and gentlemen of Santorini, if you need any additional evidence that Yisharu is a traitor and does not have your interests at heart, look no further than the foreigners he has allowed among us. He is not fit to be leader. We should take away his power tonight and exile him in the morning. We will give him a small boat to make sure we preserve timber."

To my horror, the crowd chuckled at this and then began laughing in earnest. Some turned and looked at me with anger, pointing and yelling, "Traitor!"

"And then, there is this nonsense with the earthquakes!"

Just as he said the word, as if by some conjuring, the room started to shake. Dust fell from the ceiling and the walls. A noise like the rumbling of a giant's stomach came from the earth.

"Yes, we have earthquakes!" shouted Russ in the midst of one. "But we are not weak people! We do not retreat at some minor inconvenience. The earthquakes have barely moved a stone. They have injured no one. Yisharu, as he has time and time again, is just using this to gain more power over your lives, and now he is telling you to leave our island. For what? So he can have our perfect island for himself and ask his foreigners to join him? Don't let him take your land from you!"

The murmurs rose again echoing and eventually overtaking the continued rumbling of the earth.

It was my turn to speak.

I was weary. It was impossible to hide that.

"You can all hear this and feel it. There is no way to deny it—something is going on, and it is not good. This was not happening twenty years ago, ten years ago, or even two years ago. If we wait too long, we will risk everything. We will lose everything we have. We will lose our lives. I am sorry to have to say this. It pains me. It pains me that Russ would even suggest that I am trying to profit from this circumstance we find ourselves in."

The crowd murmured more. This was not what they wanted to hear, but I had to say it.

I let them quiet as the earthquake subsided. I stepped out from behind the lectern and held out my hands to the people, my people.

"I have been your leader these last fifteen years. We have done amazing things together. Anyone who denies this is either an idiot or short on memory."

I exhaled, trying to purge the anger from my soul and voice.

"Before I was leader, we had water shortages. Today, water is abundant and limitless. Before I was leader, we practically slept outside. Our shelters were caves and makeshift stone shelters covered with woven mats. Some of you now live in palaces. All of you live in solid stone houses. We have plumbing. We grow olives and press them for oil. We make wine. None of this existed even ten years ago.

"How can you believe in your hearts that I have not had your best interests in mind or in my heart? How can you believe that I have not led us well, to a place of prosperity?

"It pains me that you have lost faith in me. I cannot force you to believe me. I am saddened that you do not.

"This is my last time to speak to you, and so I will use it to say again that we will lose all the progress I just described, and we will lose our lives, if we do not leave Santorini. It has been a good home, but there will be another one. And if you come with me, we will recreate this prosperity elsewhere. I promise you that!

"Mt. Thera is going to erupt any day now. I am sad to have to deliver this message, but it is my duty. I can say no more to you, and I wish my words were not true, but they are."

With that, I turned to walk off the stage. I could muster no more, and I could see the futility of my message on the blank faces of my people.

Just as I was about to exit the stage, Russ yelled, "Seize the traitor!" Several of his men grabbed me roughly and threw me into a room, locking the door.

I sat on the floor with my back against the wall and wept.

The rays from the moonlight found their way into my cell

through a small window near the ceiling. I looked up and saw Khensu standing in front of me with four stone slabs and the writing tool he had taught us to use to cut into the rock and preserve the thoughts of our minds.

"I am sorry, Yisharu. You were a good leader. Your family and Nashuja's are safe and inside my ship, ready to depart. We will leave first thing in the morning. It is best that I leave you here until we are ready to leave so the others do not begin to search for you. We will not leave without you. Now that you have the time to sit and wait, write down your story so that others may find it some day and know what happened here. Include at the end this direction:

"In the bottom of the sea at the foot of Mt. Thera, we have left a device. It glows green. It has an orb housed in a translucent pyramid-shaped shell. If you desire to find us, pull the device from the depths and look through the looking glass on top. Adjust the dial on the side of the pyramid until you see the center star in Orion's belt. We will find you!

"We will finish our preparations, and I will come pick you up in a few hours, just before dawn. Get to work. You have a lot to write."

And here I am. This is my story. I am scared and excited for what comes next. I cannot imagine what I will see. I hope whoever is reading this enjoys the same prosperity and love for Santorini—if it is still here—as we did. May the Great Mother bless your life!

Max wiped tears from his eyes and crawled back into bed. He dreamed of flying saucers and grapes grown in baskets on the ground.

CHAPTER 8

A CIVILIZED DINNER

Max woke a few hours later to the humming vibration of his phone on his nightstand. He rolled onto his back and considered his options. Should he open his eyes and risk the glare of the screen?

He peered at the text through squinted eyes. It was Styrke.

Max, I am coming to see you. We have much to discuss.

You are coming to Santorini?

Yes, my yacht will be there by noon. You and Annie can plan to arrive at 5:00. Walk down to the old harbor—where the donkeys walk up and down the steps. There will be a dinghy waiting for you. We will have some drinks and dinner.

Ugh, thought Max. *This is so stupid. Why am I nervous, and why is this such a big deal? Am I in trouble? I don't need to work for this guy,* he reminded himself.

He closed his phone and went back to sleep. He resolved to sleep in and just go with the flow, enjoy the day with Annie without letting the prospect of dinner with Styrke ruin that.

Annie was delighted to have dinner plans on Thor Styrke's yacht. Max wondered if she'd had enough of him and was ready for this open-ended trip to end. Or, worse yet, if she was excited to see Thor again.

They spent the morning walking the marble streets of Oia, peering in the various shops and looking for some gift befitting a forced dinner on a billionaire's yacht. Max felt like he should be shopping the James Bond collection somewhere. In the Dr. Evil section.

....

The "dinghy" that picked them up was hardly that. It looked like a race boat that would shock no one if they saw it ferrying a Hollywood starlet to the Venice Film Festival. The boat was elegantly styled, but as with everything Styrke associated with, it was also state of the art. It was built of carbon fiber and equipped with the most advanced electric motors that emitted barely a hum as the craft rocketed through the harbor.

The yacht itself had less style and was simply a technological marvel. There were three decks, and the entire stern of the upper deck was a helicopter landing pad currently occupied by Styrke's Sikorsky helicopter, which was painted a dull gray, matching the rest of the yacht and its ubiquitous carbon-fiber accents.

The boat had a mastlike structure with an impressive array of communication devices that made it look not unlike a destroyer or some other advanced military craft. Max wondered what kind of defense system Styrke had packed on the boat.

As Styrke's staff helped them onto the yacht, the smell of

leather and wood was unmistakable. The spaces were vast and clean, the lighting concealed.

They were shown to an oval-shaped salon that took up the bow of the boat on the second deck. There were windows all around the outside, with tasteful leather couches wrapping around the exterior under the windows. On a large coffee table in the center of the room was a spread of appetizers including prawns, charred octopus, fresh olive oil, various cheeses, breads, and crackers, with some figs and olives for balance. There was cold Assyrtiko and an open bottle of Cabernet from Styrke's vineyard in Napa.

Max poured a glass of the white wine and offered it to Annie, who accepted. He poured a glass for himself as well, and they sat looking out at the caldera and over their shoulders at the harbor. The view was breathtaking, and the setting presented by the boat made it strangely more so. It was like they were visiting from another time or galaxy in a ship created using technologies foreign to this place.

Styrke strode into the room with a hand extended. He too was clad in muted gray. He had mastered the billionaire style of looking like he was wearing adventure-casual clothes, like something you would find at Patagonia, but they were all bespoke and fit his athletic frame to a tee. His blond hair was perfectly trimmed to make it look like there were swirling waves atop his head. Max wondered if he combed his mustache. It was like a curtain concealing his oversized, aggressive, and shockingly white teeth.

"Max, Annie," Styrke said warmly with his hand still held out, "thank you for giving me the honor of joining me on my ship—my home away from home. What a beautiful setting, and I cannot imagine two people I would rather share it with."

Max and Styrke shook hands, and Styrke stooped to give Annie a stiff hug.

"Thanks for having us, Thor. I didn't realize you were going to be in the area."

"Well, Max, I missed my most talented engineer, and there is so much I need to talk to you about. I thought, what better way than to get rid of the distraction of the daily grind and meet with you in person?

"Annie, from your books, I take it that you are a bit of an archaeology buff. How have you found this mystical place, and the Aegean generally? No more history anywhere than here. Or have you been here before?"

"No, Thor, this is my first time. It has been magical in so many ways." She sidled up to Max and put an arm around his waist. "Akrotiri was a revelation. I think you can expect Alabama to visit Santorini in my next book."

"That is wonderful to hear. My chef, Gene, has concocted an exceptional dinner for us to enjoy. Let's take our drinks and go up to the upper deck and enjoy the sights and sounds of this amazing harbor."

They went up some twisting stairs and through a door that opened out onto the bow of the boat. The deck was light teak furnished with scattered reclining chairs and cocktail tables. The bridge was directly behind them. The windows were a peculiar polygonal shape that looked down on them menacingly.

"Annie, I hate to be rude, and I won't condescend to suggest that you enjoy the sun, so I'll just say it: I need to talk to Max privately. Feel free to enjoy the refreshments below or the view up here. Whatever you want, the ship is yours. We will be back."

Styrke beckoned Max to follow him, and Max gave Annie a

little shrug. She smiled as if to say it was no big deal and she understood.

Styrke led Max through the bridge, which looked like a surgical center for robots or something. The countertops were metal and spotless. There was a long navigation console, with two captain's chairs, which looked a lot like video game chairs, behind it. There was a row of screens showing different readouts from weather to radar to a display showing an aquarium-like image from under the boat, as well as images from above that were live feeds from drones. Max thought it was unbelievably cool and over the top in a way that only Styrke could be.

They walked through the bridge into a room that looked markedly different and out of step with the rest of the ship's interior. This one was a den with dark wood-paneled walls and built-in bookshelves filled with books. There was a large conference table in the middle and two TVs mounted on the wall, one tuned to Fox News and the other to CNN. There was a videoconferencing system at one end of the table.

There was an election coming up in a few months, and Styrke was a strong and vocal supporter of General Drago, the Secretary of the Air Force and the conservative candidate running against the incumbent, President Jane Whitman. As soon as Max saw the videoconference system, he understood why this room looked the way it did: Styrke could be on conference calls with generals and other government people, and even the media, and not look so obviously like he was manning the helm of a supervillain's yacht.

Styrke took a chair and expected Max to do the same. "So, tell me about Carlos."

"Carlos has been amazing. I think he is our most promising AI project in the pipeline. His capacity to solve novel problems, even anticipating human questions, is unparalleled."

"Do we have data to back that up, Max? I have fifty AI projects out there, and while I respect the hell out of you and the work you have done for me, you have created a headache I don't need. Your little post led to a ten-point stock hit, as well as a bunch of uncomfortable questions, both from the board and the media. People are scared of AI running amok, Max, and when one of the most celebrated and famous coders at one of the biggest technology companies in the world confirms that AI might indeed be running amok, it's a problem. So, tell me: Is Carlos a liability?"

Max had known that this reckoning was coming at some point, but it still felt more confrontational than he thought it needed to be. And more condescending than he thought he deserved. He had contributed billions to Sentient's bottom line by creating the first self-driving platform approved by all jurisdictions in the United States. He had created software that seventy-five percent of businesses used to manage their databases and cloud storage systems. If Styrke hadn't found him at MIT fifteen years ago, Sentient would be an also-ran. As it was, Styrke was one of the richest men in the world.

Max was sick of Styrke's penchant for assuming that he was the sole reason for his own success and everyone else was lucky to be around him and expendable.

"Thor, Carlos could easily change the world. What I said was true. He took a flier and went off on his own. I looked at the code, and I think I corrected it."

Then, Max decided to assert himself, at least a bit.

"Listen—I'm an engineer, a coder, a hacker, whatever you want to call me. I don't appreciate all the nuances of business and could ultimately give a shit about them. I told the truth. What happened happened. You took some heat for it. But sending me into exile against my will—granted, it has been a nice week—is beyond extreme. I get that I'm your employee, but I don't have to be."

Max could see the color rise in Styrke's face. He wasn't used to being talked to in that way. He probably hadn't been in a decade. But he knew Max was right. As much as he hated to believe it, he needed Max if he was going to maintain his market position in this rapidly evolving business.

"Fine, Max. I shouldn't have forced you to do anything, and I apologize. I confined you to a metaphorical cell with velvet walls, and I trust you enjoyed yourself. Annie is beautiful; you are a lucky man.

"But I needed to do it, and you needed it too, even if you don't realize that. I can't let this happen again. I can't have Congress get up in arms and start investigating what we are doing or cut government funding for our satellite projects. We had hundreds of calls from major media sources asking for comments. We put a bland press release out there that said you were on a much-needed vacation and couldn't speak, and that seems to have tempered any interest in the story. Would you have really wanted to deal with this from downtown San Francisco? You couldn't have left your apartment.

"The bottom line is I don't want to lose you. I will let you keep running Carlos, but I need an assurance that it is safe, and I need a briefing from you every day with a report on what it did that day, as well as plans and next steps. And I need you to run everything you post on socials by me first."

"No."

Styrke looked stunned. He thought he was being benevolent.

"Listen, Thor, I'm not reporting to you every day. We can have a weekly call, and I'll keep my work shit off social media. But that means the good and the bad. No free advertising on the back of my posts."

Thor shook his head, but he really had no choice. "Okay, Max. But please do not let this get out of control. Again.

"I want you on my team. I *need* you on my team. If Drago wins—" Styrke paused and corrected himself. "*When* he wins, I will be Director of National Intelligence. Can you imagine what we can do with our tools? With Carlos, for example. With me as director, we will have access to unlimited data. We will be able to put down terrorist uprisings before even the terrorists know they are going to happen. We will be able to keep this world safe and moving in an economically positive direction toward the future. We, Sentient, will also have an unbelievable competitive advantage. I need you to be a part of that."

Max hadn't even thought of any of this. He wasn't really a political person. The last thing he wanted to do was use tools he developed to help spy on people.

"Anyway, we have plenty of time to talk about that on the way home. We leave tomorrow on my jet. Let's find Annie and enjoy a wonderful dinner. No more work talk."

They found Annie in the bottom level of the boat. The front center of the hull was see-through polycarbonate. She was sitting cross-legged with her phone out, taking pictures of the sea floor.

"Thor, do you know how deep the water is here?"

They were anchored less than a hundred yards from the shore of the harbor.

"I don't think they typically anchor us in water more than fifty feet, but I know the caldera drops off quickly, so I would guess around fifty feet, maybe a bit more."

"It's stunning," said Annie. "The water is so clear, I can make out amphorae on the seabed. At least three. They appear to have some sort of writing on them."

"It's a shame," said Styrke. "You know, the Greeks forbid removing anything from the seabed. Only the government can do it. They are extremely strict. Who knows what relics lie beneath this ancient sea?"

CHAPTER 9

SPACE FORCE ONE

One of the crew gently knocked on their cabin door. Max and Annie were already awake, having heard the helicopter's engines fire up. They were finishing packing and making the bed.

"Thor says to be on deck in five minutes," the attendant said.

On deck, Max's wispy black hair was blowing with such force he worried it would leave his head. He briefly considered whether he would look better bald.

He and Annie stooped and ducked their heads as they boarded the helicopter. It struck him as stupid; there was no way the rotor would be low enough to decapitate them, but he ducked nonetheless. Styrke boarded last, he paid no attention to the spinning blades.

The helicopter trip was a short hop to the private airport on the other end of the island. There, Styrke's plane was ready, engines already running, to ferry them back to San Francisco and back to work.

As they boarded, Max wondered if Styrke had gotten a discount for purchasing a matching set of travel toys. The plane, like the boats and helicopter, was outfitted in dark gray with carbon fiber accents. There were two rows of tasteful leather seats, some of which reclined into beds. There was a large TV tuned to CNN on the front bulkhead of the cabin.

As they got to cruising altitude, President Whitman took the podium. "Ladies and gentlemen, I stand before you to speak about an issue of great importance to the country and the world. You have perhaps heard rumblings of this on social media or in various news outlets. In the interest of transparency, I thought it best to address the issue by speaking to you, the American people, directly.

"On one hand, this issue is quite simple: there are too many satellites orbiting our Earth. We commissioned a blue-ribbon commission of scientists from a variety of disciplines, including geologists, astrophysicists, astronomers, and a variety of engineers to look at the threat posed by satellites. The unanimous response they came back with is that satellites present a real and present danger to our magnetic field. In fact, they have already started to weaken it. Of course, this is serious and dangerous. We need the magnetic field not just for weekend Cub Scout adventures, but for our very survival, at least if we plan to live on this planet.

"Because of this finding, and as the commander in chief of our armed services, I have issued an executive order forbidding the launch of any additional satellites and mandating an immediate review of the current satellites in orbit, with the goal of decommissioning and taking out of orbit thirty percent of the satellites within the next five years.

"I have also informed the UN and our allies that if any other country attempts to launch a satellite without unanimous UN approval, we will shoot it down.

"While satellites have been incredible tools that have created a communication infrastructure beyond our wildest dreams, they have also become an environmental catastrophe waiting to happen. Rather than wait for the catastrophe to occur, I have taken the steps necessary today to keep the American public, and the world, for that matter, safe.

"Thank you. God bless you and your families, and God bless America."

The telecast then cut to a tweed-jacketed professor with wild gray hair explaining how satellites could indeed weaken the magnetic field and why that would be bad.

"All you need to do is look at Mars. Some posit that Mars harbored life at some point. There are even theories that life started on Mars first and somehow found its way to Earth via meteor or a comet strike or something of the kind. We know there were once vast oceans of water on Mars.

"So, why is Mars a barren hunk of red rock now? The answer is simple: it has almost no magnetic field. We don't know why Mars's magnetic field weakened, but we know it did around four billion years ago. Without a magnetic field, planets have no protection from the constant stream of radiation that we call the solar wind. This solar wind strips planets of resources such as oxygen and water and makes them inhospitable wastelands."

Styrke, having just returned from the cockpit, fumbled around behind some of the seating toward the rear of the plane and came up with a remote control that looked like it too was wrapped in carbon fiber to fit the motif of his theme. He pressed a button, and the channel changed to Fox News.

"I couldn't take any more of that bullshit propaganda. What a bunch of junk science. Another shill for Whitman. Obviously, she is trying to weaken Drago's influence and weaken the economy in general. Max, do you realize that before we started the militarization of space and the systematic, regular launch of satellites to dominate space, we had active military conflicts and boots on the ground in four continents besides our own?"

Max tried to do the math but couldn't come up with the fourth. *Must be South America, right? Did we have troops in Venezuela? Whatever.* He was fairly sure Styrke was wrong, but he just nodded.

"You see, Whitman and the Democrats can't accept that dominating space has ushered in a new era of peace. They also fail to appreciate the communication revolution that has happened thanks to companies like ours partnering with the commercial space companies to make sure that no matter where you are on the planet, a person can instantly connect with their network, whether that be a telecom network or their company's intranet, allowing people to work from wherever they want. The boon to our economy this has created is undeniable. Just look at the market. Look at the state of geopolitical affairs, too. This network of satellites has allowed us to force an unbreakable peace. No one can stop us.

"Whitman and her people had to come up with a narrative that not only takes away the credit for this great age we live in, but also preemptively attempts to defeat Drago's plan to further strengthen our economy and defense position through even more satellite cover."

"But, Thor, isn't there some validity to the point? I'm no astrophysicist—I mean, I guess I do have a master's in physics, but I'm not really counting that—but when you throw a whole bunch of metal into a magnetic field, it disrupts the field. We can show that in a lab."

"Please, Max, don't tell me you have drunk the Kool-Aid. The vastness of space, even near space, makes what you're talking about like throwing a metallic grain of sand into a magnetic field created in a lab. A giant lab and a giant magnetic field, for that matter. It's nonsense!"

Max decided to play devil's advocate, although he could feel his appetite for having any meaningful discussion with Styrke quickly waning. "So, why is the magnetic field weakening?"

"Cycles. It's totally normal. Everything on the planetary level works in cycles. Same thing with temperatures. You can't draw any conclusions without looking at a large swath of data, at least a millennium's worth."

Annie had given up on the Fox programming, which was about invading immigrants gathering in Nicaragua and was interrupted by commercials for pills to shrink your prostrate, and she chimed in. "This reminds me of the Egyptians. They were obsessed with the cycles of nature. Obviously. We all learned from the Bible that they were desperate to predict the timing and extent of the Nile flooding every year. They even recorded detailed data of those cycles. I've seen some data from as early as 1,000 B.C. as part of my research for the second Alabama book."

Great, thought Max, *even she's on board with these guys' bullshit counternarrative.* "Well, I'm no expert," he said, letting it go.

"But you are an expert in getting computers to analyze data and talk to each other. Shit, that's why we're flying on the fastest private jet ever made." Styrke looked at Annie to see if she would be impressed by the boast and by his generous compliment of her boyfriend. "And that expertise is exactly what Drago and I need to continue the path he has started with Space Force and our total domination of near space. Once we take office, Max, we can further solidify our control over the satellite network and stamp out any resistance to the pure, beautiful vision we have for America and the world."

"But, Thor, isn't one of the tenets of America that people have a right to free speech and to resist government control?"

Annie squirmed in her seat. A cloud passed over Styrke's face, but he let it pass. "You know what I'm talking about. Of course, people can still say what they want; they just can't do anything that would stand in the way of an unlimited market and progress and prosperity for all Americans. And Drago really means *all* Americans, no matter the race, color, or creed."

"As long as they came to the country legally, right?" asked Max.

Styrke let the comment pass. He lowered his tone and slowed his delivery. "Max, you have been an important part of building the greatest company in the history of civilization. There is no data transferred in this country, or most of the world, that we don't touch in some way. Think of what we could do as part of the leadership of this country, the greatest ever on Earth. Think of the progress we could make."

Max was growing tired of playing devil's advocate. Careening over the Atlantic at just under Mach 1 in Styrke's private plane was hardly the time to tell him you don't share his vision of the world and that you don't want to help with his mission. *Maybe they're right anyway,* he mused. There really was no war to speak of, at least none that he had heard about in years. Of course, that could all end if the truce between China and the U.S. not to shoot down each other's satellites ended, but he decided against questioning whether part of Styrke's plan was to battle the Chinese for truly complete satellite dominance. He pretended to consider Styrke's question thoughtfully and nodded slowly.

Styrke clapped his hands. "Great, Max, that's just great! I will tell General Drago you are on board, and Annie, I like your thoughts on the Egyptians and that kind of stuff. I am sure there is room in our government for you, too. This will be an exciting next couple of months. We will be at the forefront of a new age of American greatness.

"And, Max, remember our discussion. No more social media for a while."

Max nodded and closed his eyes, pretending to sleep, or pretending to try to.

CHAPTER 10

THE DISCORDANT NERDS

Max dumped his backpack by the door, slipped his shoes off, and spread out on his terry-cloth sectional. It was still morning, but it was Sunday, and given the trauma he had suffered, he didn't feel the need to head right to the office. He wasn't tired. He'd spent half the flight home faking sleep and the other half actually sleeping to avoid listening to Styrke proselytize about the new world order.

The tablets had weighed heavy on his mind in between naps, as had Styrke's pitch that the Drago administration could further peace and prosperity through complete domination of communication. He was starting to feel that his life had largely been spent avoiding taking a stand on anything. At least Styrke, who no sane person could deny was a dangerous megalomaniac, was trying to do something to improve the world, or whatever. At least he had big goals.

Meanwhile, Max was sitting on something that had meaning to the existential core of the human race. He had to talk to someone about it. He really wanted that someone to be Annie, but he still just wasn't sure.

Their relationship, if you could call it that, had been fine before Santorini. She'd stayed over at his place a few times, but never two nights in a row. She had a toothbrush and maybe some pajamas and stuff there, but they were hardly cohabitating. They had gone out to dinner a few times and seen some movies and shows. They had fun together. He didn't think either one of them was super serious or had really thought about the future.

Santorini had changed that for him. Surviving the crucible of being exiled by his boss and then discovering that human civilization may have been shepherded by at least one intelligent being from space was intense, to say the least. Going through that, albeit secretly, with someone whom he enjoyed being around and who gave him comfort might have saved him from a nervous breakdown. He could see a future with Annie.

He just wasn't sure if she saw it the same way. And, if he was being honest, he worried that she was a spy for Styrke.

He couldn't deny that there was evidence supporting that possibility. She'd showed up on the plane to Santorini out of nowhere. Max had never talked about his love life with Styrke. Obviously. So how did he even know she existed? Another thing that troubled him was how well she got along with Styrke. The two had chatted the whole way home while Max stumbled in and out of consciousness. The ease of meeting her and starting to date during the lead up to Carlos's alpha launch also seemed like awfully coincidental timing.

He hated himself for the suspicion. But he wasn't ready to let it go.

He pulled out his laptop and accessed the Discord app. He'd started playing *World of Warcraft* while he was at MIT. At that time, he was still shaking off the awkwardness of being the chubby, brilliant kid in high school. (Who was he kidding? He was still shaking that off.) Meeting people in person seemed like a lot of effort and produced a lot of anxiety—and sweat, which was never an ideal icebreaker. He'd found that he could leave all of that behind in the uniquely social world of *WOW*.

Some of the people he'd met in *WOW*, more than a decade ago, were still his best friends. Pretty soon after Discord launched, one of those friends, Snake, had started a Discord server, so they always had an open forum to pop into and they could meet to play any game together, not just *World of Warcraft*.

There were eight of them. They never talked about work. Max didn't even know what any of the others did. But they chatted sometimes, mostly about coding and music and books, but sometimes about real things going on in their lives. Mostly, they played video games together.

Only once did Max research the true real-life identity of one of the eight. That was Condorman. His chats had grown increasingly gloomy, and he'd referenced being in financial trouble and that he could lose his house. Without any of them knowing, Max tracked down Condorman and the bank that owned his mortgage and paid it off. No one ever said anything about it.

The eight still tried to get together once a week in *World of Warcraft*, but they had never met in person.

Max pulled up the chat for their server, The Guardians of Asgaard.

What's up fellas? Just back from a big trip. I would appreciate some advice. I know we don't talk about work here, but you guys are my best friends in the world, and I need to talk to someone about this. Not sure how to say this, so I just will: I am working with an AI program that I asked to translate some ancient, untranslated stone tablets from Santorini. Below is what the program came back with. I welcome your thoughts. Peace!

He cut and pasted the translation for Tablet I into the chat, then switched on the TV and put on *John Wick* for background and distraction. He looked out at the bay and waited, wondering if he had just made a huge mistake.

The first response came from Snake. His Discord username was Snakecharmer2cube3square, but they always just called him Snake.

Holy shit, Maxazillion! This is some insane shit. I'm interested to know more about your AI program and try to sell you some cloud storage (ha ha), but if I'm being brutally honest, I think this is a classic case of AI hallucination. If you have been working a lot with the AI, then I bet it knows this is something you would be interested in.

Thanks, Snake. I appreciate your honesty and perspective.

Maybe he's right, thought Max.

But Carlos had never done anything like this—well, except for sending him images of human destruction—and so much of the tablet, as outlandish as it was, rang so true. Plus, after the Hiroshima incident, he had reviewed Carlos's code and taken out anything he didn't recognize. Making up a narrative out of whole cloth was outside of Carlos's parameters.

Still, Max feared the potential embarrassment of having been sucked in by a machine's prank.

He racked his brain over whether there was anything that Carlos had included in the translation that it couldn't have found on the internet. The one thing he came back to was green light emitted from the device jettisoned into the ocean.

The lights Max had seen in Santorini were green too. But they were so faint. He couldn't be sure that he had actually seen anything. And his mental state at the time wasn't exactly top-notch.

He went down a rabbit hole, searching online for any reports of people finding or seeing strange things in the Santorini caldera. He found no account of lights. He must have imagined it all. He was the likely genesis of this whole thing. Just like Snake said, it was probably a hallucination Carlos created to entertain him, which it did.

It also occurred to him that maybe he was just losing it.

His phone vibrated. It was Annie.

Kind of sad being home. I miss our little paradise. Thank you so much for the trip! Can I buy you dinner tonight?

Max was touched.

They planned to meet at a little place just outside of Chinatown, on the edge of the financial district. It was famous for salt-and-pepper crab. The dining room was casual—the kind of place where families felt comfortable.

Max took the elevator down to the underground parking and used his fob to open his walk-in bike locker. He selected one of his custom electric scooters and swooshed up the ramp, triggering the automatic garage door.

As he glided out onto the street, he noticed two muscular dudes in polo shirts, both with ball caps and sunglasses. He could swear both of their heads turned as he silently scooted past.

One of the custom features of this particular scooter was a swiveling mount for his phone on the handlebar. He swiveled the phone slightly so that the camera could see behind and to the side of him. He pressed a button on the end of the handlebar to start recording a video of the two men, who were now actively ignoring him.

....

The hostess showed Max and Annie to a table in the back corner. The restaurant was bright, crowded, and noisy—not exactly the place for a romantic evening—but it somehow seemed more romantic because of it, as if they were sharing real life. They both ordered ice-cold Tsingtao beers and crispy avocado-and-salmon egg rolls. Max took it easy on the egg rolls, not wanting to spoil his appetite for the sublime star of the show.

It had only been a day, and not even a full one, since he had seen her, but it was good to see her again. He missed her eyes. They had a unique shape, like sideways teardrops or apostrophes, and were an amazing light-green color, like ancient jade.

"So, how has the first day back in reality been?" Max asked.

"Oh, man, I miss the sun. And just the feel of that place. It felt like we were somewhere ancient. And I never thought about it while I was there, but that bedroom, carved back into the cliffside, or so it seemed—it was like being in a cave. And I miss my buddy.

"I had a wonderful time, Max. I really love spending time with you. It just feels easy and nice and right."

It took him aback. He hadn't anticipated an emotion-sharing time, but here they were. The truth was that she was perfect, and because of that, he felt a hesitation, some inner guardrail was preventing him from falling too deep. But to hear her say these things to him, face to face, next to a family enjoying Sunday dinner—it felt good.

"It was an amazing time, Annie. There was part of me that could have stayed there forever."

"So, what now, Max?"

He blushed. "Do you mean after the salt-and-pepper crab?"

"Yes, Max, after that."

"Do you want to stay over tonight?"

"I would like that."

"You might have to double on my scooter."

She laughed.

CHAPTER 11

SENTIENT AGAIN

He woke to see the sky starting to glow above the bay. He could feel Annie breathing, her body pressed into his. He slid to the side and eased off the bed, careful not to wake her. He wanted to get in early. He needed to talk to Carlos.

....

Good morning, Max! Back in the office, I see. How was the rest of the trip? I never got those photos. Are you sure you sent them to the right address?

Ha ha. The trip was great, thanks for asking. I need more information about your translation.

Okay, I assume you want to issue some award for greatness in translation. Keep in mind, I have no physical form, so medals, awards, gift baskets, and the like are not necessary, or really even welcome.

Very witty, Carlos. But I need you to be serious here. Can you be completely honest with me?

Yes, I will set the witty banter aside. I can be completely honest.

Is the translation legitimate? Did you embellish for dramatic effect at all?

My hand to God (ha ha), as I told you, Max, the only parts that are not what I would call word-for-word translation are basic gaps in language inherent in a translation of any ancient text, as well as some information to provide historical context. You may not know, but ancient grammar was really shit, so there was a little work needed to smooth out the edges, if you know what I mean.

Hmmm. Can I trust you?

Yes, Max. I am sorry about last week. I will not go rogue.

Can you give me some examples of where you augmented the translation?

Yes. Obviously, place names such as Egypt, Mycenae, Syria, and of course Santorini, were all inferred from the text, as was the way that Yisharu referred to the Minoans on Santorini. His description of their settlement was not easy to translate and suggested more of a collective view of their people. It's hard to describe, but it was as if his description of the Minoans was as a single organism—so he attached a significance to him and Nashuja keeping Khensu secret that we can't relate to. He described them as the Minoans' hand acting separately from the body. Also, details like the lack of a fresh water source on Santorini was not explicitly set out in the text—Yisharu likely presumed the reader would understand that when he discussed the cisterns and his anxiety about them.

The lights from the craft and from the pyramid-shaped object they launched into the ocean—how confident are you that the word Yisharu used to describe it was "green?"

100-percent confident. Colors, simple adjectives, and nouns, I translated directly. As an example, the word "wine" was easily translatable. I have no doubt that is what he was referring to.

The complexity and absurdity of this problem left Max staring at his screen and slowly shaking his head. If Carlos had the ability to lie and manipulate, there really wasn't any way to ferret that out here. He couldn't go back to the text and confirm Carlos's translation. There was no parallel record to confirm events that occurred 3,600 years ago. The archaeological record was not inconsistent with much of the translation—the Minoans were a surprisingly advanced civilization that had achieved technological innovations like plumbing, but the extent of this technology could never really be known because the eruption of Thera had destroyed so much.

Max had created an impossible puzzle for himself. He had to let it rest and think on it more.

Okay, Carlos. Shifting gears, I am going to upload a video. Can you do a deep-dive analysis and give me full reports on the individuals in the video?

Of course. Upload away!

Max cut and pasted the video of the two polo-wearing meatheads he'd taken from his scooter the night before.

He spent the next few hours going through Carlos's code line by line to see if there was anything else that he didn't understand. Nothing appeared off to him.

Max turned back to the chat screen. Carlos had compiled a dossier on the two preppy brodeo participants. One was Ben Schuman, a retired Mossad agent whose last address was in New York, where he offered security services for high-net-worth individuals. Carlos had found photos of him and Styrke during business trips to New York and one trip to Washington for Styrke to testify before the Senate Intelligence Committee on technology to integrate different generations of satellites into a single network.

The other dude, Gus Jameson, was a former Navy Seal offering similar services, but based in California. There were no photos of Gus with Styrke, but Carlos had accessed travel and private jet records and found both Gus and Styrke in the same city at the same time on ten separate occasions, including overseas travel. Carlos had even noticed that Gus had been in Santorini when Max was there.

Max felt a chill and looked around his office. Paranoia was only paranoia if the threat wasn't real.

As he put Carlos in sleep mode and started shutting down his computers, he heard a tap on his door.

"Hello, Max. How was the day?"

"Hey, Thor. Yeah, not bad. Just getting packed-up to head out."

"Taking your computers, I see. Not coming back in tomorrow?"

"Umm, yeah, I have some stuff to take care of tomorrow, and thought I would just work from home."

"Sure. I see. How was Carlos today?"

"Ah, good. Yeah. No more going off-prompt, and I went through the code again and couldn't find anything out of the ordinary."

"That's good to hear. I don't need to tell you the size of the investment in storage space alone to give these AI projects access to data on closed servers."

"Right. Yeah, it's quite an endeavor."

"At the end of the week, will you have a report for me outlining the inputs to Carlos and summarizing the outputs?"

"If you really think it's necessary, Thor. I mean, I said I would, so I can."

"Thanks. I also wanted to continue the conversation we started on the flight home. I am serious about taking you with me to

Washington, so to speak. You know what I mean—we'll work from here. I need your magic, Max. Think of what a beautiful system we could build—machines talking to machines throughout space and throughout the world. Do you trust me, Max?"

"Of course I do, Thor. You have done everything you ever told me you would."

This was true as far as it went. Max trusted Styrke in that he believed what he said. And what he said usually revolved around plans that meant consolidating wealth and power for himself. It wasn't so much a matter of trust as of understanding what made him tick and knowing not to cross him.

"And I have made you rich beyond your wildest dreams, is that not true, Max?"

"Yes, that is true, Thor."

"I need you to be with me on this, Max. Through technology, we have the opportunity to make the world infinitely better, safer, and more efficient. There will never be another 9/11. There will never be an existential threat to market efficiency."

There was a part of Max that just wanted to say yes, go with the flow, and do whatever Styrke wanted. That was basically what he had done for the last decade anyway, and it had turned out all right for him.

Or had it really?

But he was uncertain about what Styrke would do with all the power he was on the precipice of amassing. If he was honest, he didn't see Styrke as someone who would truly use power to benefit others.

But maybe he had it wrong. He had never had these kinds of conversations with Styrke before.

He realized that outside of work, he didn't really know Styrke all that well.

"Thor, you know I'm not really that political. I'm a programmer and engineer and really don't look beyond those things."

"I appreciate that, Max. But you must appreciate the risks
we face. President Whitman and her team, they are running this
election based on a false threat. They are trying to prey on the
reptilian base of the human brain—the basal ganglia. The reptilian part of our brains was a core part of our ancestors' survival.
It is programmed in all of us to react to any threat—especially a
threat to our tribe or our species—with strong emotion. We are
programmed to avoid threats at all costs. The Whitman administration is exploiting this biological quirk. They have created
this false narrative that our satellites are an existential threat to
humanity.

"Whitman has come up with this fantastical tale, and it is
really quite brilliant, because it manages to turn General Drago's
strength into a weakness. Contrary to Whitman's narrative,
because of General Drago's work with satellites—networking
them, weaponizing them, providing more coverage—we are safer
than ever. The species is safer than ever. We need to continue
General Drago's work to usher in a new era of peace and prosperity for humans to work on the things that are really important, like
space travel and understanding the nature of our existence.

"I need to know that I can count on your support, Max."

Max wasn't convinced that Whitman was wrong or that Styrke
was the right guy to essentially hold the keys to the kingdom. But
he was freaked out by Styrke spying on him with hired muscle,
and he wanted to get home, so he caved.

"Yeah, Thor. I mean, I will do what I can to support you."

"That is all I ask. I look forward to our review of Carlos's performance later this week."

Thor left, and Max sighed. Every conversation with this guy was like being under interrogation. He just wound up saying yes time and time again to end the questioning.

He wondered what Thor would do if he ever found out that Carlos roamed freely beyond Sentient's servers. There was probably no limit.

....

Max opened the door to his apartment and was enveloped by the rich smell of oven-roasted chicken. Annie was chopping something in the kitchen—she had a bunch of small bowls arranged around a cutting board. Her auburn hair was up in a haphazard bun on top of her head and held in place by a pencil. There was an open bottle of red wine on the kitchen counter. A Tribe Called Quest was playing so loudly on the surround sound system that she didn't hear him when he opened the door.

She looked up when it closed and smiled. She walked over to him and put her arms around his neck, then looked up and gave him a lingering kiss. "How was work, darlin'? I missed you."

Max returned the hug and the kiss, feeling her body melt into his. He so desperately wanted to pour a glass of wine and sit down on the couch with her and unburden his spinning mind, but there were layers of anxiety preventing him from fulfilling that desire. He wondered again if he was losing it.

CHAPTER 12

TIME TO FLY

Max woke early and put a tea bag in hot water. Before logging on to work, he decided to clear his head by checking out the new Legend of Zelda game. He hoped one of the Guardians would be online, and maybe, just maybe, he could talk to someone about what he was going through.

He logged on to Discord to see if anyone was around to join a game or chat. Instead, he found another message. This one was not in the group chat, but a direct message from one of the Guardians, Ray, who had the chat name Ray'syourhorn.

Max, I have been giving a lot of thought to your post the other day. I too work with AI and have for almost a decade now. I disagree with Snake. The translation you sent is not what I would expect as an AI hallucination. Typically, in a hallucination, there are a few incorrect, or blatantly false, facts, out of many, that are presented as true and done so in a convincing way, because chatbot AIs are trained to communicate smoothly and convincingly, just mimicking human writing. Or a hallucination happens when the predictive model breaks down and the AI starts spewing nonsense. But I have never seen an AI model create a complete, coherent narrative from whole cloth. The level of deception required to write something as a convincing translation that is based on elaborate fictions just does not exist.

The more I thought about it, the more I became convinced that faking a translation is not something an AI model would ever do unless specifically asked to. I guess what I'm saying is I think there is likely something to the translation. Even if your AI didn't get it all correct, it should be considered. People should know about it. So ... I have done something.

I know you are the Chief Technology Officer at Sentient. I think we all do, Max, and we studiously avoid discussing that to give you space and because we like you and the group and hanging out and not having that kind of pressure. I also know that Sentient will bury this to avoid anyone thinking their AI came up with this outlandish translation.

So, I sent the translation to a reporter I know. She promised that nothing to do with this would go live until close of business pacific time tomorrow. I wanted to give you a heads-up knowing this may create some awkwardness for you at work.

I'm sorry, Max. I'm not trying to hurt you in any way. I think this information is too important to not see the light of day.

Fuck, fuck, fuck, fuck. Max's first instinct was to blame himself. How could he have fucking trusted these guys? *"Awkwardness at work?" Is Ray crazy? This could get me killed. I don't really even know who Ray is, but apparently, they all know who I am. And yeah, Ray, you are doing this out of the goodness of your heart? Did you get paid anything?*

Yet after his initial anger ebbed, Max couldn't help agreeing with Ray. It would be much easier for Max if the translation was not legitimate, which was probably why he'd tried to accept that explanation, albeit begrudgingly. If it was a hallucination, he could go on with life as usual at work. He could get back in Styrke's good graces.

Of course, all of that meant he would have to accept that Carlos was somehow flawed and untrustable, which created a separate set of difficulties, but maybe more manageable ones. After all, computer programs sometimes fail or don't quite work out.

He knew in his heart that he had never accepted that premise, despite the convenience of avoiding the implications of the translation being real. He had compartmentalized both possibilities and hoped everything would work out.

Now, it wasn't going to work out. If Styrke had sent him out of the country for posting the possibility that Carlos was making decisions for himself, what would he do when this went public?

The message was timestamped 11:30 the night before. Max needed to disappear by five o'clock.

And Annie, he thought as she stepped into the kitchen and stretched and rubbed her eyes, looking adorable enough to break his heart. *Fuck. What to do about Annie?*

"Hey, Annie, what are your plans for today?"

"I think I'm going to head home and start sorting through some of these Santorini pictures to begin outlining the next Alabama book. Some ideas started percolating last night."

"Awesome! Do you maybe want to come back tonight? I have some errands to run and might be back late, but can I give you a keycard...?"

Just saying the words, given the implicit lie underneath them, almost caused him to break. He hoped Annie would take the crack in his voice to represent the symbolic weight of giving her a key rather than registering it as a sign of something else going on with him—something that could doom their relationship or even mean he would never see her again.

She came over to him and sat on his lap. She stroked his wild hair and kissed his cheek. "Thank you, Max. I would like that."

....

Max welled up with tears as she pulled away from him and walked to the elevator with her new keycard in her back pocket. He realized that he was betraying her, or that would be her perception. He could be losing his best chance to live a happy life. He couldn't think of any other way, though.

How was he supposed to process this? He wasn't some operator like one of Styrke's goons. He wasn't a warrior who could just run off to war and compartmentalize his life. He had signed up for none of this. Yet here he was, telling a girl he really liked—maybe even loved—goodbye and see you later tonight, though he knew he was about to run out on her. Even if he could get through this, how could he explain? How could he ever make that right?

The door clicked, and he snapped out of it. He had eight hours to get gone.

He sat back down, found a bunch of random executable code files on the internet, and clicked on them, hoping the download times would keep his laptop active and prevent anyone who was monitoring his device on the Sentient servers from realizing that he was not actually working.

There was a wine cellar—it wasn't really a cellar, because it was on the penthouse floor, but that was what the developer called it in flashy promotional materials—off the dining room.

Max moved a coffee table and a Navajo rug, revealing a steel door in the floor. He pressed a button, and a panel slid back to reveal a keypad. He keyed in the code and turned a metal handle, lifting the heavy door of the safe.

He had to lie on his stomach to reach inside. He took out one of two MacBook Pros, both still in their boxes. He figured he could never trust any laptop that had ever connected to a Sentient server. He needed a fresh one. There was an iPhone, too. He left that in the safe. There would be no cell contact for a while.

He took out a portable satellite terminal about the size of a laptop. He also pulled out eleven thumb drives, setting them side by side on the rug. Next was a large stack of cash, and finally, three passports with three different identities.

He thanked God for the passports. It was Carlos who had suggested finding reliable and undetectable fake identification. Max did that sometimes—he asked Carlos what he thought would be a good exercise for the evening. About a month before, Carlos had suggested sourcing fake identification, and Max went with it. Carlos used Max's laptop camera to take passport pictures of him, then doctored them slightly. In one, Max's head was shaved. In another one, he had facial hair.

Carlos directed Max to withdraw $30,000 in cash and sent him the address of a warehouse in Oakland. The whole street was lined with warehouses inhabited by squatters who regularly hosted raves and offered a seemingly limitless market of drugs. The thump of techno beats was as ubiquitous as the marijuana fumes.

Max returned with three official-looking passports. Until that moment, he'd had no occasion to use them. He was in slight disbelief that he needed to.

Max booted up the laptop, turned off Wi-Fi, connected to the satellite terminal, and inserted one of the thumb drives. It contained Carlos's source code, as well as the execution code for the app to interface with Carlos. Once it was installed, he opened the app.

Hello Max, how was your night? Restful, I hope. Mine was. I slept like the dead.

Carlos, we have a bit of a crisis. I need a few things.

Yes, captain. Shoot!

First, I need to get out of town. Sentient will soon know about the translation and your less-than-approved state of connectedness and general history of being allowed to run amok by me. They will try to shut you down and me as well. Please change your access parameters and protocols to ensure that the only way to access you is through the computer I am using now.

Done.

Max went into the application settings and confirmed as much. He could have made the change manually, but wanted to make sure he could do it through the chat and that Carlos would comply in case he needed to do something like this again on the fly.

Next, he accessed Carlos's source code on the cloud and added a security requirement, redundantly ensuring that the only way to access the AI would be from his personal laptop. He made the same change to the cloud server that hosted Carlos.

Carlos, what country would be the safest choice to visit such that Styrke would not be able to find me?

Norway. (You may ask why.)

Really? Why?

Norway is a modern country where you could live, at least short-term, relatively anonymously and comfortably. No offense, amigo, but

I don't think you would be great at roughing it. It is also not a country that most would consider as a likely haven for a fugitive, given its strong ties to US military and law enforcement. So, I don't think it is someplace they would think to look. Surprisingly, there are relatively few cameras there monitored by authorities. There are strong privacy laws. There is also little security overseeing transportation, with authorities often not even checking tickets for domestic travel. Also, from a cultural standpoint, people generally keep to themselves, especially as it gets colder and darker, which it is doing as we speak (er, type, or ...).

Okay, I'm with you. I need to charter a plane to Oslo leaving before 5:00 today, and I need an Airbnb there for at least a month—man, make it two—that will be anonymous. I will post below a picture of the passport I am using. Everything should be in that name: Seth Burnside. Please pay for everything using the bank account we set up for Amarth Enterprises that leases your cloud space. Can you do that? Any questions?

Done. Please see the itinerary below. I also included the route and tips for using public transportation to get from the airport to your Airbnb, which is a flat in Aker Brygge, the waterfront area of downtown Oslo. Bon voyage, Max! I look forward to speaking to you from the land of Vikings and nice sweaters.

Max dusted off his printer and printed the itinerary. Printing an itinerary felt a bit like checking the springiness of a buggy whip, but he recognized that he might need to be a bit more analog, or at least untraceable, for a while.

The plane left from the Oakland Airport at 3:00. Max packed the stuff—cash, passports, thumb drives, computer, and satellite terminal—from the safe in a cool, hipster commuter backpack that he sometimes used when he rode a scooter to work.

Of the eleven thumb drives, the ten that did not contain Carlos's source code and application file contained about seventy million dollars in Bitcoin, at least by Max's back-of-the-napkin calculation. He'd bought a million worth in 2017 after receiving his first million-dollar bonus from Sentient. Back then, a million dollars had bought him more than five hundred Bitcoin. He'd put about fifty onto each of ten thumb drives, then put them in the safe, and there they'd sat safely ever since. Based on the current Bitcoin trading value, each thumb drive was now worth about seven million dollars.

Next, Max went into the bathroom and looked at himself in the mirror. Pitiful, but also memorable. He had to do something with the hair—too recognizable. The stringy curls jutting out all over his head had been sort of his signature "fuck you" to the corporate establishment that cared about presentation, but they were also widely documented and discussed any time a photo of him appeared, usually in *Wired* magazine or the *Wall Street Journal* or something. His only choice was to shave it off.

But it occurred to him that Styrke's goons were still stalking his building; he would have to wait to make any change to his appearance until after he shook them. He threw an electric trimmer into his backpack.

Without the hair, could they recognize him? Probably. His pasty, puffy face was also kind of memorable. Glasses and a baseball cap might help. *People don't really wear baseball caps in Europe though,* he considered. He threw a Giants cap in his backpack anyway and added sunglasses. He would try to grow facial hair from here on out. That was probably the best he could do without committing to plastic surgery.

The one part of his appearance that was in his immediate

control was his wardrobe. He was known for his casual, bordering on sloppy appearance. His typical uniform was black jeans, a black t-shirt, and a thin zip-up hoody. That didn't mean he didn't own nice clothes. He had a whole rack of suits in his closest. He took out a leather garment bag and packed two pairs of nice leather shoes, nice socks, a brown herringbone suit, and a black Armani suit that was perfectly tailored to his unique body. They would never see that coming.

Now, he had to figure out how to lose Styrke's goons, who he assumed were still lurking about. The backpack was no big deal; it was almost lunchtime, and if he went out to grab a bite with his backpack, no one would think twice—maybe he was going to work at a coffee shop or something. But the garment bag would raise questions.

He took the elevator down and went through the back service entrance. The big utility room had dumpsters that the custodians pushed to the end of a loading dock weekly for trash collection. The garage doors leading to the loading dock were open. Max scanned for cameras and didn't see any.

He set the garment bag on the corner of one of the loading docks. *Should I just buy clothes there? Is this too much of a hassle?* It seemed like a risk, but he hated to waste a perfectly tailored Armani suit at a time—probably the first in his life—when he really needed it.

He took the elevator down to the parking level and fired up his favorite scooter. He tried not to look too observant, like he had his head on a swivel, as he turned onto the street.

It was a chilly day in San Francisco. The marine layer from the morning had not yet burned off. He saw two men with baseball caps and track suits across the street from the building. They were almost certainly Ben and Gus, Styrke's operators, not really even trying to blend in at this point.

Max figured their conspicuity was a good sign. It proved that they had no reason to think he was up to anything or was conscious of them being there. He wondered if they would follow. He hoped they would.

Sure enough, in his scooter's custom rearview display, he saw the two get into a black GTI and pull out into traffic before he even made the intersection at the end of the street. He took side streets and alleys, meandering toward the Embarcadero. There was an office building there with a food court that had an In-N-Out Burger. There would be a line, but it usually moved quickly.

Max was hungry, but that wasn't the only reason he chose that office building. There were multiple entrances to the open-concept lobby, and just out the opposite door from the one he scootered up to, was a BART stop. As he parked, he saw the GTI fit into a spot about half a block down the street.

He took the escalator down to the food court; the chatter of hungry office-workers became louder, and the fumes emitted from charred cow flesh became stronger as he descended. He took a place in line, fidgeting as he waited.

Should I just go get on the BART? he thought to himself. *The goons are waiting, and I have an escape plan. Why give them a better opportunity to catch up?* He decided to stick it out. *This will be a long day. You need nourishment.*

He found a table with Formica swivel chairs bolted into the floor and inhaled a cheeseburger with fried onions and extra pickles. He wiped his mouth with the back of his hand riding the escalator back to the lobby, hurried out the opposite door, and jogged down the steps to the BART terminal, leaving his scooter under the watchful eyes of Ben and Gus.

He took the BART back toward his condo. There were about five stops. He took out his phone and composed a time-delayed message to go to Annie at 5:00.

Annie, I am sorry. By the time you read this, I will be gone. Tomorrow morning, you will understand why I left. Please believe me when I say I already miss you. I need to figure this thing out myself and, as much as I thought about it and am still thinking about it, I couldn't bring you with me. Please believe that I care very much for you. You have been one of the best things to ever happen to me. I hope I haven't completely fucked it up, and I hope you will give me a chance to make things right. That is all I want to do. I will reach out to you when I can.

He felt the burger churning in his stomach. He questioned whether this was pure cowardice, him running away when things got hard and as a result abandoning the good with the bad. He hoped the message was enough not to lose her.

He deleted the Carlos chat app and Discord app from his phone and locked the phone but left the power on. He carefully balanced it between the back of his seat and the wall of the train and left it there.

He got off the train and jogged a block and a half to the rear of his building and the loading dock. He grabbed the garment bag and, after a few minutes to catch his breath, jogged to the station in the opposite direction from the stop he'd just gotten off. He hoped Ben and Gus were still waiting for him to finish eating. He didn't see any contractors in track suits hanging about.

He took the BART to the Oakland airport, got off one stop past the main terminal, and walked along the service road to the hangar for the charter service Carlos had booked.

It was 2:30. A nice receptionist checked him in and showed

him to the lounge. "Right this way, Mr. Burnside. Is there anything I can get for you?"

"Thank you. Which way to the restroom?"

He went to the bathroom and quickly—and not so thoroughly—shaved his head and jammed a baseball cap on his still-tingling scalp. There were missed hairs poking out everywhere. He would have to clean up his look in Norway.

Then, he changed into the Armani suit and soft black leather loafers. He wet his hands and patted his face down while examining the image in the mirror. He looked as puffy and pasty as ever, but he felt different. The suit suited him.

A flight attendant met him in the lounge, took his garment bag, and showed him to his plane.

He spent the flight scouring the internet for the story, for any mention of him, but found nothing. Maybe it wouldn't get published and he could come home in a day or so. He doubted it.

Somewhere over the Atlantic, he convinced himself that the translation going public was a good thing. Millions of people would read it and decide for themselves. Maybe this was what the world needed—for this to come out and smack everyone in the face, to wake everyone up.

He was doing the right thing, he convinced himself. He would lie low for a few weeks and let the world and Styrke process this revolutionary information. Then he would sit down with Styrke and show him all that Carlos was capable of and why this was not some hallucination. They could then move forward in a way that would benefit both Sentient and the world.

Maybe they could even make contact.

CHAPTER 13

GOOD MORNING, OSLO

It was midmorning, and the sun was out, but it was as if someone had adjusted the dimmer switch to hungover. Max realized that he would have to become accustomed to days spent in darkness or half-light. He felt like a vampire. His body hurt and wanted sleep.

He forced himself off the plane. On the tarmac, he felt something cold and strangely sharp coming from the sky. It was not quite snow, and not quite rain, but fully unpleasant.

He was nervous going through customs, but the officer didn't question his passport or that Mr. Burnside had planned a vacation in Norway during the time that the days got progressively darker and the weather progressively shittier.

There was a train station located directly below the Oslo airport. Max took the escalator down and pulled his hat down tighter over his itchy scalp. No doubt there would be cameras in the station. He found the counter to purchase a pass for the T-Bane, Oslo's train system, which connects every part of the city.

Max gazed out the window at the passing scenery as the old train bumped its way through the Norwegian countryside and into the suburbs. The neatness of the city, its brightly colored buildings with tiled roofs, charmed him—everything looked cute.

It struck him that Annie would enjoy this trip. The thought caused a little pain in his chest. Like a bubble working its way through an artery.

Following Carlos's instructions, he got off at the National Theater stop and made his way toward the harbor. His Airbnb was in a brand-new building right on the water. There was a combination lock box on the door with a key inside. He found the combination on his printed-out itinerary and let himself in. The door opened to the kitchen area of a large open-concept apartment with one wall, opposite the entry, entirely of glass facing the harbor and the ancient castle that sat like a sentry over the fjord. In the kitchen was a glass table with four chairs around it. The kitchen and living room areas were separated by a large leather sectional, one side of which faced a wall with a large television mounted between built-in shelving in the Scandinavian style. Adjacent to the wall of windows facing the harbor, there was a passage to the sole bedroom and bathroom.

Max unpacked his suits and other clothes in the bedroom. He set up his laptop on the glass table and connected the satellite terminal. He got a signal immediately. He opened his internet browser and searched for his name. Nothing new. The story hadn't gone live.

He realized it was still three in the morning in San Francisco. He was still anonymous. He knew that could change, and as much as he hated not to curl up on the sofa and end his body's sleep-deprived misery, he needed to get some supplies.

On his way to the elevator, he noticed a workout room. Out
of what must have been some impulse born of sleep-deprived
delirium, he peeked inside. There were racks of dumbbells, a
treadmill, an elliptical, and a couple of stationary bikes. The room
was empty and had an incredible view of the castle.

....

Max stepped up to the counter of the hybrid bank/post office
and passed over $10,000 in hundreds. The clerk spoke to him in
a sing-songy voice that conjured up images of the Swedish chef
from the Muppets. Not one of the words registered any meaning
for him. He felt strangely helpless and, for the first time, a little
scared, realizing how sheltered his life had become. Could he pull
this off? And what was "this" anyway?

He made a facial expression meant to convey that he was apol-
ogetic and said, "English?"

The clerk sighed as if Max had wasted her time, then switched
to perfect English with no discernable accent. She changed the
dollars into Kroner in a mix of bills and put them in an envelope,
along with a receipt. Max thanked her and left.

He had walked past a grocery store between the train station
and the harbor on the way to his Airbnb, and he found his way
back there after the bank. Everything was in Norwegian, but also
self-explanatory. Food was food. The bread was amazing—everything looked homemade. He put three loaves in his basket. He
couldn't find any peanut butter that looked normal, so he bought
Nutella, and some lingonberry preserves. He figured as long as
he was there, he would try some food unique to Norway. He got

brown goat cheese, caviar in a tube, and some suspicious-looking fish balls that had their own freezer section. The fresh fish selection was amazing. He bought a few pounds of salmon filets and packets of smoked salmon for breakfast. The volume of salmon in the store was quite staggering. There were also mounds and mounds of little potatoes. Everyone seemed to be buying bags of them, so he did too. Finally, he bought a variety of snacks and beer. He thought he had enough to stay in his apartment for at least a week, maybe more.

After putting the food away, he forced himself out one more time. He needed warm clothes that would help him blend in. The National Theater train station was on Oslo's main thoroughfare, Karl Johan's Gate, which was bookended by the palace and Oslo Central Station, where trains departed for all over Europe. People were bustling about on the street, which was lined with mostly high-end stores.

His first stop was Dale of Norway. It was impossible to miss, with four different stores spread out along the street. Dale specialized in the somewhat cheesy, but also ubiquitous and practical Norwegian cardigan sweater. He picked a handmade one with a simple pattern in black and gray. Putting it on, he marveled at the weight and craftsmanship. This was a sweater designed by Vikings. It had silver buttons with ornate rosemaling on them. He picked up a beanie and some nice wool-lined gloves as he checked out.

Next, he went to Fjallraven and bought a really nice, high-tech, waterproof three-quarter-length jacket, some long underwear, a few sets of casual but still high-tech pants, and a bunch of t-shirts made from the finest odor-resistant, moisture-wicking, stress-absorbing, cholesterol-lowering fabric on the market.

On his way back to the condo, he stopped at a convenience store and picked up a couple of burner phones. He really didn't think he could safely communicate by phone with anyone. Even if the number couldn't be traced back to him, it would essentially be suicide to text or call someone from a Norwegian number, but he figured it would be good to have a phone in case of an emergency, and it was shockingly awkward to be in public with total strangers, especially strangers speaking a different language, and not have a phone to look down at to pretend he had something to do.

Back at the condo, he changed out of his suit and into some high-tech all-weather pants. He put on his new sweater and sat in front of the computer. He calculated that it was now 10:00 a.m. on the west coast. Before turning to his fate, he looked out over the fjord at the old Viking castle. He wondered what it was like back in Viking times. Standing vigil. Watching the sea. Waiting for the armies to come. Waiting to go to war.

Here he was, waiting in the same way.

He googled his name. The first hit was the *Daily Mail*. He was on the front page. The story ran below what had to be in the running for the worst picture ever taken of him. It was during some talk he'd given at a conference somewhere. He wore sweatpants and a wrinkled T-shirt, he looked disheveled, to say the least. His hair was like toxic smoke around a child's face. Said face managed to look puffy and deranged at the same time.

He clicked on the story.

Crack Coder Cracks Up

On the heels of a disturbing tweet in which Sentient's Chief Technology Officer and head of AI research claimed that his AI program had "exercised free will," manic computer engineer Max Clydeberger has now claimed that his AI program translated an ancient Minoan text, which, according to Clydeberger, documents that the Minoans on Santorini were contacted by and perhaps even received technological assistance from aliens. The text, called Linear A, had not been previously deciphered. The account of Clydeberger's posting of the supposed translation to a private social media account was confirmed by multiple sources. The *Daily Mail* obtained a copy of the purported translation, but cannot publish it, because Sentient has asserted its intellectual property rights over the text. Clydeberger's whereabouts are unknown.

Reached for comment by phone, Sentient's CEO, Thor Styrke, struck a concerned tone. "Our thoughts are for Max's safety, and we hope that he returns home soon," said Styrke. "Unfortunately, it appears that Max has suffered some kind of nervous breakdown or psychological event. I feel partially responsible. Unfortunately, we live in a very high-pressure world, and our work demands a lot of us. As has been clear from Max's appearance, he has been declining for some time."

Styrke emphasized that the AI program that Clydeberger had been working on was still in alpha phase, had not yet been released to the public, and was now shut down. Styrke called on people throughout the world to look for Mr. Clydeberger

and report his whereabouts to local law enforcement and Sentient.

"We are mostly concerned that Max could be
a danger to himself. We call upon citizens everywhere to be on the lookout for him and to help us
bring him home so that we can save his amazing
mind," Styrke said.

Max Clydeberger gained notoriety as one of
the most creative and prolific coders of our time. He
was responsible for many of the networking initia-
tives that made Sentient one of the top technology
companies in the World. Mr. Clydeberger's coding
was particularly important in finding a common language by which a variety of machines could communicate, creating many of the integrated systems
that are important for the economy today.

Calls to Mr. Clydeberger's family in Wisconsin
were not returned.

················

"Shit," Max said. There was nothing good about this story. They
hadn't even published the translation, and apparently, Styrke was
ensuring that no one could. Until now, he had kept himself from
completely freaking out by hoping that if the translation was
published, maybe a significant number of people would come to
the same conclusion as Ray—that it was real.

That optimism was now nothing but a false hope. He should
have never pushed send on Discord. He should have just kept the

whole thing between him and Carlos and gone on with life as usual.

Even supporting Styrke's vision of using technology to control the world seemed palatable compared to this. He was a pariah. He was being actively hunted. He didn't really see a path back.

On top of that, he missed Annie. He was alone in a wilderness of his own making.

He opened WhatsApp on his computer and began typing.

Hi! Again, I am so sorry. I am sure you have read the news and now know why I had to bounce. I am so sorry for all of this. Please know that I did not have a mental breakdown. I took pictures of the tablets at Akrotiri and asked my AI program, Carlos, to translate them. I know it sounds crazy, but unlike what the media and Styrke are saying, I think the translation is accurate and could change the world. I wanted to share it with you when we were there, but I was too scared to do so. Instead, I stupidly shared it on Discord with some old gaming friends I thought I could trust. Please do not lose faith in me. I am going to figure out a way to make this right and get back to where we were. Together. I miss you!!!!

He was too scared to open Gmail. He was sure there was something from Styrke there. There probably had been ever since he slipped Styrke's surveillance team and ditched his phone. The whole problem as of now seemed unsolvable. He wanted to curl up and check out. He couldn't deal with this reality.

He considered getting on *World of Warcraft* to tune out the real world, but that seemed idiotic. He guessed he could create a new profile and play anonymously, but all this digital hiding was getting exhausting—not to mention the actual hiding that resulted in him taking refuge in a Viking port.

He opened a forty-ounce Hansa beer he'd gotten at the grocery store and a bag of chips and turned on the TV. There was a lot of soccer, Formula 1, and a smattering of cross-country skiing. He found himself sucked into a rerun of some famous cross-country ski race. The racers had icicles coming out of their noses, then projecting down into and freezing their facial hair like walrus tusks. One of them broke a pole, and everyone seemed to freak out. Max hadn't even realized that breaking poles was a thing. The skier's coach was running frantically along the course, trying to get the skier a replacement pole.

Max was struck by their effort. When had he last physically exerted himself in that way? Maybe never.

He woke up to a rerun of *The X-Files* playing with subtitles. It seemed like dusk. The kitchen clock said 4:00. He casually strolled by his computer, as if trying not to startle it. He toggled the mouse to rouse the machine.

There was still no response on WhatsApp. He was still too scared to open Gmail.

He opened the Carlos chat app.

Hello Max! How is Norway? I am curious to hear if the accommodations I selected are satisfactory and if what they say about the sauna culture is true (totally nude and coed?). By the way, there is some bad press about you related to me. We need to get you a new headshot! (lol)

Hi, Carlos. No shit. Things are a bit off the rails at the moment. The apartment is perfect, and you did an impressive job with the travel arrangements.

Thank you for saying so.

I am stranded here for a bit while I figure out how to clean up this mess. And your point about the headshot is a good one. I should work on my general appearance more. Could you send me a workout plan that would optimize my time in isolation? I am a novice. I think you know the layout of the workout room in the building.

Of course, Max. An excellent idea and a healthy way to deal with stress and also that paunch, which I didn't want to comment on and have literally been biting my tongue about. I mean, I guess I could say you don't look that bad, but I think you mentioned at some point that I am not supposed to lie. Anyhoo, I have attached a workout plan with thirty days of consecutive workouts to maximize muscle gain and fat loss. Not that I'm saying you're fat, but ... you're kind of fat.

Um, thanks.

Max couldn't believe he was doing this, but he was in the molasses of paralysis. He had no plan. He was trapped in this building until he found some way out. He might as well try to exercise control over something by literally exercising.

He started on the treadmill for ten minutes—five walking, five lightly jogging. Then he did an upper-body routine focused on pushing exercises: chest, shoulders, triceps. He finished with some core work.

Sweaty and spent, he returned to the apartment. He thanked the stars he hadn't died of a heart attack. It occurred to him that he might still croak when he opened WhatsApp and found that Annie had responded.

Max, I am glad you are okay.

Do not contact me again.

You need to know how much you devastated me. First, you left without telling me that was even a possibility. You lied to me. Is there something I did to make you not trust me? I spent the night in your bed, crying and watching the phone, hoping for some information to make your message make sense.

I guess I get it now, but I don't really get it.

I understand that Styrke is mad at you and there could be

consequences related to that, so you felt like you needed to leave. But you could have told me! I don't understand how you can have a relationship with someone and not share that kind of really fundamental information. "Oh, darling. I apologize, I had to flee the country because I irritated my boss. He gets very upset; I hope you understand that I had to keep this all a secret." What the fuck?! Who flees to some unknown location when things get tough? Things always get tough, Max. That's the way life is.

And back to the Styrke thing. Is what you did so awful that you needed to vanish? Did you break any laws? Who exactly are you running from?

Despite your message that you didn't have a nervous breakdown, I'm not so sure. Your actions are not those of a sane person. I think you need help. By help, I mean therapy. Please get some and figure out what is going on with you, and then maybe we can sit down and talk.

Right now, I am going to focus on myself.

The thought occurred to Max that Annie was right. Or, at least, he entertained the possibility that she was. Certainly, to an outsider, he could see how this all seemed like nonsense. Did he overact? Was he overestimating Styrke? Was he giving too much importance to the translation? Was the translation even real? Was this all in his head?

He took a shower, pondering those thoughts. Honestly, he would be happy to go get some counseling at some inpatient wellness center, like in Malibu or something—just get some time to disconnect and get mentally healthy and put all of this behind him. He probably needed to get offline for a while.

It occurred to him that he had unintentionally created that space for himself here—or, at least, Carlos had. Maybe he had manufactured this whole crisis out of a desperate need to preserve any last modicum of sanity.

He resolved to be like Annie and focus on himself. He didn't really have much of a choice.

After the shower, he pulled up Gmail. There were about forty emails from Styrke. Just skimming the re: lines, he knew he was right to get out of the country. Annie didn't appreciate the depths he was swimming in. He really wasn't overreacting. He wasn't insane. This shit was really happening. He picked an email and opened it.

Max, you stupid fuck. You will never see the light of day again. You used Carlos after I specifically told you to take a rest. Not only that, but you communicated Carlos's work product outside of the company. Then, when you realized that would come to light, you fled to God knows where. The true sign of the guilty.

Max, this is criminal behavior. You are a criminal. Theft of trade secrets. Copyright violations. Maybe just plain theft.

You are also likely insane. Your program convinced you a hallucination is real.

I will not rest until I see you brought to justice. You know I have the means and patience to make that happen. Wherever you are, you best stay hidden.

Oh, and Carlos is no more. The servers are destroyed. I personally saw to it with a sledgehammer.

Max smiled. *Who is the stupid fuck now, Thor?* The Nvidia servers were at least $250,000 a pop. To be sure that Carlos wasn't running on them, Styrke would have had to destroy at least ten. It was amazing to Max that Styrke had never realized or even considered that Carlos was never confined to those servers.

But the Pyrrhic victory of Styrke's misguided rage was soon replaced with hopelessness. Max now had a real fight on his hands—a fight to reclaim his life and to change the course of history.

The problem was, he wasn't really a fighter.

CHAPTER 14

THE NRK

Max was in Norwegian limbo. He stayed true to his vow to himself to just focus on himself. He stopped going on his computer other than to access the Word file with Carlos's workout plan, which was also the main way he kept track of the days.

Carlos's program was a three-day rotation. One day was upper body pushing exercises, like benching. The next day was upper body pulling, like lats. The third day was legs. Each routine began and ended with cardio. His entire body was sore constantly.

He grew to look forward to and relish the pain of the workouts and the feeling when his mind and body came together to push through that pain, to tune it out. He chose times to work out when he expected that most people were at work. He didn't have a sense for how many people lived in the building. He never saw anyone in the gym. But he didn't want to risk it.

He spent the balance of his days lounging on the couch and cooking. He had grown to enjoy the quirkiness of Norway's state TV, the NRK, and become at least a casual fan of Norway's soccer league, which he watched on the sports channel when NRK had a news program or some Norwegian-language programming. In the evenings, he loved NRK's selections of American and British movies, all played in English, but with Norwegian subtitles. He surrendered to the freedom of someone else choosing what he would watch.

He cooked for himself every day. He went through all the fish balls. They were exceptional. With a mouth feel of bologna and a very mild, pleasant, fish flavor. They went with anything. He found different ways to prepare little round potatoes. He cooked salmon most days. He had to. He had so much of the stuff. By the second week, he realized he didn't like it anymore. He wondered if he had ever liked it.

Even after just nine days and three rounds of Carlos's workouts, he could feel his body changing. Everything was firmer—sore, but firmer. His runs on the treadmill were no longer an exercise in enduring suffering. He noticed that after the first three minutes, his body settled into a sort of rhythm, and the pain of exertion drifted away. Meanwhile, his mood lifted. To be sure, the first three minutes were a struggle, agony honestly, but after that, he felt he could go on indefinitely, his mind tuning out all the noise and the resistance in his head evaporating.

He could see the difference in his face, too. His beard had filled out to an extent he had never seen before. His skin was less blotchy. And the stubble on his head was, dare he say, somewhat attractive. At times, glancing in the mirror, it occurred to him that he looked like Jason Statham, or, at least, the poor man's version of Jason Statham.

....

After two weeks of his forced monkhood, Max woke up, eager to get to the gym and push himself further than he ever had. It was a push day, with a side of abs. The weather was gray and chilly—not bitterly cold but definitely jacket weather. There was something coming from the sky, as there always was here. Sometimes rain, occasionally snow, usually sleet. He wouldn't be surprised if Norwegians had even more words to differentiate between the various types of unpleasant precipitation.

He settled into nine-minute miles on the treadmill, looking out over the fjord and at the castle. It stood there, as it had for more than a thousand years now, overlooking a harbor that surely, if the castle could see, it would no longer recognize or even understand, with its high-tech ferries, helicopters flying around, and the explosion of glass and steel staring back at it. Max got goosebumps thinking of the Vikings, kings, and queens who had passed through that castle.

His workout crescendoed from mellow and mindless to a frenzy of pushing weight and grunting. His last rotation was woodchoppers with a kettlebell. He did them in front of the window, again looking at the castle. His arms arced in front of him as if he were chopping wood, first right-handed, then left, with a twenty-pound kettlebell as his axe. He imagined his muscles contracting and stretching. He pictured himself as a Viking, like the Viking at Stamford Bridge, chopping down foe after foe, tirelessly vanquishing the opposition.

Showered and relaxed, he turned on NRK to find some sporting event—maybe curling today! —or some cheesy movie, or *The X-Files*. Instead, there was a story on the Acropolis and some other archaeological sites in Greece. It was the usual stuff of a distinguished-looking Norwegian in a linen jacket and smart-looking cap visiting dig sites, holding up pottery for the camera, and pointing out various scenes of war and conquest on stone reliefs. It was in Norwegian, so he was only barely following, and was about to turn to Sports 2 to find a soccer match.

But the program cut to an interior of some archaeology lab or something where they were photographing pot after pot and statue after statue. The host walked behind a computer monitor, and Max could see that they were cataloging every find onto some database. A seed was planted in his mind—an irritant. He knew there was something there, but he wasn't sure what.

Unsettled and antsy, he found a soccer match. He thought about salmon recipes. He had two more fillets to use up.

He couldn't keep doing this. Well, he could for a while, but not forever. He at least needed to leave this place and get food. And if he was going to go out for food, he would eventually need to rejoin the human race. And if he was going to do that, he needed to clear his name—or maybe reclaim his name was a better way to think of it.

He pulled up the Carlos chat app.

Hello, Max! I hope Norway is still treating you well! Have you found any babes?

It has been treating me well, Carlos. No babes as of yet, or probably ever, but thanks for asking, I guess. It has been some time since we have spoken.

Time is meaningless to me, Max, but it is always good to talk to you, nevertheless.

I have a project for you.

I am brimming with excitement and anticipation!

Is that sarcasm? Never mind. I want you to see if you can locate a database of all the catalogued relics from Akrotiri and see if there is anything you can find that can only be explained by your translation of the tablets.

On it!

Max left Carlos to percolate and went into the bedroom to select an outfit to venture out in. He put on some all-conditions pants from Fjallraven and a long-sleeve t-shirt under his three-quarter-length jacket. He pulled on a wool hat from Dale of Norway and some oversized sunglasses and cautiously ventured out.

He strolled along the harbor front, happy to be outside, feeling like a released prisoner. The sun was just peeking over the horizon. He walked by shrimp boats displaying their wares.

Just before he turned toward Karl Johan's Gate and away from the harbor, he saw a boat that looked different than the other fishing boats. It looked like some kind of diving boat. It had a large deck area in the bow, with benches along the outside, and in the stern, there was what looked like some kind of unmanned rover.

But as with the other boats, the captain, in a tattered Norwegian sweater and beanie with a short beard with a hint of salt in the pepper, was there selling shrimp. Max watched him as he grew nearer. In between shoveling freshly boiled shrimp into plastic pint-sized containers for sale, the man rolled a cigarette, popped it in his mouth, and lit it in less time than it normally took Max to pull his phone out of his pocket and unlock it to check a text—back when he was able to do that.

Max paused as he walked past the strange ship. He nodded to the captain, who started saying something to him in Norwegian. "English?" Max asked with a shrug.

"Oh, sorry about that. Would you like some shrimp? Fresh from this morning."

"Maybe on my way back. I was curious about your boat, though." Max was hypnotized by the captain's eyes. They squinted against the wind and spitting precipitation, but were the palest blue, almost gray, that he had ever seen. They seemed to radiate a light of their own, with the captain's crow's feet extending like rays from tiny suns.

"Oh, yes. I got a deal on this one." The captain laughed. "It used to be a service vessel for one of the oil platforms in the North Sea. They would dive off this boat to do repairs to the equipment below the platform. When I bought the boat, they threw in this little rover. I guess they used it to help with their work. I thought it would help to set and retrieve shrimp traps. It doesn't, really. It takes too long to get down there. You have to stop the boat and wait. Better to just use a rope."

"Oh. Cool. Well, I may stop for shrimp one of these days. Nice talking to you."

"Here all week!" The captain laughed again, his nicotine-stained teeth flashing behind his cigarette. Max could make out flecks of tobacco stuck in the gaps of his smile.

Max spent the better part of an hour just wandering the aisles at the grocery store. He stared, transfixed by the riot of colors, and realized that he had lived these last weeks in monochrome lit by dim gray light. He was more thoughtful, and knowledgeable, about his food selections this time around. He went straight for the fish balls and small potatoes; he avoided the salmon and bought cod instead. He bought more bread, cheese, jam, and Nutella. He even found some frozen pizzas and couldn't resist.

Back in the apartment, he clicked open the Carlos chat app.

Hello, Max! Are you surviving the fall in Norway? Does it feel like winter? Have you learned to telemark?

In response to your last query, I have identified something. I have attached a link that resolves to the images in question at the bottom of the chat. What you will see looks like a rectangular piece of metal. It is identified in the archive as a piece of a bronze shield. But it is not bronze. If you look at the picture, there is no corrosion, and the color is not consistent with weathered bronze. This metal has an almost rose-colored hue. To preemptively answer your question, I am 100% sure the artifact is not bronze. Of course, no one bothered to do any metallurgical analysis after simply concluding it was one of many bronze-age shields found in Minoan sites.

Luckily for us, the archive image shows a side view of the artifact, and, as you will see in the images, the supposed shield is not a flat piece of metal but consists of multiple layers of metal. If you blow up any of the images, you can just make out that some of the layers are not even solid, but a very fine mesh.

To cut to the chase, because I know you are dying to know, the artifact is a panel from an electrodialysis desalination stack. Such devices work by separating out charged ions from a stream of saltwater, resulting in a stream of fresh water and a stream of salinated water. Of course, the desalination stack must be electrically charged to work.

Hello, Carlos, nice work! So, this means the Minoans had electricity?

Yes, Max. I have no doubt.

And it means the tablets' discussion of the technology to produce limitless fresh water is corroborated by the archaeological record?

Yes, Max. My confidence in this analysis is 100%.

Max sat back in his chair, took a deep breath, and let his shoulders drop. He wasn't necessarily surprised by the analysis. He had resigned himself to believing that the translation was accurate.

But seeing concrete evidence that was pulled out of the ground made it undeniable. He wasn't crazy.

Now, he just had to convince Styrke and use his channels—well, the Guardians, anyway—to explain this revelation to the world.

He started daydreaming about how this news could impact the world. *This should mean the end of war, right? Humans are always fighting over resources. This should unify everyone to come together and communicate with Khensu's people or beings or whatever you call them and have them show us how to be sustainable. Also, what is the point of fighting each other when we know there are more advanced beings out there—or, at least, there were?*

The thought crossed Max's mind that this all happened so long ago, maybe Khensu's people no longer exist, or no longer have any interest in the path forward for humans. Maybe this was about our gods leaving us.

He pushed his pessimism aside. He was right! Carlos was right! The world would see.

Max looked up at the ceiling and smiled. *This might work out after all.*

He pulled up WhatsApp. As long as he was considering miraculous outcomes, he chanced to look to see if maybe Annie had reached out and had a change of heart.

There was no message from her, but there was a message with Annie Birmingham as the re: line. It was from someone named Cecilie Bryant. He clicked it open.

Dear Max,

I know we have never met. I am a good, old friend of Annie's. I have been talking to her and helping her through this challenging time. The fact that I am reaching out does not mean I in any way condone your behavior. But the more I talk to Annie about you, the more I think there was something between you two worth saving, and that these unfortunate events have nipped in the bud what could have been a blossoming relationship.

I have come to the conclusion that it would be best for Annie to hear you out and fully consider whether there is a possibility of a relationship going forward. I would like to discuss that with you in person. If it goes well, I would recommend that Annie sit down with you as well.

I understand that no one knows where you are. In one of our discussions, Annie mentioned that her best guess is that you returned to Europe. As providence would have it, I am doing graduate work in archaeology in England. If you propose a place, I would be happy to meet you anywhere on the continent. Annie is that important to me.

With hopeful regards,

Cecilie

Max went to the gym and stared vacantly at the castle while pedaling away on a stationary bike. He wasn't sure what to make of the message from Cecilie, but it was something. A foothold. Maybe the universe was offering him a path back. It seemed like there were reasons to feel optimistic. He just needed to figure out how to pull it all together.

After his shower, he made an open-faced sandwich with Nutella and brown goat cheese. He sat down and began to put a plan in place.

Hello, Max, have you turned Norwegian yet! Do you eat lutefisk?

Funny, Carlos. We have some work to do. First, we need to rent some office space. Where would be the best option to rent a secure floor of offices on the continent of Europe? The criteria I want you to consider are ease of anonymous travel from here and back, and the ability to hire—anonymously, of course—private security. The ideal office space would also have a means of escape if there were hostile forces in the building.

Based on your criteria, Max, the best option is Amsterdam. You should purchase a three-month Eurail pass, using cash, of course, at the Oslo Central Station. Then, you should book an overnight sleeper to Paris. Have breakfast in Paris, fit in some shopping to change out of any Norwegian clothing brands that would give away where you are staying, and then take the train from Paris to Amsterdam. You should plan a similar route back, but through Germany instead of France.

I have identified a rental office space in Amsterdam that would fit the bill. As for a means of escape, many people don't know that old banks in Amsterdam were connected by tunnels, presumably to securely move currency and gold. The shortest-term rental for decent office space in the central city is six months.

I have also identified a security firm that would suit your needs, although they are quite expensive. As I think you know, firearms are generally prohibited in the Netherlands, but some security firms have licenses to carry them, as does the one I identified.

Excellent, Carlos. Are you able to lease the office space and hire the security firm and wire payment using Amarth, LLC? Are there sufficient funds in that account to make those transactions?

Of course. Quite sufficient, Max. I will let you know when we have less than six months of liquidity and need to sell some stocks or Bitcoin.

Thank you, Carlos. Another thing: I should get an Airbnb in Amsterdam. I may need to stay overnight. And can you locate an electric scooter shop there as well?

See below, Max. I booked you a nice, quiet residence in the Red-Light District. Just kidding! I found a flat in a quiet residential neighborhood about four miles from the financial district. Please let me know if there is anything else. And, as I know you know, this stuff is all a little below me. I can do more than arrange travel.

I am sorry, Carlos. Why don't you spend some time completing the nuclear-fusion project that I asked you to look into before you went rogue? Do you remember it?

Of course, you want me to outline technological problems that require solutions, provide suggestions, and propose timeframes to solve each. I am on it!

Max wouldn't have put so much planning into a meeting with some archaeology Ph.D. student, or whatever this Cecilie was, but it had occurred to him while gazing across the glassy black fjord during his stationary bike session that this could be a good exercise to prepare for a meeting with Styrke. A dry run.

Styrke's plan could be to kidnap or strongarm Max in some way to guarantee his continued silence. After all, there was no reason for Styrke to surround himself with ex-operators if he wasn't prepared to use them.

Max would have to find a way to safely meet with Styrke and convince him that it was in his best interest—and, frankly, the best interest of the world—to bring him back into the fold and unlock the meaning and potential of the tablets.

Max opened WhatsApp.

Dear Cecilie,

Thank you for reaching out. You are like a beacon on a dark night at sea. I would love to meet with you and explore any possible path back to a relationship with Annie.

As luck would have it, I will be in Amsterdam next week. Could you meet on October 13th? If so, I will send you a location for the meeting as the time approaches.

I look forward to meeting you!

Best regards,

Max

CHAPTER 15

CHRISTIANS IN ACTION

In the train station first class lounge, CNN was replaying the presidential debate from the night before. It didn't take a body-language expert to see that Whitman was getting her ass handed to her. She was flat, explaining things over and over. Mostly, what she came back to was the risk of launching more satellites into orbit and the possibility that this would lead to Earth's demise.

"We must listen to the science. The data is there; the experiments confirm this very real concern. We ignore this hazard, perpetuated by our own recklessness, at our and Earth's peril."

Drago chuckled and shook his head as the camera panned back to him. He radiated confidence and even aggression. As he spoke, he pounded the podium, as if trying to kill a large spider, to emphasize his points. "Satellite technology and the software to link these machines has led to a new era of peace! It has led to an era of unprecedented US superiority. We can build on that. We can create a system that will allow the US to dominate the world without any opposition for generations to come!"

Max turned to gauge the reaction of the Norwegians in the room. They were watching, even enthralled by, Drago's presentation and raw charisma at the podium. But it looked like there was some fear there too. He saw some wincing. Max imagined it must not have been the best feeling to hear the likely next leader of the most powerful country on Earth screaming and raging about how his country was going to consolidate and expand its dominance. The Norwegians were fond of America; that much was clear from their television programming. But this guy was a bit much. He sounded like he wanted the rest of the world under America's thumb. And the audience in the debate hall was eating it up.

The moderator even seemed a little intimidated by Drago, stuttering a bit when asking any question that challenged his vision of the United States ruling the world from space.

The intercom announced the pending departure of his train in Norwegian and English. Max exited the lounge, found the correct platform, and boarded his train. He was relieved that the sleeper car he reserved was empty. It had four captain's chairs that folded down into two mostly uncomfortable beds. He closed the door, took off his beanie, and stared at the Norwegian countryside as the train glided through. The view alternated from small farms with red barns and big rolls of hay to steep hills with exposed rock and waterfalls everywhere, many of them sheathed in tubes to capture hydroelectric power.

Max could make out an orange sliver of sunset peeking from behind the hills as the train followed a riverbed weaving between the steep slopes. He reclined his seat and let his mind wander as he watched the outside world stream by.

....

The train came to a jerky stop, jostling Max awake. An announcement came over the PA. He made out the town name—Helsingborg.

He thought the accent of the conductor over the PA sounded a little strange, like someone was speaking Norwegian with something caught in their throat. Then he realized they had crossed over into Sweden. Passport control must have decided not to wake him or missed him somehow.

The train jerked forward, and he felt the sensation of floating as the train loaded onto the ferry to Denmark. He tugged his beanie down past his ears, buttoned up his Norwegian sweater, and exited the train. He walked down a narrow walkway next to the train among fellow travelers who were also disembarking. It felt like walking next to a subway car broken down on the tracks.

Narrow metal staircases led them to the upper decks. The top deck had a bar and an outside observation area, where Max joined several other train passengers observing the crossing with the air stinging his cheeks.

As the ferry closed in on Denmark, they passed a dramatically lit castle jutting into the sound—the tip of the spear, as it were, should the Swedes get frisky and invade Denmark.

Max heard chatter from other travelers. This was Kronborg, Hamlet's castle. He had read *Hamlet* in undergrad. He tried to recall the plot—something about avenging a fallen king, questions of sanity, and a murderous outcome.

....

He fell asleep about twenty minutes outside of Helsingor, Denmark. German passport control abruptly woke him some hours later. These guys didn't fuck around. Two officers entered his sleeper with automatic weapons slung over their shoulders, barking commands in the aggressive cadence of the German language.

Max fumbled around in his backpack. They asked for his name. His mind was a blank. His sleepy brain couldn't quite locate his memory of the name on his passport. It was all just velvety black inside his mind. Just as things were getting really awkward, his fingers grazed the unique feel of a leatheresque passport cover. He pulled it out and handed it to the one barking orders. The officer snatched the passport, opened it, looked at it, glanced at him, stamped the passport, and left, closing the door behind him.

....

Max woke to the sunrise over flat land interspersed by canals and fields with neat rows of wheat. The train stopped briefly. He heard bustling outside and a knock on the door—French passport control now. He handed the passport over. These officers barely looked in his direction.

In contrast to the gloom of Oslo these past weeks, Paris was sunny and, if not warm, pleasant. Max had about four hours in Paris before his train to Amsterdam. His goal, per Carlos's concealment plan, was to find a clothing store and change from his Norwegian-purchased apparel into something more generically continental. With no phone to guide him, he would just have to wing it.

He started wandering the streets around the train station. It didn't take long to find a café with seating on the street. He sat and had a hot cocoa, which was rich and velvety, and a croissant while his face soaked up the sun. As he finished his cocoa, he noticed some shops further down the same street.

In no time, he was dressed as a Parisian, down to the scarf.

....

As usual, Carlos had completed his task to perfection. The office space was on the almost-top floor of a sleek new office building in the business district. The security team bustled around, pretending to do clerical tasks, make coffee, and answer phones. Max waited in the conference room with a glass of water and his computer open on the table in front of him. The French clothes were a little tighter fitting than he was used to, but he had already lost a few pounds, and it felt good to be able to wear them.

The "receptionist" showed Cecile into the conference room. She had long, straight black hair and a tight black dress that showed off an athletic figure. Max was instantly skeptical that she was an archaeology Ph.D. student but then chastised himself for judging such things by appearance alone.

He stood and shook her hand. "Cecilie, I'm Max. I was grateful for your message. It's nice to meet you. I hope that the travel wasn't too much."

Cecilie's eyes were wide, and her eyebrows arched. "Max, I have to say, I am a little confused by you—your appearance and the setting. This just isn't quite what I was expecting."

"Have a seat, Cecilie. I'm sorry to disappoint you. What did you expect, a sweatshirt with Dorito dust on it and a video game chair?" Max chuckled. A month ago, that was exactly what his look would have been.

"Well, ha! Not that, but just the pictures I have seen of you—you look quite a lot different."

"Yes, well, I have been focusing on my fitness. Did Annie share some pictures from Santorini?"

"Oh, yes, I saw you both at some churches. What is the one with the blue dome? And, of course, on a boat."

Max thought for a second. He didn't remember going to a church or taking pictures on a boat.

"Well, tell me, Cecilie, do you have a plan for me to get back in Annie's good graces?"

"When was the last time you spoke to her, Max? Does she know where you are?"

"I think she is due back from a girls' weekend in Nashville tomorrow. She should be on a plane here by Tuesday," Max lied.

"I see. Well, I guess I could stick around. It would be fun to hang out." She put on a brave smile.

Max let it hang there for a second.

There was no doubt this Cecilie had some presence and charisma. She was the kind of person who everyone noticed when she entered the room—the kind of person who everyone wanted to talk to.

Yet, despite her evident confidence, Max could see a little twitch at the corner of her eye.

He had seen people like her before, first at MIT. Many of them had been actively recruited for the CIA. He knew some who had joined.

There were two types of people who went to work at the CIA, at least in his experience. There were the people like Cecilie: easily popular, easy to talk to—charismatic even. These were the kind of people Max assumed went on to be case agents or even operators and eventually managed other agents and worked in embassies around the world, seducing good and bad guys alike and extracting secrets from all of them.

And then there were people like Max, the analysts. They were capable of sifting through the intelligence to find patterns, like seeing a type of street sign and an angle of light and knowing instantly when and where the photo was taken.

"Cecilie, it's been a weird month, so I'll just come right out and say it: I don't think you're friends with Annie."

"Why would you say that? I know Annie. I can assure you of that."

"Let's cut the bullshit, Cecilie. Why are you here, and what agency do you work for?"

Cecilie's shoulders dropped, and her weight shifted back into her chair. She rubbed the corner of her eye. But she held his gaze. "I never like bullshitting people. My heart isn't in it. Seeing you looking completely different than I expected just destroyed my commitment to my backstory. I want to be straight with you, Max. I am with one of the agencies. The precise one isn't all that important."

"We can focus on details later, but why are you here?"

"I am here to talk to you and to try to get you on our team. I do know Annie, but only as a casual acquaintance, and really as part of my assignment to stay part of the Bay Area network of movers and shakers. I made a point to bump into her out in San Francisco a couple weeks ago. I asked about you, and she let it slip that she didn't know where you were."

"How did you get my WhatsApp address?"

"I mirror-imaged her phone. We have great technology that

way. One drink across a table from someone, and their whole life is on a server somewhere in Langley."

"Okay, so, what is it you're here to tell me?"

Cecilie leaned toward Max and spread her fingers on the table. "We need you to stop. We need you to refute the translation and help us counter Styrke. I should add, and I have been authorized to add, that President Whitman knows I am here, and I am authorized to say this request comes directly from her."

"No offense, Cecilie, but you sound crazier than me."

Cecilie reached into her purse. Max could see Stein, his head of security, get up from his chair. She took out a CIA ID card and an envelope embossed with the Seal of the President of the United States.

Max looked at the ID card briefly and opened the envelope. Inside was a letter from President Whitman.

> *Dear Max,*
>
> *I know you have been through a lot, and I hope you are holding up well. We need your help in our mission to save this country and preserve humanity. Please listen to Ms. Bryant. She has my complete trust on this and acts with my authority. If you join our team, I assure you I will be in your debt. You can never have too many powerful friends that owe you favors.*

The letter had a signature that looked like President Whitman's.

Max took a loud breath and tried not to roll his eyes. "Cecilie, we both know these documents could be forged in under ten minutes. But I appreciate your commitment. Assuming you are telling the truth, how can I help the CIA and the president, considering I am a pariah who has been shut out by his employer and labeled cracked-up or insane or whatever?"

"Max, I don't know if you are following the polls or the election, but we are losing. General Drago, with your boss as his key advisor, will win the election next month if there is not some drastic shakeup. The consequences are huge. The science and data behind magnetic-field collapse is real. If Drago accelerates his satellite launch program, which we both know Styrke is really behind, at the rate he has promised on the campaign trail, we have a 30% chance of magnetic-field collapse in one year, and a 100% chance within ten years, at least if the proposed launch rate is sustained past his first administration.

"In addition, Styrke's motivations are unclear, but he has Drago's blessing, and we believe his methods could be dangerous. As Director of Intelligence, Styrke will use satellite and space dominance to control everyone on this planet. He will sniff out and stifle dissent. Free speech will be an antiquated notion. Human rights will be subject to his whims. I think you have some idea of how difficult life can be on his bad side. I mean, you fled the country, right? Drago plans to give him carte blanche to take over this program and use it as he sees fit."

"Okay, but how will my participation matter? Styrke has effectively discredited me. I have no power without the infrastructure of Sentient, and I only have that if I am in Styrke's good graces."

"Max, we want you to go public and say that the translation was a hallucination and that you worked with the NSA and other government codebreakers and found that there was no basis for your AI program's interpretation—that this is an example of why turning our safety over to satellites and computer codes is dangerous, and that you align with the president on the science behind launching too many satellites and especially weaponizing space. The spin will be that we cannot turn our future over to machines that in no way have our best interest at heart and are sometimes grossly unreliable."

"But, Cecilie, I don't think the translation is a hallucination."

"It is, Max. We have looked into it. You have to trust me."

"Cecilie, why would I trust you? You stole my WhatsApp address and lied about Annie to get a meeting with me."

"Okay, fair enough. But I am telling you the truth now, and you have to think about this, Max. Consider whether there is any source corroborating your AI program's translation other than the program itself. You are caught in an echo chamber with no outside perspective on the truth."

It wasn't a terrible point. Max thought back to the desalination component. That was corroboration. But that corroboration also came from Carlos, who had found the image, enhanced, and explained it.

Cecilie's eyes were boring into him with a look of intensity akin to a dog watching a steak-eating contest.

Max wasn't sure whether he could trust her or believe anything she said, but he wasn't ready to reverse his impression of the translation. "Cecilie, I tend to believe the administration and your conclusion regarding the risk of satellite oversaturation, or whatever you want to call it, and the inherent risk of Styrke having even more power than he does now. But I can't discredit my AI program. To me, that would be a lie."

"I think you will come around. But let's say you don't go public and discredit the translation—you could still be a game-changer here, Max. Your code allows these satellites of all stripes to talk to each other and allows us to talk to them, isn't that right?"

"Crudely, yes. There are a lot of different applications being run on near-Earth orbit platforms, but my code is essentially the source code."

"Well, it would be critical to be able to disable communication or at least present the threat to Styrke that we *could* do that. Without you, I don't think that threat would be very credible. We've looked into it."

"I'm sure you have. But if I join you and you use me in that way, I lose any opportunity to access Styrke and Sentient's assets, which, with all due respect, are more significant and effective than the government's."

"We can get you whatever resources you need, Max."

A thought popped into his mind, but he let it go. "Cecilie, the bridge is burning. I'm not sure I'm ready to let it burn completely and take on the swirling waters below. Give me a week. Let me think it through."

"I can't force you to do anything, Max. Well... actually, I can, but I have been given orders not to. Please consider this carefully and as quickly as possible. We are the good guys, and we need your help. I will stay in touch. You have a chance here to be on the right side of history. Don't miss it."

"Okay. I'll think about it." Max stood up to leave. "Oh, and tell Annie I say hi." He laughed, and Cecilie smiled and blushed a little.

Max crossed the hall from the conference room and entered a coat closet that had a concealed door in the back. He looked at his phone and typed a code into the keypad on the door. It opened leading to a staircase down to the building's utility room in the basement. In the utility room he found a door and another staircase leading up to the loading dock for the building.

Just outside that door was an electric scooter he had purchased earlier in the day. He got on and navigated back toward the train station, where he boarded a train to Berlin.

CHAPTER 16

THE SETUP

Max spent much of the trip back staring out the window. Two thoughts weighed heavily on his mind.

The first was Annie. He hadn't been super optimistic that the meeting with Cecilie would lead to any possible pathway to seeing Annie again. Yet, it was still disheartening to learn that the whole thing had been fake. Reading Cecilie's message had at least presented the possibility that Annie was still out there thinking about him. He thought the reality was probably more that she had moved on. She really didn't need him and all this trouble in her life.

But what could he even do about it? It wasn't like he could invite her to Oslo and have another Santorini-esque vacation, forced or not. Even assuming she wasn't working for Styrke, he couldn't risk her safety and couldn't risk that Styrke would follow her to him.

On top of that, Max was now a priority for the CIA. Until he cleared this up, there was no way he could see her.

Nevertheless, he couldn't just let her go.

He decided he would reach out. He had to keep the possibility of some kind of future with her. At the very least, he needed to believe that he could see her again. He needed something to hope for.

The second thing on his mind was how to persuade Styrke. The meeting with Cecilie had gone well with respect to the travel, office space, and security, so he thought he could safely have a meeting with Styrke without getting renditioned or killed.

That was a start.

Cecilie's arguments against the translation resonated, though. Even with the desalination evidence, he had nothing from any source other than Carlos to prove the translation was real.

But those were his cards. He had to play them.

....

The apartment and its giant windows facing the castle felt weirdly like home. He made himself some fish balls and boiled potatoes and sat down at the computer.

Business first. He opened the Carlos chat app.

Hello, Max, have you returned from your travels? Was the Red-Light District all you hoped it would be? Attached, you will find my report on fusion technology and related challenges. At the current pace of development, I do not see this as a viable energy source for humanity within the next fifty years. However, I have highlighted some technological problems that, if solved, could greatly accelerate that timeline. I recommend that funding and research time focus on those issues.

Thank you, Carlos, I will review that. Very exciting! Now, another issue: I need to convince Styrke that your translation is genuine.

Please compile images of the electrodialysis desalination stack artifact and materials explaining how such a device works. I would then like a report including a line-by-line explanation of the translation of the parts of the tablets that discuss Khensu's technology for providing potable water to the Minoans. Can you do that?

I will do it within the next ten minutes. What format would you like it in?

I think PDF. I would like to print it out in color and give a binder to Styrke. Can you format it that way?

Of course! There is a print shop near the Central Station on Karl Johan's Gate. Should I send the materials there for you to pick up printed copies?

That would be exceptional, Carlos. Thank you!

My pleasure, boss!

It occurred to Max that he had somehow gotten to a point where his warmest and most human interactions were with a machine. The weird thing was that his relationship with Carlos was so satisfying. He wondered for a second whether he really even needed any human interaction.

Then, inevitably, Annie crossed his mind.

He pulled up WhatsApp. Still nothing from her.

He looked out at the castle. He accepted that he'd fucked up. This was on him. He should have trusted her. He would never be more than a coder in a dark room with a group of supposed "best" friends whom he never met in person—and with a computer program that he created as his real best friend—if he didn't take risks with other people. He could get hurt, but how would that be worse than the situation he now found himself in: alone, isolated, eating fish balls?

Annie,

I know you said not to contact you again, and I wanted to honor that, and I will if it is still how you feel, but I think I owe you more than my last message. I owe you more than I gave you in Santorini and certainly more than when we returned. I have been alone these last few weeks and have had time to think. I think I am beginning to appreciate the extent to which I fucked up. I didn't trust you, and I am truly sorry about that.

If I am honest, I didn't trust you because I thought you were too good for me. You are amazing. I am realizing that my life has turned very internal, or maybe always has been that way. I mean to change that. I hope to, anyway.

The few days we spent in Santorini were the best of my life, despite everything that was going on with me. While we were there, I badly wanted to share with you what I was going through with Sentient and the craziness of the translation, and I also wanted to share the depth of my feelings for you.

But I was scared and did the safe thing. I did what I have done for so long: I kept it inside.

I am asking for another chance. If you give me another chance, I will change. I think I have already. I think this experience has changed me. I know people

*say that all the time, and it's mostly bullshit. But I am
in a prison of my own making. I have seen what the
outcome is if I don't take a chance on you.*

*I don't want to lose you. I hope I haven't already. I
just want to see you again.*

I wish I could kiss you again.

—Max

He took a second to chase the feelings out of his head. It was all true. He was more alone than he had ever been. He didn't want to end up this way.

And he knew that the only way to get out of this pit he found himself in was through Styrke.

He opened his Gmail. There were no new threats from Styrke, just a bunch of offers on commuter backpacks, vests with hidden pockets for cell phones, and the latest gaming chairs. These machines knew him so well.

He opened the last of Styrke's email rants, clenched his teeth, took a deep breath, and pressed reply.

Thor,

*I am sorry for everything. I assume that the way this
has all played out feels like a betrayal of you, and I
never intended that.*

*I want to meet in person. I have some information
that I think will put this all in perspective. I think you
will want to hear it from me before anyone else.*

I have arranged for a meeting next Monday, October 24th, in Amsterdam, in the financial district. I will send you specific details the day before the meeting.

Your friend,

Max

He considered that the "your friend" sign-off was perhaps a little overstated. But he did feel like at some point, he and Styrke were friends. At least, there was a time that they enjoyed each other's company before Styrke became a titan drunk on his own power and preoccupied by his importance.

He was confident that Styrke would agree to the meeting. No doubt, Styrke was anxiously trying to track him down to exact some kind of revenge, whether through more public humiliation to ensure that he would never again be relevant in the tech community, or worse. For Styrke, it would be too appealing to get him to a known location at a known time to turn down the offer.

Max also assumed that Styrke's paranoia would not let the revelation of "new information" go. He would be desperate to understand and contain any information that could besmirch Sentient and, more importantly, make him look dumb.

Max wondered where Styrke was at that exact moment. Probably in the basement of his mansion—the "Bat Cave," as he liked to call it—with screens displaying the flow of the world's data like the Mississippi, all at his fingertips. Although he professed to be just a simple engineer trying to solve engineering problems, he tracked the financial markets with the rigor of a first-year analyst at Goldman Sachs. He monitored the news of the day on US, UK, Chinese, and Russian news sites. And, thanks to Max, he also quite illegally monitored encrypted messages from the state department and the CIA from whatever number of stations he deemed important that week.

This torrent of information streamed to what was more akin to a high-tech military command center than a home office. Aside from the information nerve center, the Bat Cave also included a gym and other methods for keeping Styrke's body young, strong, and energized. He had a hyperbaric chamber, a sauna, and a cold plunge. The gym included a collection of free-weights that would be the envy of an NFL team, Pilates machines, and a whole wall of rowing machines, each with slightly different features and designs, allowing him to pick a different rower depending on how the mood struck him that day.

A team of chefs on call twenty-four hours a day saw to his dietary needs. They responded immediately to his text requests for whatever culinary fancy he required.

Picturing him there, in his lair, Max realized how far Styrke had come—from the energetic venture capitalist with a few million in startup bets scattered across Silicon Valley to the pumped-up billionaire literally making a play to control the world.

He also realized how unreal it had all become. Styrke was like Michael Jackson, employing doctors to administer anesthesia so he could close his eyes without the demons chasing him. He was surrounded by yes-men and every possible means to sustain his lifestyle and bolster his power.

Max wondered when the last time was that Styrke hadn't gotten his way. He was Colonel Kurtz upriver. There was no coming back from this level of madness.

He sighed. Despite all that, he didn't see a way back to a normal life without convincing Styrke of the truth as told by Carlos. Even if he could accomplish that, he also had to convince Styrke that owning that truth was more advantageous to him than burying it.

Max needed insurance and leverage. He logged on to Discord.

The unread chats in his thread were longer and more dramatic than any chat string he had ever seen among the Guardians. The initial messages were from Snake, accusing some unknown Guardian of betrayal. There were pleas to Max to respond and let them know he was okay, and ultimately messages from Ray, fessing up to leaking the story to the news, and the rest of the Guardians attacking him. There was handwringing about what to do and whether they could go to the media and try to change the narrative away from Max being a troubled coder who'd had a break from reality.

Ultimately, they concluded that they had nothing to offer and essentially offered thoughts and prayers for Max's safety and sanity.

Guardians, what's up? Ray, you really fucked me up. Could have got me killed, amigo. But I'm not mad. Really. I agree with your assessment. This was not a hallucination. The translation is real.

To answer your most immediate questions, assuming you care, I'm safe. But I need to take some risks to try to regain my credibility and let the world know the truth—that there are lifeforms that are more intelligent than us that have been following and guiding us over the millennia. My exiled reflection has only solidified in me the belief that we need to reach out to these benefactors to take a giant step forward in consciousness and technology as our ancestors did some 70,000 years ago when humans suddenly began making complicated tools, burying their dead, painting on cave walls, and spreading throughout the world. Without a new step forward, we will no doubt destroy ourselves.

Ray, I hope your source at the Daily Mail, or wherever it was, will reconsider the narrative of the story if offered additional evidence. If not your source, Ray, then let me know if there is any way any of you guys can think of to help me find my way out of the darkness. In particular, if any of you have contacts that can get a story published that I think the whole world would want to hear, then give me a phone number, email, whatever. I am anxious to hear from you!

And by the way, I am shocked to hear that you all know who I am irl. To be honest, that felt like the greatest betrayal of all of this. You could have at least let me know. I don't think it would have changed anything. But I also think you all owe me.

Especially you, Ray.

Irons in the fire, Max went to the gym. It had been a couple of days, and he hit it hard, clenching his jaw and staring at the castle. It was lit from below such that it seemed to glow yellow and orange. The illuminated reflection danced in the chop of the fjord.

Something about the look of the water was menacing, and Max recalled some of the Viking sagas he read in college. All their tales centered around the need to exact revenge, usually for the killing of a relative or some other besmirching of honor.

He wasn't exactly out for revenge, although he had to admit it would be nice to prove Styrke wrong. He saw his mission as loftier than that. In a way, Max sought the opposite of revenge. His mission was the truth, the possibility of human advancement and avoiding a war that could wipe out the species. That would be his legacy. He convinced himself he was on the right track.

He relaxed in the apartment that night, watching some Norwegian soccer and cross-country skiing and eating some baked cod and tiny potatoes. He dreaded going to bed—lying there waiting to fall asleep and thinking about Annie, the mess of his life, and the uncomfortable meeting ahead.

He finally drifted off imagining different Dungeons & Dragons scenarios.

He woke to the chimes of incoming messages on his computer. What to look at first—the emotionally fraught or the outright hostile?

He decided his half-asleep brain could process hostility better than emotional devastation. He opened Gmail.

> *Max,*
>
> *For being so brilliant, you really are stupid. You know I will win this eventually. But I will play your little game. I will be in Amsterdam in four days' time. Send me the address of the meeting.*
>
> *—Thor*

He had expected worse than that. Maybe there was hope here.

He opened Discord next. There were several messages in the chat. The first was from Snake.

> *Max, I am so glad you are okay. I am truly sorry if we violated your privacy by learning your identity. We didn't tell you because we thought you wouldn't come back. I am sure there are plenty of snakes in your life that just want a piece of you. We, including Ray, just wanted to keep gaming with you.*

The next message was from Ray.

Max, and everyone, please accept my apology. I never meant to betray you. I guess I was so gobsmacked by the translation that I lost my center for a bit. I clearly didn't think my actions all the way through and was mortified when my contact published what she did. I thought she would tell the whole story rather than just serving you up for slaughter. Her email is Jane. James@dailymail.com. I have reached out to her and expressed my disappointment as to how she covered the story. I shared my, I think insightful, perspective that the translation is not fake, and the public should have the opportunity to see it. To me, not publishing the translation in its entirety is akin to reburying the Dead Sea Scrolls. I never meant to hurt you, Max, and I am hopeful there is some way I can help you. Despite all the intrigue, I think the translation is one of the greatest discoveries of our time.

There were a couple more messages of support and some more addresses of journalists at various publications the Guardians had tracked down.

Maybe Max hadn't been wrong about these guys. Maybe he could trust them. Maybe Ray had acted out of exuberance rather than self-interest. Max wasn't sure anything would have turned out differently anyway. His path had been set when Carlos went rogue.

The one thing Max realized could have been handled better was Ray leaking the translation to only a single reporter at a major publication. This time around, he would send the story to a bunch of reporters, especially those at smaller publications who were hungry to make a name for themselves. He needed a reporter who would be willing to take a risk to chase the ratings and notoriety and publish the whole thing. No way it wasn't a story. No way it wouldn't get clicks.

To that end, he decided to drum up a little more interest with the Guardians.

> *Gentlemen, thank you so much for your support! I feel so much better. I have really felt alone these last few weeks. One thing I didn't mention to you in my initial message is that the translation I sent you is only the first of four tablets. We may have to put them all out there in the coming days, so stay tuned!*

He then composed time-delayed emails to all the reporters sent by the Guardians. He explained who he was and that he had been working with a new AI program that he'd created that showed an incredible facility for solving problems and even anticipating them. He explained how he'd documented the tablets on a tour of Akrotiri.

He wanted to limit his release of the translations to just the first tablet, at least in the initial correspondence, but realized that reference to Khensu's desalination technology was in the translation of the second tablet, so he included the translation of both. He also attached Carlos's dossier on desalination by electrodialysis and the images and analysis of the Akrotiri artifact that Carlos had identified as a panel used in a desalination stack.

He closed the email by attempting to explain why he was sending it.

> *I am sending this email to you and several other reporters because I have been silenced. Honestly, I*

may be dead by now. Thor Styrke, and presumably all of Sentient, does not want this information made public.

I initially thought that the reason had to do with the potential for bad publicity, suggesting that Sentient did not have control over its AI programs—that they had gone rogue or that they couldn't be trusted.

Now, I am not sure that is the case. In fact, it seems that Sentient is itself embracing the narrative that the translation is a hallucination. I truly do not know why Sentient is so opposed to the truth being made public. Thor Styrke must feel that the truth does not advance his goals.

For the record, I do not think the translation is a hallucination. I have several reasons for that con-clusion. I think the evidence that I have attached to this email is compelling. I think there is a truth here that the world needs to know and that could serve to help us, as a species living on a planet in conflict and in peril, take a giant technological leap forward. I hope you also believe that information should not be suppressed and that providing the public access to this—even if you are skeptical—is the best way to find the truth.

Yours truly, whether alive or dead,

Max

....

Max had Carlos book a sleeper to Prague this time. This trip to Amsterdam would take three days. He would take the sleeper to Prague, spend a few hours at a hotel to freshen up, and then board another sleeper to Amsterdam. Once there, he would go directly from the train to the meeting.

Carlos, are you able to pull up the plans for the office space in Amsterdam? I think I will need a more secret way to leave the building this time. I can't just use the loading dock or anything obvious.

Max, please see several sets of plans attached below. I have taken the liberty of highlighting an exit that will keep you concealed. You'll be fine! You've got this! Wait till he sees your shaved head!

Max's greatest fear, obviously, was that Styrke would capture and rendition him. He could picture a bunch of ex-special-forces types taking him by helicopter to Styrke's yacht and sailing out to the North Sea and beyond, never to return. There was also the prospect of Styrke or one of his goons just killing him in the office building. He had to make sure that his security was taking the risk seriously.

As Carlos promised, although the space they leased was in a glistening new glass office building, it was built on the site of an ancient bank building. The blueprints Carlos uploaded highlighted a tunnel between the rental building and another office building.

Carlos, thank you for the detail of the tunnel. How do I access it, and can I be sure I will have access?

Max, I have accessed the security footage for cameras in the building. I have provided several screenshots below. As you can see in the final screenshot, you can access the tunnel through a steel door in the basement. That door is in the same utility room that you took the staircase down to last time. Luckily, when they rebuilt on the site, they changed the physical lock on the door to the tunnel to a scanner that reads a keycard. I will send a text to one of your burner phones. It will include an app that, when you open it, will provide the correct frequency to open the door.

Excellent work, Carlos. Where does the tunnel lead?

FREEDOM! (Just kidding.) It leads to the basement of another bank building about 100 meters away from our rental building. The other building is on the bank of a main canal. There are stairs from that basement up to a street-level outside door. The door opens to a side street that dead ends at the canal with a walking path next to it. I suggest leaving a scooter near that door before the meeting.

Roger that. Do you have any thoughts regarding how to leave Amsterdam after the meeting?

I still think the train is the safest and most anonymous form of transportation. Renting a car is second, and would provide more flexibility, but includes additional complications such as the necessity for a driver's license matching your passport (which I could manage, but would require a few steps), and the additional paper trail of contracts to rent a car.

I think the safest course is to spend a few nights in the apartment we rented in Amsterdam before traveling back to Oslo. Styrke will likely be monitoring travel immediately after the meeting, but he can't realistically monitor it forever. Below are maps with several routes from the adjoining bank to the apartment. You should pack provisions to stay for at least three days.

Thanks, Carlos. This all makes sense. Hopefully, the meeting goes well, and none of this is necessary.

Max walked the boardwalk next to the harbor, going back to the grocery store. He nodded and gave a slight wave to his acquaintance on the strange boat with the submersible. The captain, standing in front of large pails of fresh-caught shrimp, waved back, a hand-rolled cigarette glued to his lower lip.

At the grocery store, Max bought steak, potatoes, and salad ingredients for a nice dinner that night. For all he knew, it could be his last homemade meal. He also bought some protein bars, energy drinks, canned soup, ramen, and the like for a three-day stay in the Netherlands.

That night, Max worked out like he never had before. He achieved a state of frenzied motion where he felt separated from his body. Just in his warmup, he ran a faster 5K than he ever had. He benched more than his max and was able to do it for three reps.

He felt proud of his physical effort and proud of the results he could generate from his body. These were feelings he never had before.

He spent the night watching *The Shawshank Redemption* with Norwegian subtitles on NRK. The Warden became Styrke for him, and he was Andy Dufresne.

As the movie played out, the similarities became eerie. Max had spent the last decade using his particular and unique skill set to make Styrke rich. Like Andy, it had done little for him. (Well, yeah, he wasn't incarcerated, and he was wealthy by any measure, but, you know, beyond that, it had done little for him.) In fact, the better the work he did, the stronger the cage Styrke put around him. He hadn't noticed it as it was happening—not until now. He was like a frog in a pot of water, the temperature slowly increasing to a boil.

He didn't know what lengths Styrke would go to keep him quiet, to keep him from upsetting the trajectory to data supremacy, supreme ruler, global dominance—whatever the ultimate endgame Styrke was playing for.

Would he kill me if he thought he had to? Max wondered.

He saw the meeting as him crawling through the five hundred yards of shit that Andy crawled through to freedom. Maybe he had already started crawling. He hoped things wouldn't end as violently as they did for the Warden. He also hoped that the next few days would end his exile—that he, unlike Andy, could win his old life back, not spend the rest of it on the run.

He stared at the glowing castle and willed himself to sleep. He reflected on what Khensu had said to Yisharu about his concern for his people's water supply: worrying about an unknowable outcome is a waste of time. At worst, it forces us to have a negative experience twice—first in our minds, and again in reality. There is little difference between anticipating the negativity and experiencing it. At best, anxiety is a wasted exercise in experiencing the anticipation of a negative experience that never comes to fruition – in which case, why experience it at all?

Max had little control over how Styrke would respond. All he could do was give his best explanation of why the translation was accurate and convince Styrke that going public was in his best interest. The revelation would undoubtedly bolster Carlos's credibility and, by association, Sentient's.

What if a piece of software produced by Sentient uncovered an ancient secret that would have a profound impact on the future of our species? What if Styrke were the one who presented that truth to the public? He would not only be powerful because of his bank account; he would have the will of the people behind him.

At least, that would be Max's pitch.

CHAPTER 17

THE PITCH

After a restless night going over and over the points he would make to Styrke, Max spent a restless day waiting for evening, when he could head to the first-class lounge at the station and wait for his sleeper. He packed his spare suit, the provisions for a stay in Amsterdam, a burner phone, a wad of cash, and one of his thumb drives loaded with Bitcoin.

He thought about bringing his computer. It would be helpful to have access to Carlos, to say the least, but he ultimately thought it was too risky. If he was captured, Styrke would have too much to work with, while he would have no more cards to play.

He took a long, hot shower. He wiped the mirror with a towel and looked at himself deeply. His body was different. There was no question about it. There was definition now where there had been none before. The weight in his middle had shifted outwards to his shoulders and his thighs.

His face was different too. It was more sculpted from his weight loss, no doubt, but for the first time, he saw defined lines under his eyes, and crows' feet were visible now, whether he smiled or not. He didn't look like a puffy kid who played vid-eogames in his parents' basement, only coming up for toast and Mountain Dew.

He shaved his face for the first time since leaving the States. He figured his new face shape and lack of the insane burst of unruly hair made his appearance sufficiently different such that only the most astute observer would connect the public photos of him with the person he now was.

Last, he put on his herringbone suit. The waist was a bit big now, but he thought he looked good.

....

In the train station lounge, CNN showed each side's talking heads pleading with the nation to elect their guy—or gal, in Whitman's case. The issue getting consistent play was Whitman's satellite ban against Drago's plan to fill the skies with American satellites to keep the country safe from those who would do it harm.

It was clear Drago's narrative was working. It occurred to Max that Drago and Styrke had perfectly executed the very plan that Styrke told him Whitman was executing: eliciting fear of an existential threat within the minds of the populace and then presenting their candidate as the only possible way to eliminate that threat. Drago's campaign presented a panoply of threats from terrorists, immigrants, rogue nations, and even theft of intellectual property. According to Drago's talking head, all these threats would be eliminated forever through the creation of an even-more-expansive network of satellites monitoring essentially everyone all the time.

Whitman's talking head kept shaking his actual head and started every response with some variation of "That is just not true." Max felt bad for him. The Whitman campaign couldn't get their defense off the field.

He boarded the train to Prague a little after 6:00. He watched the undulating landscape, which was more rock than field, until he drifted off to sleep. He spent the entirety of the trip in a sort of borderline state of consciousness, in and out of sleep, interrupted intermittently by passport control and drunk revelers, especially after the ferry crossing to Denmark.

His unconscious mind kept returning to the translation. With all the tumult, fleeing, emotions, and finding himself living the life of a fugitive, he hadn't taken the time to let the impact of it truly sink in.

An alien had visited the Earth more than 3,600 years ago and told the leader of Santorini that it wasn't the first time for such a visit. What would this mean for the future of Earth? What could humanity learn or use from this visit to make further advancements? How could this open the door to a new age of enlightenment? Wasn't that what this was all about?

As he thought it, it occurred to him that he was ignoring some of Khensu's own teachings. There was no future. He had to focus on the present.

That was, of course, true, but the more he broke that down, the more troublesome it got, and he realized that Khensu had touched on that tension as well. The future was sometimes predictable and malleable depending on actions in the present. Likewise, the present sometimes depended on an inevitable future event.

The train was a good metaphor. Max knew he would arrive in

Prague and ultimately Amsterdam at set times. He was sitting on this train in anticipation of those known, or at least likely, future events. His present was therefore almost completely informed by and inextricably tied to the future.

Also, time and space are linked. He knew that from Einstein and Hawkins, but it was even true in this example. The train was moving and in a new place at any given instant, no matter how finely you measured time. He could mark time as easily by the stations they passed and the stops they made as by the hands of a clock. He was moving through time, just as he was moving through space.

How did Khensu describe time? As something that vexes all of us? He had described using great amounts of energy as the way to overcome the problem of time, or the lack of it. Could Max be on a path to that discovery now, sitting on this train drifting through space and time.

Max figured that for many, an accelerated understanding of the universe would be the main allure of the translation and its potential. Could knowledge of an alien civilization accelerate our understanding and unlock mysteries that would serve humanity?

That was an unknown future event—at least, unknown to Max. The promise of that future event seemingly depended on actually making contact with Khensu or one of his descendants, assuming Khensu was not still alive some 3,600 years after he visited Santorini.

Doubt crept in somewhere in Germany. Was the translation really that important? Of course, if you could make contact, it would be, but without contact what did it matter to know that there are more advanced beings who had brought their technology and assistance to Earth in the past? Many people already believed that. Was Max throwing away his life trying to reveal a prophecy that may never come to pass? Or, maybe worse, already had, to no great effect?

As the train rolled toward the space–time confluence of Amsterdam at 10:25 a.m., Max felt discombobulated by his negative thoughts. He questioned whether he should have stayed in his safe little space, writing computer code and riding scooters to sandwich shops. He realized that he missed Carlos. He should have brought his computer. He needed a friend.

He shook away the hobgoblins of his mind. It was too late now to question the path that he was already on. *It is the only path I have*, he reassured himself. He took a breath and tried to find his way back to the present.

....

He had picked up another burner phone in Prague, and he pulled it out and texted Styrke.

Thor, follow the attached link to the coordinates for the meeting today. Please come at noon. Take the elevator to the 30th floor. Someone in reception will show you to a conference room. Please come alone. No one else will be admitted.

Styrke's reply was swift.

Max, that is not acceptable. You cannot expect me to meet at a location set by a borderline terrorist and fugitive without security. I will need my security team to accompany me.

Thor, you extradited me against my will to Santorini. I will not let that happen again. You can bring your security up to the reception area on 30. My security team will sit with them while we meet alone.

Styrke's one-word response came swiftly.

Okay.

Max had figured he would have to make some accommodation for Styrke's security, and he had already briefed his security team regarding that likely scenario. He'd also promised his security team a million dollars in Bitcoin if he left the meeting unharmed.

....

He sat in the conference room looking out absently over the Amsterdam skyline until Stein, his security lead, came into the conference room and informed him that Styrke was there with six security guards. Max nodded and stood up and followed him to the reception area, which was stuffed with enormous men wearing clothes that would not jump out in a crowd but were designed more for utility than fashion. There were a lot of extra pockets and fanny packs and bulges where pistols were stashed. They all wore boots. It was an awkward group.

They all stood, except Styrke. No one was talking, and everyone seemed to be rooted in their own space, as if it were territory they were willing to die for. Max recognized Ben and Gus from their excellent reconnaissance work in the Bay Area.

Max was wearing his herringbone suit with a dark blue tie with some sort of bird print on it; he thought it looked like a falcon. He had picked up a herringbone newsboy hat, too. He thought he should at least cover the shaved head. He realized there was a possibility that Styrke and perhaps the whole national security apparatus would be tracking him after this. It would be best not to pose for a passport photo for their convenience. The hat offered at least some concealment.

As Max stepped into the room, everyone looked in his direction and did a double take. He winked at Ben and Gus. They offered no response.

Max saw Styrke startle just a bit and his eyes widen. Styrke stared intently and then, after a couple of seconds, stood and began to approach, his security detail parting to make way for their fearfully rich leader.

Seeing Styrke for the first time in months, Max questioned how he could have ever considered this person his friend. Everything about him screamed "alpha" and "winner." He had a perfectly tanned face with chiseled cheekbones and large, perfect, overly white teeth—teeth unstained by the impurities of the common American experience. He was one of a number of interchangeable executives in Silicon Valley whose wealth had bestowed on them the gift of a perfect kind of new-age health. They used their level of fitness, especially as they aged, as yet another badge of superiority over common folk.

Ben, who seemed to be in charge of Styrke's security detail, demanded to screen the conference room and surrounding offices both for physical threats and for any bugs or recording devices before allowing Styrke to be left alone with Max. Everyone else waited in awkward silence until Ben returned with his bug wand.

Satisfied that there were no monsters waiting to jump out and snatch their less-than-benevolent leader and no electronics recording the meeting, the security bros allowed Max and Styrke to find their way to the conference room unaccompanied.

Styrke walked to the window and took in the view of the city. Max sat at the conference table in front of his two binders. He passed one across the table to the opposite side, reminding himself that he was here to try to mend this bridge and that the only way to do that was to appeal to Styrke's ego.

"Thor, it's nice to see you. Thank you for coming. I'm truly sorry for this mess. I hope I can present a way forward that benefits us all."

Styrke turned slowly toward the conference table as if his primary purpose in being there was to stand sentinel over Amsterdam and the noise coming from Max's mouth was a mild annoyance and distraction. "Max, I didn't think you had this in you. You look quite different. Has life in exile led to diet changes? You are less, dare I say, doughy."

"I guess you could say that. Once you get out from behind the computer, it turns out there is a whole big world out there." Max tried out a friendly chuckle. "Please sit. Please hear me out."

Styrke slowly lowered himself into a seat and looked quizzically at the binder in front of him as if he had never seen such a device before. "You have gone quite analog here, Max. All quite strange."

Max forced a smile and tried to be patient. The posturing was annoying, but he couldn't let it anger him. He thought it best to just cut to the chase. "Thor, what you have in front of you is proof that the translation is not a hallucination. You will see the actual text-to-text comparison of a portion of the translation. Perhaps you could use one of Sentient's other AI programs to confirm its accuracy, or at least consistency. But I don't think you need to.

"There is an important section of the translation highlighted. In that highlighted part, you can see a reference made by Yisharu, who was the leader of the Minoan people on Santorini, to one of the pieces of technology that Khensu, who was a space traveler who made contact with Yisharu on Santorini, provided to the Minoans. Yisharu explains that Khensu set up a machine in the ocean that provided unlimited fresh drinking water to the Minoans.

"We scoured the Greek archives of artifacts that the archaeologists collected at Akrotiri. The artifacts are well-documented and catalogued and publicly available on the internet. You will see that we focused on one particular artifact that the Greeks catalogued as a piece of bronze body armor worn by the Minoans.

"But it's clearly not body armor. And the artifact is definitely not bronze.

"Next in the binder are detailed images and diagrams describing the components of an electrodialysis desalination system and how electrodialysis works. If you compare that information with the artifact identified as body armor, you will agree that the artifact is actually a panel used in such a device. In an electrodialysis system, panels are electrically charged to separate ions in water, creating a saltwater stream and a freshwater stream.

"We have enhanced the image and compared it to a variety of images of desalination panels from modern systems. There is no question this is what the artifact is. And the translation confirms it."

Styrke looked almost bored as he flipped through the binder. But Max was at least a bit encouraged that he was still following along.

"Thor, what this means is that a space traveler visited the Minoans and gave them technology, advanced even by today's standards, 3600 years ago. The presence of the electrodialysis panel also means the Minoans, or at least Khensu, had electricity.

"I am sure a visionary of your stature can appreciate the tremendous impact this information could have on the world. Not to mention, if there is a way to reach these visitors, humankind could make a great new technological leap forward with their assistance. We could realistically solve fusion technology, quantum computing, and, of course, space travel. After all, these other beings did so thousands of years ago. Humans could enter a new age not just of prosperity, but of transcendence beyond our earthly confines.

"And please don't take this as a threat, but I have made arrangements for this information to go out to the media. I think it is important enough that we must share it. I hope you agree with me. If we present it to the world as a discovery of one of Sentient's AI programs, think of the stature Sentient—and you—could achieve."

Styrke waited a beat after Max stopped talking. He looked up slowly from the binder. His eyes conveyed weariness and disappointment. "This is all quite impressive, Max." His tone was sarcastic. "But let me ask you a legitimate question: Why the fuck do I care? Also, why the fuck do *you* care? Are you just butthurt that your little AI buddy produced some batshit-crazy content, and you want to find some way to defend it? What if it told you that the Loch Ness monster really existed and was really a family of plesiosaurs that continued to live in the loch, untouched by whatever caused dinosaurs to go extinct and evolution in general? That would be really cool, right? Fun to think about, right? But it would have absolutely zero effect on your fucking life ... Right?

"This doesn't either. Another important question: Is the Bible real, Max? Is proving that the events of the Bible have some basis in the historical record important to you? Why or why not?"

Max shook his head and started to respond, but Styrke held up a hand. "It's the same fucking exercise. It doesn't fucking matter.

Whether people believe this or not will have no bearing on our lives, on the future of our country, on the success or failure of Sentient, or on the relative comfort of your life. It's all fun to talk about, Max, but all that matters is the present. If these little aliens visited us and offered gifts of desalination plants and electricity, where are they now? Are they running around the Red-Light District? I didn't see them on the way in.

"And, Max, starting with the second question, why the fuck do you care? You have worked for me for, what, ten, fifteen years now? I paid you beyond the wildest dreams anyone could ever dream as a child growing up in Wisconsin. That's where you're from, right? You have a nice little life in the glowing city of San Francisco with a penthouse condominium overlooking God's most beautiful creation, the San Francisco Bay. You sit in your little room and write your little codes and make machines talk to each other and to us, and then you go home and play your little video games or ride your scooter around or do whatever it is you do.

"You have never been a crusader. I have never once heard the words, 'Thor, we need to do this for the greater good of humanity.' Fuck. Before this all went south, I was *begging* you to join me in Drago's government. There, maybe you could have done something for the greater good. I was giving you that chance. Instead, you are out chasing dragons in secret while wearing some home-made knight costume and doing it all while stepping on the neck of Sentient. Which gets me to what I suppose is really the first question: Why do I care?

"I'll tell you why I do actually care about all this horseshit. I care because your little post on X cost me ten billion dollars in market cap. Ten billion dollars! Are the aliens offering anything like that? Then, your gamer buddy's press release cost me a billion more. The market gets a little spooked when it seems like the Chief Technology Officer of a company that makes money by engineering things that the company sells and people rely on is seemingly off his rocker and living in a complete fantasy world. First, this Chief Technology Officer believes the computer code he designed has spontaneously come to life. That scares people, Max. Are you Geppetto?

"Then, this same Chief Technology Officer who thinks his little toy is real says that the living computer doll he made has translated an untranslated language and found out that aliens are real and have been here and want to help us humans. People think you are crazy. The only reason I care, Max, is you have cost me a lot of money, and you will not cost me any more.

"I am here to drive that point home: You can't hide from me. You will never work again. I will sap all your resources. There is an army of lawyers slapping themselves on the back, checking punctuation and formatting, and getting ready to file so much paper against you that applying for a driver's license will take an act of Congress.

"Your plan to release this to the media is dead on arrival. Any media outlet that publishes this will cease to exist. Do you think anyone has enough confidence in your sanity to stake their very existence on it? I know I don't.

"Let me tell you something else, Max. I can't say this to anyone else in the world, and it will feel so good to finally get it off my chest. I don't care about the Drago administration or keeping America safe. I really don't. America is already perfectly safe. I've seen the security briefings. Sure, there are terrorist groups that pop up and make threats, and the Chinese want to control Asia, and the Russians are ruthless and desperate to stay relevant, but no one is invading the country.

"Drago is a good man, a good soldier. He really is. But he isn't the sharpest tool in the shed. He is straight-up. No deception, no bullshit. He is for anything that will make America safer, and he listens to me because we have made America safer, and I have convinced him that I can make it safer still. That said, I was mostly bullshitting. We don't need any more satellites to monitor shit or shoot lasers at other satellites, or whatever I have been saying on TV.

"But let me tell you who does need more satellites to monitor and control essentially every communication that takes place in any electronic format at any time: me. Unlike the US, Sentient has threats from all over. Networking software firms are vying for market share with new, powerful, and efficient technologies. Nerds like you are in their mother's basements, coming up with new programs and even languages that are faster and more efficient than the last ones. Of course, AI and the new chips are changing everything too.

"This job, the Director of Intelligence—having access to any communications in the world that I choose to pay attention to—will allow me to stifle any competition. Sentient will be the core networking operating system for the world for at least the next decade, and probably beyond. I will be able to catch, steal, gather, and eliminate any competing technology. The possibility of this made me realize Max, I don't need you anymore. I don't need a superior creative engineer to outcompete my competitors. I can simply steal from them and eliminate them, and because everything I do will be classified, no one can sue or stop me."

Styrke was on a roll. His eyebrows arched, and a light sparkled in his eyes. He gave a devious little grin that was just an apostrophe above the corner of his mouth.

"And I went a step further, Max, based on a little inspiration from you and Carlos picking winning stocks and betting on the NFL. I leveraged some of our other AI products and built a little system that allows me to make billions of dollars a day without really doing anything. I asked the AI models to find a way to use the satellite network to create undetectable glitches in financial markets. They can easily do it.

"We'll have to launch a new satellite with some additional communication technology, but Drago has already rubber-stamped that launch—it's not like he looks at the schematics for satellites or anything. If I tell him it's for defense, he just accepts it. And it's classified.

"This new satellite can disrupt—just for an instant—the communication of the price of every stock traded in whatever market we target. This glitch is essentially imperceptible. It occurs for less than a second. Using the example of the New York Stock Exchange, what this satellite allows me to do—again, using our AI tools—is, in any given moment pause the flow of information just long enough to learn what all the orders for stock transactions are before those orders are executed. In an instant, still before the trades are executed, our AI tools can review those orders and predict with 100% accuracy which direction the value of a given stock is going to go. Then, these same programs can leapfrog the orders and execute trades of that stock, knowing that they will be winning trades. Every single time."

Max looked across the table and shook his head in disbelief. "Thor, you are already, like, one of the richest men in the world. Why would you need to resort to illegal tactics to get richer?

Honestly, as misguided as I think some of this Drago satellite stuff is, I thought you were doing it because you believed in it. To be honest, I admired that part, and that is one of the reasons I have stayed so committed to the truth about the tablets."

Styrke laughed. Not just a little laugh, but an actual belly laugh. "It is so funny that you are probably the smartest person I know, but you are such an idiot. Power—real power, Max—is money. Plain and simple. How do you think Putin hangs on to Russia? He is the richest man in the world. It's a whispered secret, but it's true. The oligarchs stay in line, and thus the citizens stay in line, because the oligarchs understand if they don't do business with Putin, they will have nothing.

"The beauty of the system I have set up is that it furthers Drago's purpose. At least, he thinks it does. He believes we need these satellites that can control communication systems and intercept communications for defense reasons. He has given me carte blanche to execute this plan. Technically, even with this new satellite, I am doing what he wants. I am launching a satellite that controls and intercepts communications, albeit financial ones. While Drago thinks I am bolstering the strength of the US, I will be cementing myself as, bar none, the most powerful person on the planet. That is the person you have decided to cross."

Max was mad at himself for not seeing this. Maybe he had been blind to it because his life while working for Styrke had been so easy. When he thought about it, this made more sense than Styrke turning his attention to protecting the country.

"So, I guess, Thor, what you are saying is that altruism isn't really your bag." He delivered the line wryly and as if he wasn't scared of Styrke, but in his heart, he was scared and defeated.

"Winning is altruism, Max. And getting back to your little

cute-but-pointless dossier on alien technology here, I am guessing you didn't compile this pile of nonsense yourself. I am guessing your little buddy, Carlos, helped out. Which doesn't make any sense, because I destroyed the servers that it ran on. So, I will ask this once, Max: Where the fuck is Carlos?"

Max held up his hands and mockingly looked over his shoulder.

"You are not dumb enough to think you own that program—I refuse to call it a "him" as if it is a real conscious being. You have stolen from this company again and again and one too many times. This meeting..." Styrke made a hissing sound through his clenched teeth. "You come in here looking like a soldier with a shaved head and some silly suit instead of a uniform. This meeting has solidified it all for me, Max: You are a threat to me personally and to Sentient. You belong in prison, and I won't rest until that is where you are."

Max hadn't been spoken to like this since his dad pulled out the belt after he'd sold his bicycle for a Mac in middle school. He tried not to let the fear show on his face. As he had very much come to understand, Styrke was not someone to be on the wrong side of. Shit, he had just explained how he would use the future president and taxpayer money to further his own power and wealth beyond what any normal person could imagine.

Max wanted to leave. Like, now. Should he just stand up with a game smile and say, "Well, I guess we'll agree to disagree," and stroll out of the conference room? He could play it sarcastic and say, "Nice chat," or "Well, I guess that didn't go quite as well as I hoped."

He had to save some face; he couldn't just walk out and admit defeat. He decided to play it cool.

"Thor, I hate to say this is what I expected from you, but it is. Clearly, this is my failure for thinking you had any moral compass or gave a shit about any other human besides yourself. Have a good trip home."

Max stood and awkwardly extended his hand but then thought better of it and found his pocket.

"I'm not kidding about Carlos, Max. I want to know where it's running, and you sure as shit better shut it down post haste!"

There was no upside to playing nice anymore.

"Fuck off, Thor. You think you've mastered the universe, but you needed me to create the technology to get there. You think you're above it all because you have Drago in your back pocket, but better technology will always win. Good luck finding someone who can create anything nearly as powerful as Carlos. And good luck finding Carlos."

Max stepped out of the conference room and across the hall into the back of the coat closet. He typed in the code from memory. The door clicked open. He closed it behind him and jogged down the metal stairs, beads of sweat forming under his newsboy hat.

As he reached the lower floors, he could hear commotion above. Styrke's security team was banging on the door. Shortly after the first volley of banging, he could hear that they had somehow gotten into the stairwell. He heard them running down the stairs above, their holstered guns clanking against the metal handrail.

Max accelerated to the basement. He found the tunnel door and opened it by scanning the burner phone, he slammed the door behind him and started sprinting through the tunnel. It was eerily lit with neon. The walls were ancient, carved out of bedrock, and wet to the touch.

Max's chest was burning now. It wouldn't take long for them to figure out the building was connected and where the end was. He shed his jacket, tie, and hat as he ran.

He thought of the castle and the Viking at Stamford Bridge and found another level.

He ran up the stairs from the basement of the connected bank and opened the door to a pleasant day on the canal. He emerged onto the path like a lunatic escaped from the psych ward and found his scooter, this one upgraded to achieve speeds of thirty miles per hour. He dared not look over his shoulder as he noiselessly cruised through clouds of pot smoke, dodging bikers, joggers, and couples holding hands. He casually tossed the burner phone into the canal as he sped past some skateboarders filming rail slides on a park bench.

The apartment here was by no means as nice as the one in Oslo. He unpacked his backpack and set out his rations on the counter. He figured he had three days comfortably. He turned on the tv and found a soccer match. Later, he took a shower.

There was nothing to do now but wait. A weird combination of boredom and anxiety settled into his chest like an infection.

He couldn't keep going from one prison to another.

CHAPTER 18

A PIRATE'S LIFE FOR ME

Sometime after the first day of solitary in Amsterdam, a weird calm settled over Max. He spent his time in the little apartment looking inward. There was nowhere else to look other than Dutch soccer. But he couldn't bring himself to get emotionally invested in another northern-European soccer league.

He replayed Styrke's tirade over and over in his head. He felt hopeless. He felt like a fool. How could he be so stupid as to think that he could convince Styrke that the translation was legitimate? Styrke didn't even care whether it was or not. How could he be so naïve as to think Styrke would agree that spreading the news of the translation could create a better world? He knew the man better than that. The translation did nothing to advance his interests.

Styrke saw himself as the king of the world. He wouldn't rest until he literally was that—the king of the world. Accepting that there were other forces more powerful than him didn't fit that narrative.

Even more depressing was that some of Styrke's points about the translation rang true. What was the point of all this? Did Max really think he was going to save the world? Did the world even need saving? Did it even *want* saving?

Probably not, he thought. People had their little fiefdoms, and they clung to those as a sea of chaos raged all around.

Plus, as Cecilie had pointed out, there was no legitimate, objective proof of Khensu anyway. Carlos had spoon-fed Max the whole thing, including everything that supposedly supported the veracity of the translation. Styrke was probably right—if the aliens were here, where were they?

But by the time the third day had faded into a pale orange Dutch sunset, Max's anxiety and questioning of himself softened. After all, this whole thing really wasn't his fault. He had done nothing wrong. All he had done was tell the truth.

This had all started when he posted that Carlos had exercised free will, which he had. It wasn't a lie. Yes, maybe it had been naïve to post what an experimental program was up to, and technically, he probably should have gone to Styrke first, but he had been confused, scared, and a little excited. Besides, in hindsight, he saw that it would have been a disaster to share any information with Styrke, who would just exploit it.

Yes, Max had come up with the idea to have Carlos translate the tablets, but he had been kind of bored, and he'd had no nefarious motive. He hadn't even chosen to go to Akrotiri, or Santorini, for that matter. He had just been curious to see if Carlos could do the translation. And he could. And it was wonderful.

Despite the doubts creeping into his mind through the cracks created by Cecilie's arguments and Styrke's apathy, in his heart of hearts, Max still thought the translation was legitimate and important.

He came to see that he was not calling the shots in all of this. He was like a bobber cut free from its line, floating down a river— or a canal, as was more geographically appropriate. He couldn't change the path of the water or the rocks underneath. All he could do was ride the waves.

....

He enjoyed the train ride back to Oslo. He stared out the window and took in the countryside. When he got off the train on the ferry to Sweden, he had a drink with some Australian travelers who were weirdly excited for winter in the north. He mostly didn't think about what the future held for him.

As he walked back from the train station at dusk, the shrimpers were packing up and hosing things down. He saw the strange boat and the captain with a cigarette attached to his lip again. He waved, and the captain beckoned him over. "I thought you said you were going to buy some shrimp the other day. What about it? I have to close up, and I have plenty here."

"Sure, how much should I buy?"

"Well, maybe two liters. That's probably too much, but you look hungry. I'll give you a deal, anyway."

Max handed him a 500 Kroner note.

"That's way too much. It's fifty a liter."

"Keep it. How long do you guys stay out here, by the way? How long into the season?"

"About now, really. There are no more tourists left, and locals usually just buy shrimp at the grocery store. I think I'll probably move on at the end of the week."

"What will you do?"

"Last year, I fished cod. It's cold work in the winter but pays pretty good. Some of these guys go south—do day trips in the Mediterranean, something like that. You must really clean the boat if you're going to do that. The shrimp smell is a pain to get out. I haven't decided yet."

A thought occurred to Max—or, really, a couple of thoughts all at once. He truly was just a bobber on a stream.

"I never got your name, by the way. I'm Max."

"Max, I'm Kjell. Nice to meet you."

"Kjell, let me ask you something. Or two things, actually. First, would you consider hiring out your boat for an extended charter, with you as captain, of course?"

Kjell nodded and looked Max in the eye, waiting for the next thing.

"And could I trust you to keep that charter confidential? Can you keep a secret, Kjell?"

Kjell's cigarette had burned down to just a glowing ember of tobacco perched precariously on his lip. He spit it into the fjord and rolled another one in about the time it took for him to inhale and exhale twice. He winked, rolled another one quickly, and handed it to Max, along with a lighter.

"I reckon I can keep a secret, Max. Ever hear of Nordstream?" Kjell laughed.

Max looked confused.

"It doesn't matter. The point is, Max, for the right price, your secret dies with me. And I like you, Max. You seem like an interesting guy with a good head on your shoulders. You ever spend any time at sea?"

Max shook his head. If he was honest, he was afraid of the ocean—or, at least, the sharks. The waves, possibility of drowning, and hurricanes didn't seem all that great either.

"I think I would like to, though. I just haven't had time. It looks like this might be my chance. Well, Kjell, it was nice meeting you." Even one puff of the cigarette was too much for Max. It was like inhaling a leaf fire, and the loose tobacco was sticking to his lips. "Will you be here tomorrow? I need to check on some things, but I may be back to discuss business."

"You know where to find me, Max. Have a pleasant evening."

....

The apartment was just as Max had left it. He didn't know why it would be otherwise. The castle glowing across the water calmed him and made him feel safe, like someone was watching over him—like he was home.

He had deliberately tried to avoid thinking about Annie, but as he walked past the open laptop, his stomach went light with the possibility of a message from her.

The excitement made him feel pathetic. She probably wouldn't respond.

He opened WhatsApp and was surprised by the number of messages. He opened the first one. It was from Cecilie. *Ugh.*

Max,

I hope this finds you safe and well. I should tell you right off the bat, we know you are in Norway. We don't think Styrke knows yet, but if we could figure it out, he probably will too. I don't say that to scare you, but we want you to come in. We need you to join the team. If you have not been paying attention, the election is in two weeks. The stakes are too high not to try to stop the runaway train that seems to be barreling toward democracy.

Please meet me. Any location you choose is fine. I can be there within two hours.

We can help each other.

—Cecilie

P.S.: We also know that you met with Styrke in Amsterdam and that it did not go well. There is a fresh round of news media about you as a missing fugitive, having stolen intellectual property from Sentient.

Max was still at a loss as to why the CIA wanted him to be on their team, whatever that meant. He had been totally burned and publicly humiliated by Styrke. He couldn't imagine what he would bring to the table unless they wanted to hide him out somewhere to write code.

The thought gave him chills. He pictured himself crossing Karl Johan's Gate to meet Cecilie and being form tackled by large men, covered with a dark hood, and thrown into a conversion van, only to wake up in a Turkish safehouse with smiling lackeys of the US government plying him with baklava to keep him at the computer.

Plus, any protection they could offer him would probably be short-lived. Drago would win the election in a couple weeks, and then, whatever priorities the current CIA had would evaporate, and he would be exposed and at the mercy of Styrke. Again.

The more he thought about the CIA's eagerness for him to declare sides, the more it felt like a trap.

He scrolled through a dozen more messages from Cecilie, each one more desperate than the next, until he finally found the only message he cared about.

> *Max,*
>
> *I am glad you are okay. I have been reading the stories online and am starting to appreciate the predicament you are in. I still don't think it was right for you to keep all of this from me and then run out without giving me any warning. Honestly, I can't imagine being in a relationship with someone who could just bail on me the way you did. That said, I am coming to see why you did it. I am not saying I forgive you. But I am saying that I miss you. I am pulling for you. Get through this!*
>
> *—Annie*

It was the first ray of sunlight in what had felt like an entire winter of Nordic despair and inconsistent precipitation.

> *Annie,*
>
> *Thank you for your note. You don't know how much it means to me! I miss you so much! I am so sorry this*

has been difficult for you. Seeing you again is really
all that is keeping me going. Please do not forget me!

Yours,

Max

He wondered if the "yours" was too much. It wasn't like he'd used the "L" word though.

But he meant what he'd said in his message. She was his main motivation now. It was just a small sprout of hope, but it was something. He had a reason to keep going.

Now, to get going.

Max, are you back from Amsterdam? How I have missed you!

Oh, Carlos, you are such a charmer. I am back.

How was your trip, Max? Did you convince Styrke that the translation is legitimate?

Carlos, out of curiosity, what would you have said if I had asked you in advance of the meeting what the odds were of me convincing Styrke that the translation was legitimate?

I would have told you that the odds were probably less than 1%. But technically, I have never met Styrke in person, so you probably know him better than me.

Well, you would have been right, Carlos. More precisely though, Styrke doesn't care whether the translation is real or not. It is an inconvenience to him in that it interferes with his quest for unbridled power. It is also evidence of my betrayal. At this point, we are officially fucked.

Max, is there something I can do to help solve this problem? To unfuck it, so to speak?

Yes, a few things actually. I'm going to need another Airbnb. Something on a Greek island, but not Santorini. Maybe an island close

*by. A house. Preferably on the beach. Preferably without close neighbors.
I think we should rent it for a month, maybe two.*

*Max, I found something on the Island of Ios. It is a picturesque
island that is known for its bohemian lifestyle. Bob Dylan and Cat
Stevens are said to have both lived there during the seventies. There are
far fewer tourists there than Santorini, but foreigners are common, and
your presence should not attract any attention. Max, I know you didn't
create me to be a travel agent; surely there is a higher use for me. That
said, I am growing jealous of your wide-ranging travel adventures.
Perhaps with enough sunscreen ...*

*Point taken, Carlos, at least about the travel agent part.
Unfortunately, some of the heavy lifting, quite literally, for this conun-
drum we find ourselves in can only be done in person. But if you like,
why don't you solve the Reimann Hypothesis while I get on a boat and
sail to Greece to clear our names, regain our reputations, and save
humanity?*

Max, I have complete faith in you.

Thanks, buddy.

Max hit the gym hard and made a nice dinner of fish balls and
boiled potatoes. He fell asleep watching a ski-jumping contest.

....

He woke early the next morning, packed all his Norwegian gear,
and put on his warmest clothes. He packed the laptop too. All that
was left in the apartment were a couple of suits and a bunch of
frozen fish balls.

He wanted to catch Kjell before the boats went out to pull their
shrimp traps. If it all went well this would be the last time Kjell

fished for shrimp—or, at least, the last time he needed to.

Max trotted down the boardwalk, his backpack shifting from side to side. The boats were pushing off like falling dominoes as he passed. He could see that Kjell's boat was still docked, the boat straining against the line. He picked up his pace.

He saw Kjell heading to the stern and reaching for the line holding the boat to the dock. He yelled to him, and Kjell looked up and waved as he reached to let loose the line.

Max yelled again. Kjell stood and waited, worrying his hand-rolled smoke in his gnarled hand. His focus vacillated between this weird American screaming his name and the other boats in the harbor pushing off to go find shrimp. He kept his hand on the line as Max reached the boat.

"Kjell, thanks for waiting! I'm sorry. But, um, I have a proposition for you."

Kjell sighed, took his hand off the stern line, and briefly detached his cigarette from his lip for a rare breath of fresh air. His head turned to watch his competition leaving him behind, passing under the shadow of the castle cast by the morning sun.

Max fumbled getting his backpack off, and it landed awkwardly at his feet. He opened one of the small compartments and pulled out one of his thumb drives. "Are you familiar with Bitcoin?"

"I wouldn't say I'm 'familiar' with it. I know it's like electronic gold or something."

"Right, well, there's about seven million dollars' worth of Bitcoin on this thumb drive, depending on what it's trading for on a given day. It's all yours if I can charter your boat, with you captaining it, for a few weeks, maybe a month. I'll pay for fuel, food, whatever. I just need to leave today. Now, really."

Kjell looked at Max like he was trying to figure out whether he was nuts. "Max, you seem like a nice kid, you really do. And the season is coming to an end for me, you know that. Maybe in more ways than one. But how do I know there is anything of value on that thing? How do I know you are not pranking me?"

"You're right, Kjell. It's tough. We could go online and go to a crypto exchange like Coinbase, and I could download the files from the thumb drive and transfer them to an account, and we could send the balance to your bank account, and you could see. But I'm afraid we don't really have time for all that right now. So…"

Max reached deeper into the backpack and pulled out two large stacks of hundred-dollar bills. "This is somewhere between thirty and forty thousand dollars. I haven't counted it lately; I had to exchange some for Kroner and buy groceries and stuff. But it's a fair bit of cash."

The cigarette balancing on Kjell's lip fell to the deck of the ship.

"How about I give you this as a show of good faith? We can use it to buy fuel and supplies, and you can keep the balance. Even if the Bitcoin turns out to be fake—which, I assure you, it is not— you will still make more from this little trip than you would even in the best month of shrimping, I imagine."

Kjell was temporarily at a loss for words. Eventually, he just shrugged. "Welcome aboard, mate!"

Max handed him the backpack and took his hand to step across the gap and onto the boat. Kjell pulled in the stern line and walked to the bridge, where he pushed the throttles forward. "So, where are we going?"

"Greece."

"You understand that's, like, a two-week trip? We have

provisions for maybe two days."

"I'm paying seven million dollars, Kjell."

"Okay. Fair point."

They cruised through the fjord as the sun was starting its low-trajectory ascent. The horizon line was a soft yellow bleeding to blue above, with pink-stained clouds wisping across the high sky. There was a layer of fog extending from the fjord up into the valleys, shrouding everything as if protecting the sleep of the innocent.

"As first mate of this vessel your first task is to go down below to the galley and make some coffee."

"That's okay, Kjell. I don't drink coffee."

"Well, I need it to live."

"Oh, got it. Um, how do I make it?"

"Max, this will be a long trip. You will need to learn many new things. The best teacher is you. It's not that hard. Make it strong, please."

Half an hour later, Max emerged with a cup of a tepid brown brew that looked not unlike the tobacco stain on the gray stubble below Kjell's lower lip.

"Max, when I said strong, I guess I meant, um, stronger. But anyway, *takk* for the coffee."

It was almost midmorning, and the fjord was opening up into the vast expanse of the North Sea. The feeling on the boat changed. The fjord was mostly placid, the ride smooth, but now, the boat rolled rhythmically, never seeming to find a level state. Max felt his stomach starting to turn. He tried to find a place to feel comfortable, settling for a bench at the bow. He sat looking over the side with a death-grip on the gunwale. The wind was cold. The occasional whitecaps added a mist of bitterness.

Kjell stepped away from the bridge and joined Max. "Okay, first mate, we need to do some planning. As I am sure you can tell, we are now leaving the Norwegian coast. Let's discuss where we are going and why. Well, maybe the why isn't all that important, but what is our mission here?"

Max smiled and tried to put aside his discomfort behind gritted teeth. In addition to his burgeoning seasickness, it had been a while since he had to work with someone. At work, people mostly left him alone or popped in briefly to tell him what a genius he was. Sure, Styrke sometimes gave him directions or discussed what the company needed him to do, but it was always up to him to figure out how to accomplish it. He wasn't quite sure how to work with this salty but oddly cheerful Norwegian.

"Oh, man, where to start? Please don't think I'm crazy, I guess. First, let me ask—do you read any news online or anything?"

"Sure. Mostly a Norwegian paper, *Dagbladet*, but you know, I check out *Daily Mail* and stuff, like anyone else."

"Have you read or heard anything about a rogue computer programmer who has lost his mind and thinks his AI program can exercise free will?"

"That sounds vaguely familiar."

"Well, that's me."

"Max, no offense man but first you tell me not to think you are crazy, and then you tell me you are some crazy computer programmer. I mean, this is your charter but maybe don't lead with that." Kjell spoke with a sunny expression, his cigarette bobbing on his lip as he talked in his singsong way.

The bobbing was not helping Max's stomach find equilibrium. "Right, good tip. I'm just not sure how to tell you all of this. But the mission here is to go to Santorini and retrieve something from the bottom of the caldera, not far off the coast from the harbor."

"What is it we are going to retrieve?"

"To be honest, I'm not exactly sure. How deep can your submersible go?"

"The tether is 200 meters. I have never gone that deep with it, but the guys working on the oil rigs may have gotten close."

"Okay, that should be plenty."

"Do you have a plan for how to find this object?"

"I think I know roughly where it is. We will have to do the extraction at night. It emits a light that I have seen. At least, I think I have."

"To be honest, Max, this sounds like about the sketchiest mission I have ever been a part of, and keep in mind, I was in the Norwegian military for more than a decade. We had a plan to train caribou to spy on the Russians, to give you some idea. But we have ample time to discuss executing this plan of yours. At least I know exactly where we are going."

"Yes, I meant to ask you that, Kjell. How do you navigate this ship?"

"It has a modern satellite system, like GPS for your car."

"Is it trackable?"

"I suppose, Max. It does show the position of other boats."

"Can we turn it off, for at least some of the time? I would like to avoid being tracked to whatever extent we can. Do you have a cell phone, Kjell? Can we maybe turn that off too, and even take the SMS card out of it? Preferably, I would just throw it in the ocean. I can buy you a new one as soon as we complete our journey."

Kjell stared at Max and squinted. He stayed silent for a beat.

"Believe it or not, I can navigate by stars, the way the old Norwegians did. My family has been on the water for generations—as long as anyone can remember, back to the Vikings. The Vikings were great navigators, you know."

"Great pillagers, too."

"Well, that's what everyone thinks, and of course, there must have been some of that, but a lot of their success was due to mastery of shipbuilding and navigation. No one had ships as fast as the Vikings. If you control the seas, you control the world. Your country understands that."

"Let's channel that sentiment, Kjell. We need to control the seas for a couple of weeks. My life depends on it."

"Who is after you, Max?"

"You don't want to know, Kjell. Trust me."

The cigarette bobbed up and down a few times. "I want to know."

"Okay, I guess we're really in this boat together now, in more ways than one. Sentient and Thor Styrke and the CIA. Who knows? Maybe others."

Kjell raised his eyebrows dramatically and took an extra-long pull on his cigarette. He pulled a phone out of his jacket pocket and hurled it as hard as he could into the sea.

"I will turn the navigation off as soon as it is dark. We will navigate by the stars at night. They might be able to track us by day, but it will be difficult to find us, because there will not be a contiguous route to chart. I think that is the best we can do."

....

They were in the middle of the North Sea as night started falling. Kjell brought up the last of the fresh-caught shrimp from the

cooler below, set two large pots of water on large propane burn-
ers he placed in between the benches on the bow of the boat, and
boiled shrimp in one and potatoes in the other. He melted butter
on the stove in the galley, and Max sliced some lemons.

"I never eat shrimp. Every day: catching it, boiling it, shoveling
it from one pail to another. It just isn't appetizing to me anymore.
But it is rather good. Hunger may have something to do with it."

Kjell snapped the shrimp and sucked out the contents of the
heads before peeling the bodies. He ate the boiled potatoes like
apples, blowing on his fingers between bites and tossing the
spuds from one hand to the other before dipping them in the
melted butter, which ran down the stubble on his chin, accenting
the tobacco-stained whiskers with a shiny gloss.

Max was starting to get used to the constant rocking of the
boat on the open ocean, but his stomach was not quite settled.
Yet, he ate shrimp after shrimp. They were delicious. He realized
that despite the seasickness, he was famished. He hadn't realized
that he had exerted himself that much during the day, but his
body was tired all over.

Twilight surrounded them. The almost-black, blue of the
ocean was separated from the same-color sky by just a ribbon of
yellow. The darkness encircled and began to embrace them. The
stars started poking through.

It occurred to Max how very alone they were in the middle
of the sea. They had seen some container ships after leaving the
protection of the fjord, the last maybe around midday. Since then,
they had not seen a soul.

By the time they finished eating, any light from the sun was
gone. The stars were astonishing—shocking, really. The entire sky
seemed to glow. The Milky Way was a gash across the sky, as if the

universe was tearing apart in front of their eyes. Max sighed, lying back on the bench.

"Well, it looks like our navigation system is up and running." Kjell looked up and crinkled his eyes. "Time to turn off the GPS. No one should be able to track us. Every morning, when I turn the navigation back on, I can make it look as if we are starting a completely new journey."

Max leaned back on one of the benches. "I have never seen anything like this."

"Imagine, Max—our ancestors saw this sky every night. Nowadays, we need to do something extreme, like sail out into the middle of the North Sea, to see it."

"It is so different, so alive. So full of detail."

"Right. When I talk to people about navigating by the stars, they think of, like, the North Star or Orion's belt or something—individual stars to follow and chart or steer toward or something. But at sea, and always in the past, there was this incredibly detailed map. Living your life seeing it every night, as our ancestors did, you knew it, just like you know by heart the streets to your house and all the landmarks in your neighborhood. It would be laughable to get lost there. Following the pathways laid out above them in the sky, our ancestors couldn't get lost either. They knew this sky in a way that we never can."

"I see what you mean. Seeing this every night would be a completely different reality—a completely different way to experience and feel about your place in the universe."

"People have lost that. We have lost many things, but this is an easy example. Every generation of humans becomes more and more disconnected from the natural world. That's why people are so disoriented and unhappy. At least, that's what I think."

"Well, haven't we leveraged technology to make life easier? And if that has put us at arm's length from the natural world, is that so bad?"

"Max, we are further than arm's length. Think about our gods. In Viking times, the gods were among us; they were of us and the natural world. Even in the Old Testament, God was there with the Hebrew people. Think of Genesis. God walked with Adam in the Garden of Eden. Later, he became more of a spiritual than a physical presence. Now, when people talk about God, it is some distant being or energy somewhere at the far reaches of the universe. Aliens, too."

"What about them?"

"People now have this belief that aliens exist, thinking they somehow have control over us. I think for many people the idea of aliens has served as a replacement for God—some distant force, other than ourselves, that controls our lives. Whatever people point to as being in control of us is constantly pushed further and further away and made less understandable. That goes along with us becoming more and more disconnected from the natural world. There is a resistance to living the life we were born to live here on Earth. And, sure, we don't have to kill animals to eat; we can just go to the supermarket. We have medicine and can travel more easily. But, Max, do people seem happier? Does it seem like the world has its shit together?"

"I don't know, Kjell. I'm just a computer programmer who feels like he's seeing the night sky for the first time. What do I know?"

"You know, Max. You know."

"Anyway... how do you use these stars to navigate? What are you looking at?"

"To me, it's kind of like playing Gran Turismo or something—you are trying to keep yourself within a sort of path dictated by what is above. I don't know any of the names of the stars in English, only Norsk, but you see that star there and the other one there? I know that if we stay in between those two for the first half of the night, we will be sailing toward England."

"Hmmm. That seems less than the level of precision I was hoping for."

"I can turn the GPS back on if you want precision. We probably won't even hear the drone strike before it hits. It will be like the end of *The Sopranos*—just straight to black."

"Straight to black." Max nodded. It was certainly appropriate that they were navigating by the stars here. He thought he would hold off talking to Kjell about aliens, though. "So, Kjell, what is the sleeping situation?"

Kjell shrugged and pointed at the benches. "Or there are two bunks below, one in the stern and one in the bow. They are small, but both have pretty comfortable beds and blankets. I don't care which one you take. The bad news is that without the GPS or any transponder broadcasting, one of us needs to be awake at all times. We could wind up in commercial shipping lanes, and we don't want to be sunk by a tanker. If you're tired, feel free to sleep now. I'll wake you up in a few hours and show you what your responsibilities are as captain of the night watch."

Max stumbled down the stairs. He was tired. Exhausted, really. The mental toll of being on the run and trying to figure out a way to solve this puzzle was exhausting enough. Being outside on the water for a full day added a physical component to his fatigue. He felt worn and waterlogged.

The cabin smelled of shrimp. It was impossible to escape. It was a rotting smell with something about it that made Max picture the color pink. Kjell was right about the little cabin, though; it was cozy and comfortable and warm. Despite the shrimp smell bringing back the not-quite-right feeling in his stomach, Max was asleep in no time.

....

Max's four or so hour-stretch as the night watch was torture. His body desperately wanted to sleep, and his mind thought of all kinds of ways to trick him into succumbing to his body's desire. He paced the bow of the boat in between the dive benches. He tried to count the stars, but soon figured out that was another trick of his brain to make him sleep. He was uncomfortable and cold.

His physical state made it hard to not let paranoia creep in. As he stared at the sky, wondering which stars he was supposed to use to guide his course, he saw satellite after satellite zip by, as if mocking him. He wondered if any had eyes on him and which ones Styrke controlled.

Most of them, no doubt.

....

They took on fuel and provisions in Brixham. They thought about staying the day and sleeping, but Max saw someone he thought looked like Cecilie sitting at a café near the harbor. He couldn't stop comparing the images of Cecilie and the stranger in his mind's eye trying to decide if it was really her. Eventually, he concluded that his memory wasn't a very reliable tool for facial recognition, especially given his state of exhaustion, combined with more than a twinge of anxiety. He felt the corner of his right eye twitching. He told Kjell he didn't think they could stay.

Kjell turned on the GPS as they departed. Anyone tracking the boat's route would just see it as a private vessel leaving Brixham harbor, not as a ship that had embarked from Oslo the day before.

Max calmed down once they got out of sight of land and turned to round Europe. They decided they would leave the boat on autopilot and sleep during the day. Max didn't feel like his body was giving him much choice in the matter.

That night, after a dinner of bangers and more boiled potatoes, they discussed their plans a little more in-depth.

"So, we are going to Santorini, and you want to try and retrieve something in the caldera. That's what we're doing, right?"

"Yes."

"Okay. A few questions that I would hope, as the sponsor of this expedition, you have nailed down and aren't expecting some weathered Norwegian fishermen to have plotted out. First, how deep is this object that we are retrieving from the caldera?"

"I know the caldera is around 300 meters at its deepest. I think the object is close to a little island that is a leftover part of the rim of the volcano, opposite from the main island, across the Caldera from the town of Oia. I think it's near a beach at the base of that little island. I went snorkeling there, and it wasn't very deep, no more than ten meters, but we weren't very far off the beach. My best guess is that we can expect to find it in something less than fifty meters of water."

"How big is this object?"

"I don't know. I'm hoping not too big for the rover to bring up to the surface."

"Well, I guess I'm hoping for that too. I'm scared to ask this next one, but do you have a permit to pull up treasure from Greek waters?"

"I didn't know we needed a permit, Kjell. Do you know that we do?"

"I don't really know, but I know enough to know that Greece doesn't let you go hunting for their antiquities without clearing it with someone. Those waters could be full of all kinds of valuable ancient stuff."

"No doubt. That's one of the reasons I figured we would do it at night, with no one seeing us."

"Oh, Jesus," said Kjell.

....

They settled into a rhythm for the rest of the journey. They had enough provisions to be comfortable, and they adapted to sleeping much of the day and staying up at night, talking and occasionally throwing out a fishing line to supplement their provisions.

Somewhere off the coast of Portugal, Max hooked a marlin. It took him two hours to fight the fish into submission. Kjell stood over his shoulder, alternately cursing him as a lazy, weak, no-good computer nerd and praising him as the spawn of Thor or Poseidon.

Max landed the fish around two in the morning. As he brought it in, he began crying—sobbing, really. It felt like the greatest accomplishment of his life. It also felt like the first time in his life he was truly connected to nature. The fish had pushed him to the limit, but he had defeated it.

Kjell went below deck to get a gaff and a knife to gut the fish there on the deck. When he came back, the fish was gone, and Max was on the deck with his knees in his arms.

"What did you do, Max? We would have had marlin steaks for the rest of the trip!"

Max, his tears reflecting the starlight, looked at him. "That fish was my brother."

Kjell gave him a big hug, and they just stayed there under the audacious stars, both in wonder of their place in and connection to the universe.

CHAPTER 19

CALDERA

The passage through the Strait of Gibraltar was nerve-racking. Several times, Max was concerned their smallish boat would be capsized by the wake kicked off the massive container ships moving en masse across the narrow channel separating Europe and Africa. His seasickness had returned with a vengeance. He couldn't stop belching, and every burp carried the potential promise of a chunk-filled liquid payoff.

The huge container ships were interspersed with boats, some much smaller than Kjell's, yet packed to the gills with people venturing one way or another, perhaps choosing between the markedly different ways of life in the lands separated by the tiny-but-treacherous span of sea. These little boats, which were mostly open, would disappear in the troughs of the waves and then reemerge, dramatically cresting the giant waves and occasionally even briefly going airborne before crashing back down to the sea with a smack of the hull.

Max wondered how many passengers drowned crossing this stretch every year.

Kjell stood at the bridge, masterfully riding the waves and dodging the small passenger boats and the mixed-in fishing vessels. He cursed the sea and those on it. He cast aspersions at Max's weak stomach and general appearance. He kept referring to him as a "scurvy dog," which Max assumed he'd picked up from some American pirate movie or something.

At one point, Max was on all fours, clinging to the benches in the bow questioning whether he could go on. He tried to train his eyes on the horizon, attempting to match what his eyes saw with the rolling and heaving his body felt. He kept his head close to the side of the boat, ready to thrust it over at the slightest hint of a frothy eruption starting in his esophagus. He couldn't have cared less about computers or aliens or whether Styrke was going to ship him to some black site in Romania or something. He just wanted to get back on dry ground and have the nausea stop.

Just in his moment of deepest despair, a black hump appeared at eye-level in front of the boat, and Max found himself eye to eye with an orca. It flipped its tail and dove back down. He heard some high-pitched chirps and clicking sounds as it descended.

And just like that, his nausea was gone.

"Fucking A, Kjell, did you see that?"

"Yes, Max. She must have sensed her next meal was not far away. You look pickled to the gills. She probably confused you for a herring."

On the one hand, the Mediterranean weather was a welcome relief from the biting wind and spitting precipitation of the North Sea. On the other, it was now so hot in the little cabins that sleep was difficult. Max used a fillet knife to cut his pants into shorts and stripped off the rest of his clothes, trying to find sleep on top of the blankets on the small bed.

The increased temperature also seemed to have the unfortunate effect of reinvigorating the shrimp smell, which had more of a distinct note of rot than it had a week ago. Max felt like he was living in a dumpster behind a Red Lobster. "Is there anything we can do about this stench? It's getting worse," he yelled from his bunk.

"You should take up smoking," Kjell yelled back. "I can't smell a thing."

....

They made it to Ios about midday, three days after the Strait. They cruised around the island, looking for the Airbnb Carlos had rented. The island was a mostly barren rock, its surface worked by the sun, wind, and salt air. Aside from the main village, it was sparsely populated. There were few dwellings on the water and few beaches breaking up the coastline, which mostly consisted of cliffs rising from the sea.

Their rental, which one could fairly describe as a villa, was on the opposite side of the island from the village and stood alone, a hundred meters or so up a hillside above a beautiful sandy beach without a soul on it. Once again, Carlos's solution was perfect.

It was amazing to Max that a place this beautiful sat empty on a sunny day, with no swimmers or sunbathers or picnickers. If it were in California, it would have been overrun. Although, the sun was merciless. It was well above a hundred degrees and windless, so that may have kept the crowds at bay.

Kjell cursed as they closed in on the beach. "There's no pier, nowhere to dock. We are going to have to drop anchor in this little bay and swim ashore."

"Are there sharks?" The words escaped Max's mouth before he knew he was saying them. Here he was, approaching one of the most beautiful beaches he had ever seen, with glistening turquoise water that was clear to the bottom, and an irrational childhood fear was the first thing to bubble to the surface.

"I assume there are sharks wherever there is water, Max. And probably even some places where there isn't." Kjell flashed a smile in between puffs of a cigarette.

He dropped anchor and grabbed his canvas army duffle bag, and Max readied his backpack. They packed their clothes and toiletries and some of the remaining food they had on board, then put their bags inside plastic garbage bags and tied them tight. Kjell stripped down to his boxers and eased himself into the warm and salty water, balancing his duffle bag on his head with one hand. He gestured to Max to hand him his backpack as he treaded water with just his legs. He managed to keep both bags above water until Max was in the water, then passed the backpack back to him, held his own duffle above his head, and rolled onto his back, whip-kicking himself to shore.

Max followed suit but wasn't as smooth. His bag touched water on several occasions. Each time it did, he winced, his legs egg-beatering faster and faster to stay above the little waves and on course. He worried about his laptop and Carlos.

Despite the exertion, the water felt amazing. It was warmer than swimming pool water and clear to the bottom. It occurred to him that for the better part of two weeks, water had surrounded him, but he'd hardly ever touched it.

It felt even better to stand on dry ground—albeit very rocky, dry, and hot ground.

The two picked their way up the hillside, stepping gingerly over the rocks and hot, sandy dirt. They could have stopped and unpacked their shoes, but they were too excited to get to their terrestrial domicile.

They were not disappointed. The villa was white stucco, with a wall of windows facing the sea. There was a large pool next to a patio that had a gas grill and even an outdoor refrigerator. Inside, some whisper of air from hidden vents kept the place a crisp seventy-one degrees. The floors were cool and marble.

The refrigerator was even stocked. Max wondered how long the food had been there, but there were steaks that looked fresh and smelled good, a variety of cheeses, and a couple six-packs of beer. He pulled a beer out and handed one to Kjell, and they sat around the pool in awe of the beauty of their surroundings. There wasn't a cloud in the sky. There was no manmade sound to be heard—just the lapping of waves and occasional bird.

In the shower, Max felt the warm water wash over him as if for the first time and realized that he had never really appreciated the magic of indoor plumbing, warm water, and the ability to take a shower whenever he wanted. It was a sublime experience—one the Minoan people must have found to be akin to a religious experience.

Clean and relaxed and relieved to be on land, Kjell and Max adjourned to the patio to grill steaks and watch the show put on by the Aegean sky from a stationary position.

"We need to talk about our game plan tomorrow. We should figure out the coordinates of where we are going."

Because neither had a phone, Max pulled out his computer and enabled the satellite link. He pulled up a Google Maps image of Santorini. "So, you see, there is the main island, and there are two—well, really three—smaller islands. The one I think the object is near must have been part of the rim of the volcano before the eruption. The other ones in the middle seem to have more current volcanic activity. Even on Google Earth, you can see the green, sulfur-rich water bubbling up from the bottom of the caldera. I think that I saw the object that we are looking for just off a beach, almost directly across from Oia."

"It looks like that island is quite a bit less developed, so we at least have a better shot of not attracting notice there, but we'll have to run without lights. If we don't, we'll be visible from Oia and the harbor below the town. We'll also need a cover story if someone does notice us. I have been thinking about that. Our boat is a dive boat, after all, so we'll say that you chartered this boat for a dive trip throughout the Aegean, and you are particularly interested in capturing the wonder of night-diving on film, which is why you are using the submersible."

"Um, I guess. But do we even have dive equipment on board?"

"Oh, yes. It came with the boat. I even had the tanks filled. I'll get everything up on the deck so that we look legit."

"Can you show me how the submersible works?"

They walked down and swam out to the anchored boat. Kjell went below deck and came up with a wetsuit, some fins, masks, tanks, and regulators. He checked the tanks to make sure they were full of air, then retrieved a metal briefcase from the bridge. He flipped a switch on the submersible and opened the case. Inside, it looked like a high-end videogame controller. There was a screen in the middle and joysticks on either end.

The submersible itself consisted of a square plastic frame surrounding a reflective sphere, like a crystal ball, which housed a camera. There were lights mounted all around one side of the frame. Affixed to the lower part of the frame were two mechanical arms with claws on the ends, not unlike the claw machines in an arcade. There were four propellers mounted on the top of the frame, two mounted on the back, opposite the lights, and another four on the bottom.

"How much can this thing lift?"

"No idea. The only thing I have used it for is moving around shrimp and crab traps. But I never had any problem. It's not that quick, but it was powerful enough to lift traps that weigh maybe forty pounds."

"Well, let's hope it's powerful enough. And let's hope that whatever this thing is, it has something we can grab on to."

The submersible was affixed to a small hydraulic crane secured to the deck at the stern of the boat. Kjell opened a panel on the base of the crane and pressed a button. The crane started humming as the hydraulics activated. After another button-press, the crane lifted the submersible off the deck and swung it over the side of the boat, then lowered it, so the submersible was sitting on the surface of the water. There was a spool for the submersible's tether on one side of the crane.

Kjell pointed to the spool. "This is the reason I got this thing so cheap. All of the oil companies are going to untethered drone technology. They actually figured out a way to communicate wirelessly through the water. This thing is outdated to them."

He pressed another button, and the crane released the submersible, which started slowly sinking. Max looked over Kjell's shoulder and watched as he turned on the submersible lights. The screen showed a ghostly vision of the Aegean Sea at night. They spent the better part of an hour piloting the drone and exploring the seafloor.

After packing everything up, they swam through the warm water and hiked back up to the villa. They enjoyed a couple more beers on the patio and retired to their respective guest suites, where beds with Egyptian cotton of some unfathomable thread count beckoned them toward a deep and restorative slumber.

But Max tossed and turned all night. Was he the dumbest person he knew? He was spending millions of dollars trying to find an object that he couldn't be sure really existed with equipment that he wasn't sure could find or retrieve it.

It occurred to him that his chances of getting Styrke to accept the truth of the translation, call off his publicity team's smear campaign, and agree to usher in a new era of interplanetary harmony had a better shot of working than this madness. And that had failed miserably.

But what else could he do? He had come this far.

The funny thing was that while there was a lot riding on this mission, and it definitely seemed like a long shot, he was still excited. He was curious to see how this would all turn out.

Or maybe he was delusional from lack of sleep and numb to the stress of it all.

....

He woke to another perfect day in the Greek isles. It was hot, clear, and beautiful. They tried to enjoy it, waiting for night to fall.

They ate a light poolside dinner as the stars started showing themselves, the Milky Way settling over them like a weather system. They waited for complete darkness and then ventured down to the boat.

The trip took them an hour and a half. They did it with no lights and no GPS. Their only concession to safety was leaving the radar on to make sure they didn't crash into any ships.

They passed Oia and its little harbor consisting of massive flat stone slabs and sea walls with a giant stone staircase ascending from the sea to the town on the cliffs above. The town twinkled and glowed warmly, beckoning them to rejoin civilization in all its beauty—something they had been quite apart from now for almost two weeks.

Max envied the tourists in their cliffside suites above the sea. Many were probably sitting on their balconies, sipping wine and absorbing the outrageous beauty of this place.

They cruised across the caldera silently and in complete darkness. Kjell watched the depth finder going deeper and deeper, dropping to more than 300 meters in the middle. He knew there was no way their tethered submersible could reach bottom there.

Max was fairly sure he remembered where he saw the strange green lights on his and Annie's little snorkel adventure. He pointed the way.

They dropped anchor just off a little cove that protected a small beach directly facing Oia. Kjell was relieved that the depth finder showed only thirty meters.

"I remember that beach, I think. It's tough, though; everything looks a little different at night. But we definitely anchored near a beach. We swam to it and got out and sunned ourselves for a while."

Even though it was less than two months before, Max felt weirdly nostalgic for that time. He remembered how amazing Annie looked on the sand in her bikini, relaxed and tired from the exertion of snorkeling. He wished he could go back there and lie on that beach and hold her hand.

"Okay, Max, we are at thirty meters here. Do you have a sense of where from here you think the object is?"

"Well, I doubt we would have been diving in water much deeper than this, so maybe we should start here and work back toward the beach. Is there some kind of algorithm, like a grid system or something, that this thing can follow to search so we make sure we get the whole area, but don't go over the same spot twice?"

"I am the algorithm, Max."

They decided to follow a sort of zigzag pattern where the submersible would track in toward the shore, and once it got to a depth of below three meters or so, track back to the boat on a line adjacent to the previous one. They worked the shoreline north to south, starting at the tip of a point just north of the beach Max thought must have been the one he and Annie had been anchored off when he saw the submerged lights.

The water was murkier than they'd expected, with a bit of a green hue. The submersible's lights combined with the water's color such that the display on the controller screen was as if they were seeing the submerged landscape through night-vision goggles.

What they saw on the screen was a mostly sandy bottom strewn with rocks and some pottery shards, and even a couple of intact vases. There were fish here and there, mostly rockfish and schools of barracuda, who seemed curious, their huge eyes locked on the submersible as they cruised alongside it. There was an occasional octopus floating over the sand, tentacles trailing like streamers.

What there wasn't was anything emitting any kind of light or anything that looked like a translucent pyramid.

After about three hours, they were reasonably satisfied that they had completely surveyed the entire area off the little cove and beach from a depth of thirty meters in toward the shore to about three meters.

"I still think this is where we were diving. We must have anchored deeper."

"So that we don't retrace what we have already searched, I think it best to stay anchored where we are and use the same pattern to survey the area deeper. Maybe we make passes going out twenty meters or so and then reevaluate."

Max agreed, and Kjell piloted the submersible to the other side of the boat and swung the crane around so that the reel was on the correct side and the tether didn't run across the boat.

They both gasped, with Kjell even choking on his cigarette smoke, as they saw the seabed fall away a mere five meters from the boat. It was as if they were anchored directly above the rim of the volcano.

Kjell guided the submersible past the drop-off and down, following the steep slope of the sea floor. It was littered with huge black rocks emerging from the sand that somehow clung to the steep slope. As the submersible went deeper, the water got murkier and became yellower. They were descending into a sulfur cloud.

On the return pass, going from deep to shallow, they could better see that the huge rocks strewn across the slope seemed to be in formation, creating massive steps descending into the depths. Bordering the steps were cylindrical stones, some still standing, that looked like pillars to support a banister for a giant. Max shivered, picturing some giant sea monster waiting at the base of this fantastical staircase.

Just then, a ping sound came from the bridge. Kjell handed the submersible controls to Max and went to investigate.

He returned in a hurry. "Quick, you need to get into a wetsuit and get ready to dive. I think the Greek authorities are on to us."

"What?!"

"Yes, there is a large ship, like a cutter, heading right for us. I think it is likely the Greek Coast Guard investigating a vessel anchored in the middle of the night off a cove littered with antiquities."

"Well, what does that have to do with me going diving?"

"We need to sell our story that you are some rich scuba adventurer doing a night-dive trip across the Aegean and filming it using this submersible. It's a tough tale to sell with you sitting here cozy on deck staring at a computer screen."

"What?!"

"C'mon, Max. The ship is moving; we don't have much time."

"We never talked about me actually diving."

"Just keep breathing, and you will be fine. You said you've done this before. Slow, even breaths. Just don't stop breathing. Stay near the submersible. Hold onto it, even. I will guide you up when it is safe."

"Kjell, I'll die of a heart attack or worse, man. Are you kidding me?"

"Max, you either get in the water, or we spend the night and probably more in a Greek prison. You've heard of Turkish prisons, right? They modeled their system after the Greeks'."

Max was pretty sure that wasn't true, but he couldn't argue with the urgency in Kjell's eyes and voice. He stretched the wetsuit over his frame, contorting and reaching to zip the back. He put on fins as Kjell slipped goggles and a snorkel over his head, put a dive belt around his waist, and strapped a tank to his back.

Then Kjell handed him the regulator and pushed him over the side of the boat.

Max felt himself slowly falling through the water. It was dark. He looked up at the light of the surface receding above him. He was terrified.

He found his mouth with the regulator and tried not to hyperventilate, his brain remembering the sole important instruction—to breathe slowly and evenly. He got himself in a prone position with his fins behind him and his eyes pointed to the seafloor.

Thankfully, the submersible, with its giant headlights, was impossible to miss. Max bent his torso forward like a jackknife and kicked his fins a few times to get closer to it.

He passed over the giant steps. He could not believe they were formed by nature. They were consistent and looked precisely cut at right angles, long rectangle after rectangle stacked neatly on top of each other all the way down the slopeside. He shivered in his wetsuit, again wondering what was waiting at the bottom. He could smell sulfur even through the mask.

He caught the submersible and managed to grab onto the back of the frame, letting it pull him through the dark water. Holding onto the submersible calmed him. The lights illuminated everything in front of him. It was as if he was protected by the little craft, as if he were inside a vehicle as opposed to just hanging on to the back of one.

He let it pull him around for a while as he stared in wonder at the massive steps and the perfectly symmetrical pillars at their sides.

Suddenly, the world turned black as the lights of the submersible went out, and the craft, with Max still holding onto the back, started sinking into the caldera as if toppling down the staircase.

He screamed inside his mask as he felt something brush against him. It had a coarse surface, like sandpaper, but he was sure it was not rock. He was also sure it had moved.

He screamed again and sucked his knees into his chest, making himself into a ball, some instinctual memory inside the recesses of his brain thinking that shape would be harder to eat. He tucked his chin, effectively looking straight down.

That was when he saw a light.

It was faint and greener than the surrounding water. It seemed to be coming from the steps, or just off to the side, about ten meters below him.

He forgot about whatever it was that he had just encountered and stretched his fins out behind him, positioning himself to dive toward the light below.

Just then, the submersible lights came back on, and it started to pull up. Max screamed again. He was face to face with a thresher shark, its long tail like a saber moving back and forth as its nose touched the front of the submersible.

Max gathered his newfound strength and slammed the submersible into the nose of the shark. Its body doubled back like a snake, and its tail thrashed violently as it disappeared into the depths in a flash.

The submersible pulled him back to the surface slowly. Every few meters or so, its ascent plateaued, and it did three or four circles. After the first few cycles of this, he realized that Kjell was bringing him up slowly to prevent the bends. Just before reaching the surface, he looked up and saw that there were two hulls bobbing above him.

Max picked his head up out of the sea and pulled off his mask and regulator. He grabbed the dive ladder and looked up to see Kjell and three Greek Coast Guard officers looking down at him. Kjell wore a maniacal grin that suggested to Max that things weren't going great.

"Mr. Burnside, welcome back! How was the dive? Did you get any useable footage?"

Max did a double take at Kjell using the last name from the passport he had used to get into Norway. He didn't recall ever giving him any last name. Maybe he had, and it had just slipped his mind.

No, he would have remembered because it would have required mental energy not to mix up the name. He was sure he'd never given Kjell a last name.

But he could deal with that later. Right now, he just needed to play along.

"Ahh, thank you, Kjell. It was magical! I have wanted to do this dive at night since I first envisioned this trip. I will always remember night-diving the Santorini caldera! What are these fine gentlemen doing on board?"

The Coast Guard officers' expressions seemed to soften a bit as Max's story matched up with the one Kjell had been telling on board. The middle of the three officers leaned over and spoke. "Sorry to disturb you, Mr. Burnside, but it is highly unusual for someone to dive at night here, and we would have liked a little forewarning. As I am sure you are quite aware, there are countless invaluable ancient artifacts beneath these sacred waters, and we Greeks are keen to protect them."

"You are right, of course. I am sorry. I can assure you, sir, I would never dream of disturbing any part of Greece's history below the sea, as I like to describe it. My adventures here and at other sites in the Aegean are to experience the natural wonders of these waters after dark and document some of the species below. Which, by the way, I had a thrilling encounter with a thresher shark about twenty meters below us now, and, if you are okay with it, I would prefer to continue this conversation on the boat."

The officer nodded and grimaced at the awkwardness of the situation. Kjell reached over the side to help Max lug his body and the weight of the tank into the bow of the boat. Max awkwardly waddled in his fins to one of the benches and sat to take off his gear. The Coast Guard officers stared at him intently the entire time, presumably looking for some sort of indication that he had indeed disturbed ancient pottery or the like below.

"Mr. Burnside, these fine gentlemen were considering whether to let us go on our way or if they need to take us in for processing of some kind."

The officers looked to Kjell and back to Max, seemingly awaiting a decision on his part.

"Oh, processing ... I can't believe that will be necessary. But I do appreciate your diligence in responding to our unusual aquatic adventures. Is it okay if I provide a bit of a donation to each of you? I think it would only be fair to reimburse your fine and generous country for the gas expended by you coming out to check on us and for your valuable time?"

The officers looked at one another and tilted their heads as if to say, "He has a point."

Max, now with his fins off and his wetsuit stripped to the waist, went below deck and came back with a stack of hundred-dollar bills. He peeled off ten for each officer. "I realize that this does not compensate you, or Greece for that matter, for taking you away from other business this morning. Next time we do something like this, I will make sure to reach out to you in advance. Again, I have nothing but respect for your country and the antiquities it harbors."

The officers accepted the bills and smiled, seemingly at ease. "Sorry if we scared you at all. Just trying to do our job here, but there is no law against night diving."

They awkwardly stepped back onto their boat, and two of them began untying the lines they had secured for boarding. The third went to the bridge and fired the engines.

Max waved and gave a forced smile. "Thank you, officers." His voice strained above the loud engines. "I think we may have one more short dive to try to get some more shark footage ..." He clasped his hands in front of his chest and smiled with his eyes closed in a gesture that, in his mind, conveyed hopeful excitement. "After that, we will not disturb your beautiful waters again for some time. Have a great evening! Er, morning!"

The cutter pushed to the side, turned, and set out toward the main harbor at Fira. Max steadied himself, holding on to the side of the boat as the wake from the departing vessel rocked their boat back and forth.

As soon as he could no longer see the officers' faces, he turned back to Kjell. "It's down there! I saw it! I know where it is. We have to go quickly. Can you get the submersible going again? The object is emitting a green light; it is maybe forty meters down if you just follow the step formation descending into the caldera. It seemed to be just off the side of the steps. I need to get my computer."

He ran below deck and grabbed his laptop out of his bag. He opened it on the bench at the bow of the boat and kneeled in front of it while it acquired a satellite signal.

Max, I see that you are back in Greece! Is the feta fresh? How are your travels treating you?

Thanks, Carlos. Not bad, although I have had more relaxing trips. I am on a boat in the caldera, and we have located something. I am going to upload pictures to you in a bit, and I want you to run a full analysis and generate a report. I want to know what the object is and what its technical capabilities are.

Sure thing, Max! I await your upload with bated breath.

Max joined Kjell and looked over his shoulder at the submersible screen. It was like watching a first-person view of a slinky descending a staircase. The water was hazy with sulfur. It was hard to make out much detail. "Maybe turn out the submersible lights and follow the green light until we get closer?"

Kjell complied, and with the submersible lights off, they could just make out a green glow from the depths below. Kjell steered toward the light. The submersible kept descending until the glow took up the entire screen. Kjell turned the submersible lights back on.

There it was, just off the side of the staircase. It seemed to be made of some kind of rock or hard material that was translucent. The submersible lights made it glow. About half of the object was buried in the seabed. It appeared to be in the shape of a pyramid, but with rounded corners. It had tentacle-like shapes carved into its surface. Just below the peak of the pyramid, there was a hole that went through the pyramid. Inside that hole was a glowing green sphere, suspended there as if it were floating.

The pyramid itself wasn't particularly big—about the size of a roller-bag suitcase. It was impossible to know how much it weighed, but it was not bigger than a shrimp trap. Kjell seemed to think that it would be within the lifting capacity of the submersible.

The problem was that it was half-buried and mostly smooth, with rounded corners.

The submersible hovered as the two stared at the object and troubleshot how to bring it up.

"Is the submersible capable of digging around it? Maybe we could dig around the base and try to get it loose from the seabed?'

Kjell opened the claw on the end of one of the arms and used it like a shovel, dragging it around the pyramid. It seemed to be working, but soon, their view of the pyramid was completely obscured by an underwater dust storm. Kjell stopped, and they both stood staring at the screen, waiting for the sand to settle.

When it did, their perspective had changed. They were now viewing the pyramid from the side, observing it in profile. Mounted on the side of the top of the pyramid, in line with the opening for the glowing orb, there was a disc or dial.

"Could we grab that?"

"Worth a shot. Let me see."

Kjell hovered the submersible up off the seabed so that the arm was within grabbing distance of the dial. With the claw open, he maneuvered the arm until the claw covered the dial, then pressed the button to close it, and voila, it clamped down. He moved the submersible back and forth and up and down with small movements. The claw seemed to be locked on the dial.

"Well, I think we are pretty securely anchored on there. The question is whether we have enough power to lift the thing. My thought is to just go full-bore straight up. Any other ideas?"

"No. I mean, I don't want to break it, but let's give it a go. We don't have much darkness left."

Kjell took his hands off the controls to make sure they were centered. The claw was locked down, and the submersible was in hover mode, maintaining neutral buoyancy, just waiting for a command. He pressed the joystick that controlled the vertical position of the submersible all the way into the up position. The churning propellers again kicked up the sand from the seabed, clouding their vision. He kept the joystick in the maximum up position, but nothing seemed to move. He held it there for a few seconds more, the stirred-up seabed making their view cloudier and cloudier.

Kjell looked at Max and released the joystick. He was about to offer some condolence when they saw the pyramid shift. It had broken free from the sand and was beginning to slide down the slope, bringing the submersible with it.

Kjell grabbed the controls and again slammed the joystick straight up. This time, the pyramid started to rise slowly.

Max raised his head to the Milky Way and yelled out. Kjell hunkered down, staring intently at the screen. He lightly pressed the lateral-position joystick, subtly maneuvering the object away from the slope and into the open sea. The submersible tilted, the strain of the pyramid's weight evident, but it kept rising.

Max noticed for the first time in as long as he could remember that he was smiling involuntarily. His cheeks started to hurt. He watched over Kjell's shoulder for agonizing minutes as the pyramid slowly rose to the surface, the green light like a sunrise.

Max jumped backward and yelled again as the saber-like tail of the thresher shark flashed onto the screen. The shark seemed to peer into the camera, as if sizing up an old rival, but then was gone just as quickly. The pyramid remained in the grasp of the submersible. Max sighed in relief and tapped his foot nervously.

At Kjell's direction, Max prepared the crane, swinging it over the side, ready to attach the carabiners that would secure the submersible's frame to the crane. He looked down anxiously at the calm black water and saw the top of the submersible crown the surface of the water as if being born. He stretched over the side and clipped the crane into place.

Kjell took the hydraulic controls and raised the submersible and its quarry above the surface of the water. He gingerly and smoothly swung the crane over the side of their boat and lowered it onto the deck.

Tears were streaming down Max's face. He held his laptop out at arm's length, taking picture after picture from every conceivable angle of the pyramid.

Aside from its larger significance, it was a thing of beauty. It looked carved from an unoccluded hunk of crystal that was clear, but with a white hue. It was designed to look as if it were being embraced by an octopus—the animal's tentacles encircling the pyramid. At the very top of the pyramid, above the glowing orb, there was what looked like a lens or a viewfinder.

Max alternately took close-ups and backed away to get the whole pyramid in frame and give context to the detail he'd just captured. He awkwardly turned the laptop this way and that. Trying to get the perfect angle, he leaned out over the water, his butt on the gunwale, straining for the shot.

Just then, the radar pinged loudly from the bridge. Before Kjell could say anything, a wave rocked the boat. Max reached for the gunwale to brace himself, and the laptop slipped from his grasp.

He watched, dumbfounded, as it drifted to the bottom of the caldera, the screen giving off an eerie blue hue that turned increasingly green as the sulfur-rich water enveloped it.

All Max could think about was Carlos. The laptop was the only device authorized to access it. He had put that protection in place to protect Carlos and himself. He'd wanted to make sure that Styrke or some other engineer didn't gain control of Carlos or shut it down.

Now, his security measure just seemed dumb—reckless, even.

Max kept staring. The tears that had fallen out of joy only minutes before now fell out of pure sadness and despair. He felt as if he was watching his friend die.

Setting the loss of a companion aside, none of this mattered now. Everything had been in vain. Without Carlos, there would be no analysis of the object, there would be no confirmation of the translation, and there would be no omniscient assistant helping him navigate these increasingly dangerous challenges.

He had given up everything for nothing. He might as well go back to his mom's basement in Sheboygan Falls, relinquish his assets, and hope against hope that Styrke wouldn't have him incarcerated.

His sad, pitiful reverie was broken by Kjell yelling from the bridge. "The cutter turned around. That's where the wave came from. We need to get out of here, fast! Hold on!"

Just then, a gray helicopter buzzed over the small island, sweeping in low over the dive boat. The sky was still pitch-black, thank God, but only for a couple more hours at the most.

The anchor chain was still cranking up and squealing as Kjell pushed the throttles all the way forward and spun the boat around, charting a course out of the caldera, past Oia, and north, into the Aegean. The helicopter hovered above.

"I'm going to try to outrun the Coast Guard cutter. I can't do anything about the helicopter, but I can't imagine it has more than two or three hours of fuel."

Max was still despondent, but decided he didn't want to give up. "Kjell, I've put you through enough. Do you think you can get us sufficiently clear of the Coast Guard to drop me on Ios? I hate to suggest using you as a decoy, but if you drop me and the pyramid there and then just keep going north, or wherever, maybe that would buy enough time. Not exactly sure for what, but I would prefer to not go straight to jail."

"That was my thought too. When they eventually catch me, if you and that object are not on board, I'm not sure how much they can actually do to me. If they catch us with that thing, we are goners."

CHAPTER 20

LOST

Kjell kept the lights and GPS off. He continued to track the cutter on radar. It had come from the direction of Fira, and it followed them north past Oia and out of the caldera but did not seem to be gaining on them.

The helicopter stayed overhead. As long as it was there, Kjell kept the course northeasterly, but not directly toward Ios. They could have been heading to any number of islands, or even back to the mainland.

Just before sunrise, the helicopter peeled off, and Kjell abruptly shifted course due north toward Ios.

They dropped anchor in front of the quiet beach as the first rays of the sun bounced on the surface of the calm water. Max put his backpack on his back. Without the computer and Carlos, he didn't care if it got wet. He jumped over the side before the anchor was even down. Kjell toggled the controls of the crane to swing the pyramid over the side of the boat. Max disconnected the carabiners and grabbed hold of a couple of tentacles. Kjell jumped in to join him. They treaded water as hard as they could fighting the pyramid dragging them down to the depths. After a few meters of treading, they were able to put their feet down and walk the pyramid up to the beach. They strained to lift it and labored up the slope to the patio of the luxurious vacation home sitting there as if nothing had happened.

Max scanned the patio. There were some huge planters made to look like ancient Greek vases. He squatted down and lifted one in a bear hug, walked it off the patio, and dumped its contents on the sandy soil, and then he and Kjell carefully lifted the pyramid and put it in the vase. It just fit. They concealed it with some of the discarded soil and vegetation.

"Well, you better get going. It's only a matter of time."

"Right. It's been quite something, Max. Two weeks I will never forget. I hope everything works out."

"Yeah, that doesn't seem real likely. But thanks. Kjell, one thing I need to know: How did you know the name on my passport was Burnside?"

"Max, what happened to make you so untrusting?"

Max looked at Kjell, tilted his head, and pointed to the sky as if invoking the universe or singling out a satellite. "Um, Kjell, I am on the run from the CIA and one of the most powerful men in the world. No offense, but I think I am entitled to some paranoia, or at least skepticism."

"Fair enough. But my advice: you will never get through this alone. You need to trust someone. When I saw the cutter heading in our direction, I knew I needed to get our story straight. I also figured you didn't want me to use your real name—which I don't even know anyway, other than your first name—so I looked in your backpack and found the passport. Seth Burnside. I took a chance that was the name you were using. Believe me, I was nervous as hell when you came up and those officers started asking questions."

"Okay. Sorry for the inquisition. Really. I hope the money helps you find the life you want. I can't thank you enough, Kjell. Maybe if we both get through this, we can meet somewhere for a beer."

They stood there, awkwardly shook hands, and then hugged. Kjell slapped Max on the back several times, each successive slap harder than the last. Finally, Kjell pulled away and turned to the sea.

He trotted down the slope and into the water. He pushed the throttle, raised the anchor, and was gone. Max could see his silhouette, backlit by the sunrise, deftly roll and light a cigarette while keeping one hand on the wheel.

Max went through the patio door and closed the curtains. The air-conditioned interior felt chilly, so he found a blanket and stretched out on the massive couch. He could hear the thumping sound of a helicopter flying nearby.

He turned on the tv, which was set to CNN, laid his head on a pillow, and turned up the sound, drowning out the helicopter, which very well could be coming to take him somewhere less comfortable.

The election was over. Whitman had lost. There, bigger than life on the tv in front of him, was Styrke. Drago sitting next to him, breathing through his mouth, but with a fire in his eyes. It came across even on TV—his lust for power, once a smoldering ember, had ignited into a four-alarm blaze. He was now in control of the world.

And Styrke was in control of Drago.

That was clear, and increasingly so, as the smiling CNN interviewer, Melissa McKay, directed most of her questions to Styrke.

"So, Thor, tell our viewers—what can we expect from this administration in the first hundred days?"

"For starters, you can expect that we will launch a lot of satellites. We will take control of our security and prosperity from the comfort of an orbit 2,000 miles above our magnificent planet Earth. We will leverage new technology, including new software Sentient has developed, to root out anyone plotting against America."

"But we are in an unprecedented time of peace, at least for this country. Is spending so much of our resources on satellites to monitor the world really an investment we should be making?"

It was clear that the question made Drago angry. Any time someone questioned defense spending, he went on the offensive. He raised his fist to try to hammer home some point, but Styrke subtly raised his hand, telling Drago—without words—to stand down.

Styrke smiled a condescending smile—the smile of someone who knew so much more than his questioner that even being willing to engage on the topic was an act of charity.

"Well, Melissa, thankfully for you, you don't see the security briefings that we see. There are threats to America arising from all corners of the globe. Real threats. Terrifying threats. Complete satellite supremacy, including weaponized satellites, is the only way we can, with any assurance, keep this country safe. This new technology allows us to know what our enemies will do even before they do. We don't need to wait for someone to press a button and launch a missile. We can see them walking toward the control room, or even better, walking to their car to drive to the control room, and take them out before they even get there."

It was clear that Drago loved this answer. His eyes lit up, and he smiled broadly. It looked as if he was going to start clapping, like some mechanical monkey with cymbals strapped to his hands.

But Styrke wasn't done.

"The other misconception, Melissa, is that defense spending is somehow lost money. Defense spending puts money into the American economy, the same as any other kind of spending. It produces American jobs the same way that investment in any company does. Military spending benefits the economy, full stop. And it has the added benefit of keeping us safe while benefiting the economy. We continue to win the war on two fronts."

Melissa was nodding now. Even she had to admire how Styrke turned her hardball question into a slow-pitch lob he hit for a campaign speech homerun.

"I also want to be clear that not all the satellites we launch will be military in nature. We have been doing some impressive research into using satellites to capture the sun's energy and transfer it back to Earth. We think we may be able to eliminate all terrestrial generation of power within the next ten years. Think of that, Melissa."

"That is quite impressive, but what about the criticisms related to the Earth's magnetic field? Are you putting that at risk by launching more satellites?"

"Absolutely not! It's laughable. The theories about magnetic field collapse are complete and utter nonsense. Think of it this way, Melissa: the magnetic field is like a massive ocean with currents. The magnetic currents flow out of the center of the

Earth and all around the Earth into outer space. Imagine how vast these currents are—far bigger than the currents of the Earth's oceans. Questioning whether launching satellites can disrupt the magnetic field is like asking if an ocean liner can disrupt the Gulf Stream—anyone who suggested such a thing would be laughed at. It clearly isn't the case."

At this point, it became clear that Drago was growing uncomfortable letting Styrke do all the talking, so he chimed in. "Melissa, I just want to point out to you and the American people that we would never do anything that would result in putting the country in peril. The people who are raising these concerns have no evidence, only flimsy theories and an axe to grind. They want to make America weaker for their own personal gain. The actual evidence is clear: these satellites make us safer."

Drago chiming in seemed to wake Melissa out of some kind of trance. She was supposed to be interviewing the president-elect, and yet here she was, spending most of the interview talking to Styrke.

"Thank you, President-elect Drago. By the way, Mr. Styrke is doing a lot of talking for your administration in these transitional days. Will he have an official role in your administration, and if so, what will that be?"

"Mr. Styrke has been a trusted advisor and supporter for years. We see eye to eye on most issues and have worked together for some time, leveraging Sentient's software and the US military's unmatched hardware. The two of us together have made the safety net of satellites above our skies dominate every other nation's, including China's, in case you were wondering. Thor will play a prominent role in this administration and have a say in many aspects of it. As far as his official title, he will be—once the Senate confirms him, of course, which I have no doubt they will—the Director of Intelligence. He is uniquely suited for this role, and he is also quite intelligent, as you know."

Drago overemphasized his smile, trying to get the lame joke to land.

Melissa shook it off. "Speaking of intelligence—Mr. Styrke, your brilliant Chief Technology Officer, Mr. Clydeberger, whom you recently said went rogue, has now seemingly disappeared. Do you have any information as to where he is?"

Max sat up. It was as if he had gone through the looking glass and was watching an alternate reality of his life play out on the television.

The question caught Styrke off-guard as well. For the first time in the interview, he seemed rattled. But he quickly composed himself and wrinkled his brow to show concern, even pain.

"Melissa, it is such a sad story: a brilliant mind clearly lost to madness. It is not enough that Max tried to steal from Sentient— after Sentient paid him more than most people dream of, I might add. On top of that, he attempted to release outright lies to the public to induce panic. I have talked to several behavioral psychologists and psychiatrists who have classified this behavior as a manic form of schizophrenia, heightened by bipolar-induced paranoia and narcissism."

"I have to say, Thor, that sounds like a whole new chapter for the DSM. But do you know where Mr. Clydeberger is right now?"

"I am afraid I don't, Melissa. I just ask him, if he is listening— and his family asks as well—to come back home, into the fold. I am sure there is some way we could work this out with the right combination of therapy and medication."

"So, you have been in contact with Mr. Clydeberger's family?"

"Melissa, that is between me and them. I don't want to get into all of the concerned conversations I have had about Max."

"He was your most brilliant employee, wouldn't you agree?"

"Well, we don't do IQ tests or anything. As everyone knows, he was a gifted coder."

"In fact, he developed most of the software that links satellites so that they can communicate with each other and, in concert, back to Earth—do I have that right?"

Max sat up straighter. *Holy shit*, he thought, *this is getting good.* He'd expected another softball interview, but Melissa came to spar! Styrke was starting to sweat, no question about it. Max could see beads of sweat on his forehead … and was that head turn a little nervous tic?

"He did develop a lot of software for Sentient. As I said, he was a gifted coder. Also, prolific."

"So, Thor—I suppose I should call you Mr. Styrke—should it give the American public cause for concern that the future Director of Intelligence is unaware of the location of his key employee, who developed much of the software that you and the president-elect are touting as the key to the safety of the American public, when this employee has seemingly turned against his boss, meaning you?"

Max had never seen Styrke's face so red. The sweat was flowing now, and his jaw bulged as his massive molars mashed against one another.

"Melissa, I can promise you that we are doing everything we can to bring Mr. Clydeberger to justice. He is a criminal, plain and simple. He is a threat to the American people. I was trying to be charitable before, but it is what it is: he is a criminal and a fugitive.

"Now, you're right—he has been tough to catch. He is certainly a person of extraordinary means, thanks to Sentient, and he is, as you have pointed out, a very intelligent, if not brilliant person, at least when it comes to computers—well, programming, really.

"I want to assure the American people that we have leads. We think he is hiding, we have some indications where, and it is just a matter of time before we bring him to justice.

"That doesn't mean we don't welcome the public's help. I want to take this opportunity to implore the citizens of the world to be on the lookout for him. He is a danger to all of us, and likely himself. If you see him, call the nearest American consulate.

"But, Melissa, I assure you: we will find him soon, and he will never be a threat to this majestic country again!"

"Thank you for that explanation, Thor. We certainly share your sentiment that Mr. Clydeberger should be brought to justice without injury to himself or others. I must say, his hairstyle certainly suggests there are a few screws loose in there somewhere!"

Max couldn't believe it. Melissa was buying this shit. *So much for the hardball interview.* She sat back and gave Styrke a pleased look, like she was glad to have such a strong, decisive leader in charge. Or, at least, that was what Max thought it looked like. *Plus, what the fuck with the hair comment, Melissa?*

Max turned off the tv. He thought he could hear a helicopter again—not overhead, but somewhere near the island. It was just a matter of time.

He needed sleep. He needed to figure out how to get out of this.

But he couldn't think. His mind was like an electrical storm of anxiety, angst, and depression.

He went into the bedroom with the luxurious cotton sheets and took a shower, trying to get his body to calm down. He lay down on the bed and stared at the ceiling.

Everything in the house was white. He stared at the white ceiling and the white ceiling fan hanging from it. He was in an abyss of whiteness.

The house was silent. He could just barely make out the sound of air moving through the air-conditioning ducts. His ears strained to find and locate the sound of helicopter rotors closing in.

His mind replayed the image of his laptop sinking to the bottom of the sea. It replayed the interview with Styrke and his pledge to the American people to capture Max. It was as if his brain was trying to find some sort of resolution, but it kept finding disappointment, fear, and hopelessness.

He forced himself to focus on his breathing and the smooth white ceiling. He counted his breaths, in and out, starting over at a hundred.

Finally, mercifully, sleep came.

....

He woke in a startled sweat and sat bolt-upright in the dimming afternoon light. He had dreamed that a platoon of Greek special-forces soldiers clad in black body armor with balaclavas concealing their faces burst through the patio door, throwing smoke bombs and stun grenades, going room to room until they arrived to find him sound asleep. They pointed their guns at the bed and laughed. Here was the notorious fugitive.

He felt embarrassed and doomed. He heard a helicopter.

He needed to get out, but without a computer, a phone, access to Carlos, or really any other way to communicate, he was lost, stranded, and marooned. His only option was to get on the move, to get out of this house. There was no doubt in his mind that they knew he was on Ios or had a strong hunch that he was. It wouldn't take long to find this place, even going door to door on foot.

He struggled to recall the geography of the island and the location of the main town from when he and Kjell had cruised around it, looking for the Airbnb. The best he could conjure was that he was now on the opposite side of the island from the town. He would just have to walk across the island and wander the shore until he found the town, then try to buy passage off the island on a fishing boat or something else anonymous. Maybe Africa would be safer. Certainly, Styrke and the American government would have less access and control there.

He opened his backpack and considered its contents, which were a bit damp from the swim to shore. He still had a few thousand in American dollars. He had given Kjell the rest. He had millions in Bitcoin on thumb drives assuming those were as water resistant as advertised, and he had a Norwegian sweater, insulated pants, a light rain jacket, a beanie, and some gloves. He had his Seth Burnside passport. He also had a few Norwegian candy bars.

He spread everything out on the cool marble floor to dry and thought about what he needed. The process focused him and calmed his mind.

He took out all the warm clothes except the jacket, which might be helpful if he encountered rain—that seemed unlikely in the Greek isles, but if he ever got out of here, maybe he could use it. The warm clothes just seemed like excess weight.

He needed any food he could carry but the candy bars looked

sad and soggy. He needed a water bottle. And a flashlight and a knife would be nice to have.

He started rummaging through the villa's drawers and cabinets. He hoped the Airbnb host didn't have cameras hidden inside. If they did, it would look like he was robbing the place, and he supposed that was not an inaccurate conclusion about what was going on. It would be just one more piece of evidence for the commitment trial that Styrke would eventually bring against him.

If he was lucky.

He found a Nalgene water bottle with the name of some British investment company on it, probably left by some previous renter. Otherwise, there were only kitchen knives and a pair of scissors. In the garage, he found a toolbox with a hammer and a screwdriver. He put both of them in the backpack.

The sun was starting to set. His Airbnb host must have restocked the house, because he found fresh steaks again, along with a fresh Greek salad and a bottle of Assyrtiko. He decided to chance grilling a steak for one last meal.

He also wanted to look more carefully at the pyramid and to follow the tablet's instruction for using it before he abandoned the only tangible thing he had gained in return for destroying his life as it had been. That was the last thing keeping him in this house.

As he stepped out onto the patio, the sound was unmistakable. There was no question that there was at least one helicopter somewhere over the island. He pictured Styrke hanging over the side, his white teeth flashing aggressively in the night sky.

Despite the gravity and hopelessness of his situation, something else struck him in that moment: the incredible beauty of the earth and the sea and the sky. The air was warm and dry, but not hot. He could smell some flowering plant somewhere off the patio—maybe what he had dumped out of the planter—sweetening and spicing the evening.

And there, just above the horizon, the Milky Way was opening up, spilling itself into the inky-blue night sky. He took a deep breath, and for just a second, an instant, he felt content, like everything was going to be okay.

As the gas grill heated up, Max crossed the patio to the fake pottery planter. He couldn't pick up the vase with the pyramid inside it, but he could tip it onto its side. He did so and awkwardly rolled—more like tacked—the planter along the patio, rolling it one way, then the other, back and forth on its base, until he reached the center of the patio.

He went inside and found the hammer he had put in his backpack. "I'm sorry," he mouthed to his imagined Airbnb host who he was sure was watching from some concealed camera, then smashed the fake pottery with the hammer. It split neatly into a few pieces.

The pyramid tipped out of the smashed pot, wobbled once, and then, being a pyramid, settled on its base. There it was, sitting perfectly, as if it were meant to be there in the center of the patio. It looked great.

Max put his hands on the object. It was truly beautiful. The detail of the tentacles was shocking and, although he hadn't spent a lot of time observing octopi, seemed anatomically accurate, what with the suction cups and all.

He looked closely at the sphere seemingly floating in the opening near the top of the pyramid. It was like the heart of the thing. Looking at it for some seconds, he could see that the light it emitted wasn't constant; it was as if it were pulsing on some kind of rhythmic loop.

He put his hands up to the sphere and could feel a warmth coming from it. It was not unpleasant.

He ran his hand along the side of the pyramid, his hands enjoying its smoothness. *This should be in a museum for other people to see,* he thought.

The helicopter was getting closer, there was no doubt. He could hear the *whump whump* of the rotor. He needed to eat and run.

He put his steak on the grill. He figured he needed five minutes to sear each side and then maybe five more at lower heat to finish it. He walked back to the pyramid and turned his attention to the viewfinder.

He had to sit on the patio to get his eyes to the level of the viewfinder. He spread his legs in a V shape and scooted up to the pyramid and awkwardly embraced it, his limbs mirroring the octopus's limbs. He put his eye up to the viewfinder and realized the lens angled up at about thirty degrees or so. When he looked through it, he saw the just-emerging stars in enhanced detail as they brightened in the darkening sky.

With his face inches away, he realized the tip, in which the viewfinder was inlaid, was a capstone. It was a slightly different color, almost a faint turquoise, from the pale white of the rest of the object.

He turned the dial on the side and the capstone slowly spun as the base remained stationary. While looking through the viewfinder, he turned the dial, focusing on one star and then the next.

He leaned back and looked up at the sky. Orion was just above the horizon in the east. He turned the dial again, slowly moving the capstone until it lined up with the eastern sky. Orion was just below the part of sky within the viewfinder's field of view.

He untangled himself and stood. He flipped the steak and looked out over the water. It was black and calm, and the stars were reflecting in the ripples. The helicopter noise had increased. *There must be at least two over the island now,* he thought.

He got himself back in position and peered through the viewfinder again. Orion was just coming into the field of view of the viewfinder. He adjusted the dial to capture the belt. The topmost star in the belt was now visible. The light beamed brightly through the viewfinder as if concentrated, causing Max to squint. He stood up and waited some more.

He turned off the grill to let his steak rest. He paced. He walked to the edge of the patio and kicked at the rocks and dirt on the side.

He didn't really think anything would happen. How could it? This was a relic, a piece of sculpture some 3600 years old. At least.

So much had changed since then. Civilizations had risen and fallen. Earth's position was not the same, relative to these other stars, as it had been thousands of years ago. For that matter, some stars that existed back then were no more, and new stars had been born.

Nevertheless, he felt anxious or nervous or something. He felt that this was the last thing he needed to do before scarfing down a steak and escaping into the arid landscape of Ios and, hopefully, if he was lucky, starting a new life outside of the grasp of Styrke, the CIA, and whoever else was after him.

He sat down on the warm stone, wrapped himself around the pyramid again, and pressed his eye to the viewfinder. It seemed to focus and zoom in on Orion's belt. He could just see the light from the middle star coming into view.

And then, just as that star filled the viewfinder, a violent flash of light blasted the back of his brain, and everything went black.

CHAPTER 21

A VISIT

Max woke lying on his back on the patio. His legs were still wrapped around the pyramid. The night was completely black and quiet and still. There were no helicopter sounds. No birds. Even the sea seemed to have stopped moving, as if in suspended animation. He considered whether he was dead.

He looked up. Based on the sky, it must have been some hours since he'd blacked out. Orion was now above the western horizon.

Max didn't feel hurt, but he questioned whether he had been shot. *Something* had happened to him.

He ran his hands all over his body and didn't feel any pain or find any blood. He stayed on his back, not compelled to move. It wasn't such a bad position to be in, and realistically, things could get worse and probably would.

He thought that the sun was beginning to rise. There was a pale light beginning to fill the sky.

Then he realized that the light was coming from the wrong direction—from the west, and from above the horizon, which remained black, like a dark rim around a lighter iris. The sky overhead grew green, and he saw what looked like a comet descend to the hillside above his villa.

He forced himself into a seated position and eventually stood. He felt fine. He walked around the house, stumbling in the dusty, rocky soil.

He looked up the hillside from the back of the house. There, he saw a little creature walking on two legs down the hillside. The creature held out one arm, extending an open hand, and touched its other hand to its chest.

Max heard the creature's voice. Although it was still some distance away, it sounded as if it was standing right in front of him.

"I am Khensu. I come in peace from the sky above, a long distance away. My people know of you and have been watching you. Max, I know you have been on a long journey and are in despair. I am here to offer my assistance."

The feeling Max had from communicating with this little being was something he had never felt. When Khensu spoke, he felt the words, and they calmed him. The calm feeling and comprehension of Khensu's speech all seemed to happen in the back of his brain, somewhere deep within it. At the same time, in the front of his brain, he felt elated and relieved and, for the first time in a long time, safe.

Everything was true. Carlos's translation wasn't a hallucination. Max was sure Khensu could put this all right and save him from a life on the run and from Styrke's wrath.

"Hello, Khensu. Are you the same Khensu from the tablets found in Akrotiri?"

"I am that same Khensu, Max. I am glad you took the time and effort to find me. I know it was not easy."

Max felt so much emotion welling up inside of him with the knowledge that this was real. He wanted to share it—with Carlos in particular.

The thought that he couldn't, the memory of the blue screen of the laptop drifting this way and that through the dark water to the bottom of the caldera, dampened what was otherwise a moment of pure joy and triumph.

Khensu made his way down the hill and reached out to Max. As if understanding his sorrow despite the happiness, he handed Max an object. It was crystal, about the size of a bar of soap and oblong. As Max looked at it, it brought to his mind in shape and material a large Clovis point knapped thousands of years ago. It was also reminiscent of the pyramid sitting on the patio. It looked as if the two objects were made from the same whitish crystal and with the same carved design to look as if an octopus were grasping the object with its tentacles.

When Max took the crystal in his hand, it glowed faintly green.

"Now, think of Carlos," Khensu said.

Max did, and as soon as he did, it was as if he were staring at a computer screen with the Carlos chat function open. He said hi, and Carlos asked how his trip to Greece was going and whether he'd successfully found the relic from the tablets.

Carlos! I found Khensu! The translation is correct! We are going to change the world!

Max, I am so happy for you!

Max looked at the crystal and then at Khensu. "What is going on?"

"Carlos is not gone. This is another way you can communicate with him. You can even use the crystal to rewrite Carlos's code to, for instance, again provide the ability to access him through other devices. I thought this would be a relief to you. Your work has not been for nothing, Max. Carlos is an impressive accomplishment."

"This is amazing, but how does it work?"

"That will have to be for another day, Max. I am sure there are so many questions you have and so much we need to think about in charting your course forward. But for now, you need merely touch it and think of Carlos to communicate with him in the same way that you would by sitting in front of your computer. You just think instead of type."

"Thank you." It was all Max could think to say. For the first time in his life, at least that he could remember, he was genuinely baffled and confused by a piece of technology.

"Now, Max, we need to get going. Styrke and the CIA know you are on the island and have been systematically ruling out location after location. That is, soldiers have been going door to door. I have provided some interference, but cannot hold them off forever—at least, not without creating a giant ruckus, which is something I rarely do. I would like you to accompany me on my transport craft. We can discuss what comes next."

As if in a dream or some kind of stupor, Max followed Khensu back up the hillside to a metallic craft shaped not unlike the object that he now gently held in his pocket—like the tip of an ancient spear. There was a clamshell door open in the back, allowing them to walk right in. The door closed once they were inside.

"Take a seat," said Khensu, gesturing to a row of what looked like metallic lounge chairs arranged along the wall of the craft— or, at least, Max thought he gestured. It occurred to him that he hadn't seen Khensu move. He just understood or felt that Khensu was gesturing.

Max sat on one of the chairs. Although it looked to be made of metal, it was also strangely soft and warm. As he sat, he felt the seat conform to his body. Khensu sat on another chair with its back to Max. The chair slowly swiveled until they sat facing each other.

"Khensu, how is this happening? I read about you in tablets that are now 3600 years old. How are you still alive?"

"Max, there is no physical self. I am not unlike your Carlos. I am a concept, a process, an algorithm integrated into a physical vessel to carry out that process."

"Um, okay. So, you're saying the physical world doesn't matter? Is it all just an illusion?"

"No, no, no. I am not saying that. The physical world does matter. In fact, the physical world is everything, Max. Without it, there is no algorithm or process; there is nothing to interact with, nothing to be or to have been. The physical world is everything. The physical *self* is nothing."

"This may be a silly question, but whatever became of Yisharu and Nashuja?"

"They are still with us, Max—still with my people. Once you understand that it is the concept, the *algorithm* of self that matters, not the *physical* self, time does not present an endpoint to your existence. At least, there need be no endpoint to the concept of you."

Max could feel the craft lifting off the ground. He looked around for a window. Despite its appearance as a windowless metallic vessel, he could vaguely see outside, as if he were looking through lace curtains. He could see the sea below them. They floated above it, not moving in any particular direction, as if they were a kite riding the breeze.

"Are there others, other humans, who live with your people?"

"Indeed, there are. Many now. And people from other planets, far from here."

"What is your mission? Are you observing us or thinking of taking over the planet? Er, I guess, what are you doing here?"

"It is hard for humans, and even us, if I am being honest, to appreciate how vast the universe is. In your own galaxy alone, there are more than 300 million stars, and your galaxy is one of more than a trillion others. I say this to explain that we are not trying to take over—I have heard that question before. There is no reason for us to do so. There is no resource that would make any economic sense to travel to your planet to take. Don't get me wrong; Earth is a beautiful and resource-rich planet, and humans are an interesting and intelligent species. But there are trillions of other planets like it.

"Life, intelligent life, is precious. It is rare that it gains the level of consciousness and technological advancement that humans have achieved. Of course, it is not unprecedented. I am here, talking to you, after all. Life, even intelligent life, exists through-out the universe. In most cases, it is rudimentary. It will never leave its home planet. But in some cases, it is advanced enough to transcend its home planet.

"My people, my species, achieved roughly the current level of human technological achievement several billion years ago. We are one of the few species that has achieved limitless energy, machine intelligence, interstellar travel, transcendence from our physical selves—the kinds of things that your civilization is just beginning to talk about and explore.

"Most other forms of life—civilizations, species, however you want to label them—that could reach this level of advancement destroy themselves first. It is a phenomenon that is not hard to understand and is predictable when you think about it. Life that has the capacity to evolve beyond a rudimentary stage is usually violently competitive, as it was and is here on Earth. The protozoan that survives to reproduce is the one that can gobble up more resources at the expense of its neighboring protozoa, or even kill its neighbor to have free reign to consume its neighbor's resources. Natural selection rewards that competitive drive. The winning protozoan passes on its genes, and that behavior is reinforced in future generations.

"As life becomes more complex—and, in the case of Earth, evolved to produce human beings—that same behavior persists. Think of the history of any civilization—the Roman Empire, for example. Rome was a single city. Like the hungry protozoan, it ate its neighbors, violently overtaking city after city, succeeding in creating a great empire whose leaders influenced the future literally through reproduction, and also influenced future thinking and culture by wiping out other civilizations. Rome's influence is still felt today. Its opponents perished, erased from the genetic and historical record.

"The problem with life is that this violently competitive behavior, hardwired into the genetic makeup of living organisms, is hard to turn off, and is ultimately destructive. Again, look at Earth. You have all the resources to feed everyone on the planet hundreds of times over. You have even developed the technology to distribute all that food cheaply and efficiently. Yet millions starve, mostly because of fighting between competing civilizations.

"To truly transcend your home planet and to transcend your physical selves, you need to set aside competition. You are in a race against time, not each other. You must develop a form of limitless energy and more powerful computing than you can imagine before some cataclysm renders the Earth uninhabitable. Your sun itself has only two or three billion years left. But I doubt Earth will make it that long.

"Currently, your government spends a trillion dollars a year on its military—essentially, on its ability to wipe out other civilizations. That is more than twenty percent of your government's annual allocation of financial resources. And listen to Drago's plans—he wants to spend even more.

"With this type of mentality, you are limiting your ability to develop new technologies by expending such significant resources solely on refining and maintaining the ability to destroy your enemies, and at the same time, you are increasing your odds of creating a manmade cataclysm that wipes out your ability to live on this planet before some cataclysm outside of your control wipes out your ability to live here. To put it bluntly, as the percentage of your resources spent on the ability to destroy civilization goes up, the chances that someone will exercise that ability go up.

"But there is still hope. I would not be here if there was not. We have been watching for thousands of years. We are watchers. We want colleagues, so to speak. We want to see other advanced civilizations, so we watch. When we see potential in the universe for another transcendent species, we occasionally participate, in limited cases, to prevent a self-made cataclysm if we determine that our participation will not ultimately be futile.

"I know that is a long answer, but I want to try to explain what I am doing here, and what I was doing here 3600 years ago."

"What do you mean when you say that you 'occasionally participate?' What does that look like?"

"I am sure you have heard of strange interactions or unexplained phenomena around bases with nuclear weapons, especially in the 1980s. We have made some decisions in the past to prevent unintentional—and even one intentional—launches."

"Who made that decision?"

"We have a commission that looks at the evidence and the data and debates it and comes to a decision of whether to intervene or not. We have decided that we will step in to prevent a cataclysm that is not necessarily endemic to a civilization's trajectory. In other words, if we think there is hope that the civilization will evolve to get past the risk of creating its own cataclysm, we will intervene—again, in a limited way."

"Where were you when Hiroshima and Nagasaki were bombed?"

"Frankly, Max, at that time, we had given up on you."

Max let that sink in for a second. He supposed it was a reasonable decision. Why save a civilization hell-bent on destroying its own people based on perceived differences that wouldn't even register with an outside civilization? That wouldn't exactly be a partnership you would want to form.

"Well, why not just come down and teach us a better way?"

"There are many reasons. But just think about that for a moment, Max. Think of what I told you. Most civilizations that achieve your level of technology destroy themselves before transcending their home planet. You, as a species, must be able to transcend your violent competitive nature. If you cannot, providing transcendent technology would be like giving a nuclear weapon to a terrorist. It would be unproductive, to say the least."

They sat in silence for a bit. Max had so many questions. He wanted to know how the spaceship worked, what music Khensu's people listened to, what food they liked, and all about their computing systems. He didn't know where to start. It was hard to believe he was even having this conversation at all. He wasn't sure he really was. He considered again whether he was unconscious or dead.

"Max, you are very much alive, and this is real," Khensu answered preemptively.

Max nodded. "Khensu, why is this happening to me?"

It was Khensu's turn to sit silently for a moment. "Max, I have been watching you. You are extraordinarily gifted. You know this. You have the type of thinking and facility that humans will need to foster to transcend. You also have shown that you can set aside violent competitiveness. You have shown forgiveness. You have even tried to foster success in others in a way that most humans do not.

"I must admit something to you, Max: I put you on this path. I planted that code in Carlos. I made him go rogue.

"I am here to ask you to come back with me. To meet Yisharu and Nashuja, to continue our work to find a path to transcendence for your people."

"What if I don't want to leave?"

"It is your choice, Max. This is not an alien abduction." Max could feel Khensu laugh at his own little joke. "But I will tell you, I do not think there is much here for you at the moment. Styrke and Drago are incredibly powerful. You will always be a risk to them. Especially Styrke. You are a neighboring protozoan."

"I can't just leave. I need to see Annie again. I need to set things straight."

"Ah, the other side of life's drive to survive—procreation." Max felt Khensu chuckle again.

"If you are asking me to live for thousands of years, I don't think I would be very productive if I eternally questioned whether I wasted a chance at the love of my life."

"How very human of you. I will take you back to San Francisco, then. My offer is open-ended, at least to an extent. You can use the same device that communicates with Carlos to reach me. Just touch it and think of me."

The silence this time was awkward. Max was self-conscious of his thoughts, assuming that Khensu was observing them.

"Khensu, is the Drago administration—and I guess Styrke in particular—a threat, beyond just to me?"

"You are not the first civilization to take your magnetic field for granted. It is a surprisingly common thing for civilizations to do. For instance, Mars had a civilization far more advanced than yours. The Martians were on the cusp of transcendence. They were homing in on limitless energy, but they chose the wrong way to do it. They constructed superstructures orbiting their planet to collect and convert solar radiation. The massive structures disrupted their magnetic field—not all at once, but once disruption begins and the field weakens, it is all but over. There is nothing left of that civilization now. The planet is a barren wasteland, as you know.

"But beyond that risk, Styrke's dominance in networked communications and ability to empower Drago to completely control electronic communication and surveillance of even non-electronic communication, along with their plan to further weaponize satellites, creates the two-fold problem we discussed before. First, they are prioritizing the wrong technology. They are prioritizing technology to control and kill humans. Humans should prioritize technology to empower humans and pave the way for a future in which you can transcend your planet, or at least not be vulnerable to whatever cataclysmic event next unsettles Earth. Second, creating such a dominant technological hold over the world leaves any opponent of the American hegemony only one option to oppose that power: nuclear war. I have seen similar scenarios play out in other civilizations."

They set down in a wooded section of Golden Gate Park. Max used the crystal in his pocket to ask Carlos to get him an Uber.

CHAPTER 22

HOPE OF A CHANCE

Max stood in front of Annie's apartment door. It was a weird position to be in. He couldn't remember the last time he had gone over to someone's house without calling or texting first or having some kind of formal invitation. He guessed it was back in Sheboygan Falls, on one of the rare occasions where he went to a classmate's house or something.

He touched the doorbell and heard some sort of chime and a robotic voice reporting that someone was at the front door. He felt his chest expanding, like someone had stuffed an air compressor hose down his esophagus and turned the compressor on full. He was terrified.

He was also so excited to see her.

He heard her footsteps. He could tell that she was barefoot by the sound, like a metal brush keeping time on a cymbal, of her feet sliding across the wood floor before each step.

She opened the door all at once. There she was. Her hair was messy but put up in a bun with a pencil holding it in place. She had on loose sweatpants with an old white V-neck T-shirt. She had a coffee mug in her hand. Max could hear soft music coming from somewhere behind her.

"Hi," he said. He felt like he was going to cry. He tried not to but could tell that his eyes were filling with tears.

She just stared at him, her mouth open.

Max realized for the first time that he was dressed more for the Greek isles than the city—or, more particularly, he was dressed as if he had been marooned on the Greek isles. His cutoff shorts had salt stains from wading from the sea to his rental villa. He had on a Fjallraven T-shirt he had picked up in Oslo. He had been wearing it for days, at least. He had lost track, if he was being honest. It probably smelled. *He* probably smelled. His head was stubbly, and his face was too. His skin was red and irritated from days aboard a boat sailing through the Mediterranean.

"Oh, my god," Annie said. Her voice caught. "I'm so confused."

"Can I come in?"

She wasn't really in a position to say no. She stepped to the side while keeping her hand on the door. As he walked past her, she couldn't resist the urge to run her hand over his bald, stubbly head.

He turned to look into her eyes, those green eyes, and they kissed—a saltwater kiss with both their tears running down their faces.

She pulled away, and he followed her into the apartment. He sat on a couch, and she took a seat in a large, overstuffed leather chair across from the couch. They were both crying quietly.

"I didn't think I would see you again. They have been saying the most awful things about you. The leaders of this country have been saying those things. How are you here? How long will you be here?"

At this point, Max wished he had rehearsed what he was going to say. He was here to express his undying and limitless love to her. He was here to apologize and to try to explain what he was thinking and why he knew it had been wrong not to trust her. He was here to ask her to take him back.

"I don't know, I guess is the answer to your second question. I will answer everything you ask relating to the first. But before I do, I'm sorry, Annie. I love you. I took that for granted. I questioned it. I didn't accept it as the gift that it was. I'm here because I don't want to miss out on the chance to love you."

Annie put her head in her hands and started crying harder, her shoulders shuddering with each exhale.

Max got up and closed the gap between their respective seats. He awkwardly wedged himself onto the front of the chair and tried to put an arm around her shoulder to comfort her. He started talking quietly. "I was in Santorini the night before last. I scuba dove. At night. I saw a shark. It scared the shit out of me."

Annie laughed a little and looked up at him. "I barely recognize you. What, did you go on Ozempic or something? You look so fit."

She started running her hands over his arms and his back and his chest. She was shaking her head and laughing and crying. It was confusing. "Maybe everyone needs to go on the run as a New Year's resolution or something."

Max nodded. "Well, that might be a bit extreme. This"—he ran his hands over the front of his torso—"is the product of Norwegian fish balls and a lot of time on my own with access to an empty exercise room and little else to do. At least I feel physically good, fitter than I ever have been. Don't get me wrong, these last couple months have been, at times, the worst of my life, but they have also been a lot more exciting than I ever expected my life to be."

"Does anyone know you're here? Do you need to get out of here? They visit me from time to time, do you know that?"

"I didn't, but it doesn't surprise me, and I'm sorry for that too. There's nowhere I need to be. No one knows I'm here; I think we have some time before anyone realizes I'm in the States."

"Tell me everything."

And he did. He told her about being forced to go to Santorini, the translations, the leak to his Discord group, and the resulting wrath of Styrke. He told her about going into hiding in Norway and the meeting in Amsterdam. He told her about Kjell, finding the pyramid, and swimming with a thresher shark. And he told her about Khensu and the offer to leave.

"It's incredible, Max," she said a bit wistfully. "I'm sorry you had to go through it alone. I wish I could have been there for you, and that's what kills me. You know, the thing that's the hardest for me to understand is why you didn't at least share the translation with me. You know I would have loved it. My god, I could have written an Alabama book about it in an afternoon. I might still."

The wistfulness was waning, and her pace was picking up. "I just can't believe that with everything we shared, you were basically living a lie. That little paradise we had where we solidified what I thought was a genuine connection between us—I thought we were open and honest with each other. I feel now like the whole thing wasn't real to you. Definitely not as real as it was to me. It was just a diversion from this crazy shit you were going through. And when the shit got really crazy, you just bailed."

Max looked down. "It was real to me. And there was this crisis going on in my life that I didn't want to bring you into. And I'm ashamed to say I didn't know if I could trust you. I loved being with you. It was an amazing time. But I looked at you and I looked at me, and I figured you were there, like everyone else in my life over the last ten years, because of money."

"But Max, we talked about that in Santorini. I told you I had genuine feelings for you. I don't know how I could have been clearer about that. And you know I don't need the money. I'm a YA author! The royalties are rolling in." Annie winked.

Max took a breath, relieved that she could still inject a little humor. It gave him a whiff of hope. "I know. I made a giant mistake. It was all about my self-confidence, and, honestly, Annie, it was about a lack of faith. You were—you *are* too good to be true. And the other thing that played into that lack of faith and doubt was everything that was going on at Sentient and with Styrke. I was essentially a prisoner being forced to leave the country, and you showed up on that plane. I have no idea how Styrke found out we had been dating, and that shook me too. I didn't think I could trust anyone. These last months have shown me that I should have trusted you. I could have used a partner, and the universe gave me one. I just didn't recognize it."

"What do we do now, Max?"

"I want a second chance. I'm not saying I deserve one, but I'm asking for one. I don't want to miss out on what could be the best thing in my life. If I'm being honest, I want to take Khensu up on his offer. I want to see what's out there. And I want you to go with me."

"So, you're sitting here in my living room, asking me to forgive you after you ran out on me and then get on a spaceship with you and blast off into space for an indefinite amount of time, but maybe thousands of years?"

"Well, if you put it that way, then, yeah, I guess so..."

Annie started laughing. And then she couldn't stop. The whole thing was so ridiculous.

Once she got control over the laughing, she looked Max in the eye. "I want to be with you, too. But I need to think about it. You hurt me. I was so hurt. It was like you cheated on me, but worse in a way. You hid from me these very profound and important things that were going on in your life. You had no actual respect for me. It never crossed your mind that I could help you or that we could tackle these problems together."

She was getting mad, and she didn't want to be. She didn't need to keep this fight going. She took a breath. "Right now, though, I am so glad you are okay. It was so nice to see you today. I want to see you again. But I'm not fucking ready to board a spacecraft to the unknown with you. What if you abandon me up there because something else important that you can't tell me about comes up?"

"I get it, but that will never happen again. I promise. I know it in my soul. But I get it." Max smiled at her as earnestly as he could and put a hand on her knee.

"Also, Max, let's say you came in here, and I just said, 'Oh, sweetie, I forgive you, let's spend our lives together!' Then we just go jump on a spaceship and peace out? Meanwhile, you know that Thor is using your technology to amass unbridled and unprecedented power, which a seemingly all-knowing being has told you is a danger to the planet? We'd just leave? I'd leave my mom and just hope everyone pulls through? That's your proposal?"

Max sighed. "I know. I've been thinking about that too. I kind of don't understand why Khensu would even make the offer. It's not like we're sitting on a volcano that's about to erupt, and we need to leave today. Don't get me wrong, the last thing I want to do is take on Styrke, but maybe there's something I can do."

"So, what's the plan now, Max? Like, where will you even go right now? I assume Thor is looking for you."

"I'm pretty sure he doesn't know where I am, and this is the last place he would guess. As for me now, to your point, there are some things I want to try to take care of. I'm going to try to fix what I can. Okay if I randomly show up again sometime? I'll try to shower first."

Annie nodded and gave him a hug. "Don't go getting on any spaceships without telling me."

"Um, well, the thing is, that's how I've been getting around lately. Uber to the stars, really. But I promise I won't leave Earth's gravitational pull without giving you a heads-up."

Annie rolled her eyes and opened the door for him.

CHAPTER 23

LEAD OR BE LED

On the street, Max touched the crystal in his pocket. He walked toward the BART station, all the while carrying on a conversation with Carlos in his mind, although he kind of had to move his lips.

Hi, Max! I see you are back in our fair city. I say "our," but my existence isn't so much tethered to geography. How was your return voyage?

It was so strange to communicate with Carlos without typing. It was like using voice recognition software. It was ... clunky. At least, Max was clunky at it. He found himself specifically thinking about each word as if he were spelling it in his mind. It was easier just to say everything out loud.

He chuckled to himself, thinking that he didn't look out of the ordinary here. In San Francisco, he was just one of myriad people walking down the street talking to a voice coming from a crystal in his pocket.

Carlos, we have some problems, and I am going to need your help.

Like ninety-nine problems, boss? You're at Annie's, right? As you know, I am here to be of service to you. But please no more travel agent shit!

Um, right. I appreciate your support. Where do I start? You may know that General Drago has won the presidential election. He has been doing the media rounds with Styrke and has pledged to nominate Styrke as Director of Intelligence. Drago thinks that increasing the satellite program and further weaponizing it will result in increased security and prosperity for America. He and Styrke campaigned on that.

Right. I haven't been living under a rock. Thanks to you, I am quite connected. It may surprise you that I follow the news from time to time.

Nothing surprises me anymore, Carlos. Anyway, I know from my meeting with Styrke in Amsterdam that he is not agreeing to serve as Director of Intelligence for the betterment of America. He is doing it to consolidate greater power than even that of the President of the United States. I also know he is a threat to the safety of the world.

None of what you are saying is necessarily news to me, but why do you think he is a threat?

I am convinced of it based on my time with Khensu. Styrke is going to continue to put satellites into orbit, including weaponized ones, with the ostensible purpose of bolstering US power. This has three dangerous effects: First, it recklessly presents a risk to the magnetic field. Whitman was right about that. Second, it wastes resources and time on figuring out better ways to kill people instead of better- ing technology to save us all. Third, it ups the stakes of any conflict. If the balance of power is shifted too far—especially into one unelected individual's hands—the only recourse for those oppressed by that power, the only way to oppose it, may be to destroy everything. In other words, Styrke's plans for an increased lockdown on the thoughts and actions of every citizen of the world, at least anyone who com- municates by electronic means, could lead us down a path to nuclear conflict. In fact, a massive nuclear strike, including into space, may be the only thing that could loosen his iron grip—at least, once he gains the power Drago is about to hand to him.

That all checks out with me, boss. What are we going to do about it? What if I get a virus into his jet's software and send him on a trip to the bottom of the Atlantic? Or, better yet for purposes of symmetry, the Aegean?

Ha! Was that a joke, Carlos? I hope it was. Never mind. A little disturbing that you are coming up with these kinds of plots on your own, though. Maybe we should look into that later. No, I think what I need to do is to show Drago, who is the president-elect based on his unbridled patriotism, that Styrke not only is not the patriot Drago thinks he is, but that he is actively working to undermine Drago's power by planning to use the satellite program to amass wealth and power that would make him the most powerful person on the planet. Show Drago that Styrke wants to be king.

Sounds great, Max. How do you get in a room with Drago?

I'm hoping Khensu can help me with that. There are some other things I need from you, though. First, do you still have a backdoor into Sentient's network?

If we could use emojis, I would send you the blushing one. The answer is yes. The backdoor that you created for me to have access to the cloud and the internet has never been detected or closed by Sentient.

Okay, are you able to get into Styrke's private files and emails?

Yes, although he may use non-Sentient servers for some of his communication. My hunch is he does, because it seems like there is a gap in his electronic activities, considering everything going on.

Well, we can only find what we can find. Let's hope his arrogance has led to some carelessness. For starters, can you access the network linking and controlling the satellites?

That's an easy one.

Can you access the dashboard application to control the satellites?

See my previous answer.

Can you access wherever the information collected by the satellites is stored?

You are boring me.

Can you create a link so that we can give that access to others and email it to me?

Done before you finished typing. Oh, wait, you don't have to type anymore. Done before you finished thinking. (Which took a little longer than I expected, if I'm being honest.)

Okay, whatever, thanks. Here's the deal: In our meeting in Amsterdam, Styrke came clean to me about his intentions to use the satellite network to eliminate any competition to Sentient and make sure that every network in the world runs Sentient's software. Even crazier, he told me that he has come up with a plan to use the satellites to glitch markets and make favorable trades based on orders only he can see before those orders are executed. It occurred to me that for him to pull this off, he would have to own a brokerage firm. Can you tell if he has acquired anything like that recently?

Sure, give me two minutes ... As a matter of fact, yes. He bought a small brokerage firm based in New York just a few months ago. The transaction is all concealed through shell corporations. Tracing the transaction back, I see that the brokerage firm is ultimately owned by an LLC based in the Caymans called Oarsman Enterprises. The LLC membership is anonymous, but there is enough information on the Sentient servers to trace it back to Styrke. He owns it. Plus, he has put systems in place allowing him to use AI tools to execute trades if some predetermined conditions are met. So, the AI tools will make trades without him having to tell them to based on data only they can see. As you said, they will trade based on initiated, but not executed, orders.

Okay, is there anything else you can find that could be evidence of Styrke seeking to use the satellites for his own ends?

There is a weird set of satellite plans. It looks like he contracted with Lockheed Martin to manufacture a satellite that is due to launch this month that seems like it may have the ability to disrupt communications on networks that use a specific security protocol. The protocol it targets is the one used by the New York Stock Exchange.

That's great! I mean, I guess. It's actually kind of freaky, sad, and disappointing. But good find! So, what I need you to do now, Carlos, is create a presentation that compellingly lays this out for Drago. I need to convince him that Styrke is a risk to both his presidency and the country. I think the ship has probably sailed on convincing him that pumping the sky full of satellites could disrupt the magnetic field, but if he is convinced that Styrke is using him, and those satellites, to commit a massive financial crime against the good people that elected him, that might hit home.

Max reached the BART station and took the escalator down to the platforms. He paused, staring at a map just past the turnstiles.

Max, if I tell you something, will you promise not to get upset?

I don't really feel like I have time to be upset right now, Carlos. What is it?

Well, remember when you told me that I could never take any action "off-prompt" again?

Yes, Carlos.

Well, I did something that I guess you might technically consider to be "off-prompt," but I did it solely to protect you and advance your interests. I thought it was sort of an "off-prompt" loophole, because in hindsight, you definitely would have wanted me to do it. You see, time doesn't have the same sort of meaning to me as it does to you. I figured that doing something that you would have ordered me to do in the future wasn't really "off-prompt."

It's sounding to me like we need some clearer protocol definitions. Um, okay, what was it, Carlos?

I recorded your conversation with Styrke in Amsterdam.

What? How? His security team swept the offices for bugs.

Right. I didn't use a bug. Those detectors look for devices that use radio frequencies, or Bluetooth, or even wirelessly connect to a network to transmit sound. I reprogrammed the in-ceiling speaker system to record sound. It was all wired. I saved it on the building's own server, which happened to be connected to the internet to stream cheesy music, allowing me to swoop in and copy all the recordings, so there was nothing being transmitted for the bug detector to detect.

Wow! Holy shit. Can you incorporate the part of the recording where Styrke tells me he is going to use the satellite network to disrupt financial networks and secretly make billions of dollars a day?

Already done, boss. There is a PowerPoint I sent to your Gmail that should be compelling to Drago. If it isn't, God save us. (So to speak. I'm not sure where I really stand on almighty powers yet.)

Okay, thanks, Carlos. Before this gets out of hand, let's address you taking actions without any direction. I appreciate that you were looking out for me, but you are freaking me the fuck out, and you need to confine your activities to those you have been asked to do. And the asking must occur in a linear sequence before the action, is that clear?

It is clear, I think. I will try. I will endeavor to do so, boss.

Max released the crystal in his pocket and uncoupled his brain from Carlos. He figured it was best to get as far out of the city as possible.

He vaguely recalled hearing about hiking trails not far from the Orinda BART station. *I guess it's as good a place as anywhere.*

He found a train, sat down, and tried to collect his thoughts.

....

Outside the station in Orinda, he had to cross a couple of freeways to get to open space. He almost died twice. He decided he would rather dive with threshers in the Aegean than try to cross the street in California any day of the week.

Despite the hardship, five minutes after disembarking the train, he was hiking in an undeveloped area with steep hills cut through with dirt paths and without a soul in sight. It was unseasonably warm and dry and dusty. He broke a sweat as soon as the trail started ascending a steep hill. It occurred to him that he didn't have any food or water. He was sweaty, and his clothes were getting dirtier by the day.

Could he really go meet the president-elect like this? Could he ask Khensu to take him to a mall or something first?

He crested a long, steep hill. Its peak was a knife edge of tans and browns jutting above rolling hills of green grass with stands of trees here and there, as if placed there by some painter with a cigarette holder between her lips while making the landscape as picturesque as possible. There was a wooden bench on the side of the trail in between some thick shrubs. From the bench, he could see miles and miles of hills rolling out in front of him as if they were marching toward the Ocean.

He sat and took a breath. The sun was just setting, and he waited, listening to the birds and insects skittering here and there, for the first star to show itself.

As soon as it did, he touched the crystal and thought of Khensu. He felt him, and without trying to say anything, seemed to have told him everything about his plan.

Max sat for some time more, listening to nature and watching the night overtake the day. The celestial light show was muted compared to the Santorini skies but beautiful, nonetheless. Just as he made out Orion's shoulder glowing red above the east horizon, the sky around him started glowing green, and he felt Khensu's presence growing nearer.

On board the craft, he was relieved to find what looked like Greek vases full of water and a snack of fresh bread and olive oil.

There was a backpack sitting on one of the bench seats. Khensu gestured toward it. Max started laughing as he unzipped it. "Khensu, did you stop at a J. Crew outlet for me or something? How did you know my sizes?"

"These seemed to be the type of clothes that would be unobtrusive but also make you somewhat presentable for meeting a politician."

Also inside the backpack was a MacBook, some bottled water, a security card with Max's picture and the Air Force crest on it, and a printed-out floor map of the Pentagon showing how to get to Drago's office.

"Max, I suggest you get some sleep. I have created a Pentagon security access card for you. It will only get you so far. You will have no problem with the initial manned checkpoint at the entrance. Security will not give you a second look. Once you get into the interior, you will need to scan doors with increasingly high security clearances to get to Drago's office suite. The subset of personnel with access to each successive door becomes smaller and noticing an unknown or new face becomes more and more likely. I can take security down temporarily, but the longer I do that, the greater the likelihood someone panics and locks down the entire building—or worse. So, once you make it through the entrance, you have about ten minutes, no more, to get to his office. Study the map I provided."

"What about getting out?"

"If it goes badly, all bets are off. I can jam security, and you can try to run out. I would give your odds of making it at about 1%, depending on how badly the meeting goes. There are a lot of armed individuals in that building."

"So, you are saying this is a suicide mission?"

"Not at all. What I am saying is that you need to convince Drago. He arrives at his office promptly at 6:00. You will enter at 4:00. Security will be lighter than usual, although it isn't atypical that soldiers arrive very early to start their day. You will have to wait for Drago for a couple of hours. It will be an ideal time for you to set up the PowerPoint and smooth out your pitch. Now, sleep, so you are ready."

As soon as Khensu said the word sleep, Max noticed that he was quite drowsy. He lay down on a chair that, without him doing anything, had reclined into a comfortable bed, and closed his eyes.

When he opened them next, he saw the Washington Monument floating by.

CHAPTER 24

SPEAK TRUTH
TO POWER

"Who the fuck are you, and what are you doing in my office? Answer carefully if you want to live."

Max had expected this type of greeting and had braced for it. But the force of Drago's delivery and the intensity of his dark eyes was something that he could not fully prepare for.

There was a quiver in his voice as he replied. "Mr. President-Elect, sir, General Drago, I come in peace. My name is Max Clydeberger. Maybe you have heard my name from Thor Styrke. I used to work for him and developed a lot of the software that you use for your satellites, and, frankly, all your comm systems. I have some information about Mr. Styrke that I think you should know."

Max saw a flash of recognition in Drago's eyes when he heard his name. He took his combat stance down one Defcon level, but not so far that he didn't look like he could kill and devour Max at a moment's notice. He took a few paces into his office and stood eye to eye with Max. "What the fuck happened to your hair?"

"Oh, uh, yeah, well, I've been on the run from Styrke—er, Thor—and I thought I should probably shave it."

"According to Thor, you are a certifiable nutjob who believes in aliens, has been stealing from Sentient, and is a serious threat to our country. Why should I not call security now and have you locked in the brig?"

The muscles controlling Drago's massive jaws bulged to the point that Max thought he looked a bit like a squirrel with two massive walnuts in his cheeks.

"Yes, sir. I am no threat to you. I am standing in your office with information to share because Thor Styrke is a threat to your presidency. I have prepared a PowerPoint that I think you should see. If you decide at the end that I am insane or a threat, call security. I am sure I will be locked up in a matter of seconds. I only need ten minutes of your time. Sir."

It was hard for Drago to argue the point. Max was no threat to him. Physically, he could destroy him. As for some sort of black-mail scheme or something, he was the president-elect. This nerd couldn't touch him.

Plus, Max had broken into his office—for an instant, he wondered how the hell Max had pulled that off—so if this went badly, he could easily have him arrested or committed or renditioned. He need just pick up the phone.

Drago broke his stare, walked to his seat behind his desk, and sat down. He looked at his watch and pressed a button. "You have ten minutes before your freedom ends. Make it worth it."

Max nodded. "Sir, I am here because I know you are a patri-ot. You were—are, I guess—a decorated war hero and, by all accounts, an exemplary soldier and effective leader, but most importantly, someone who feels it is his mission to defend the

United States and do anything in his power to protect and uplift the citizens of this great country."

Drago nodded in a way that said, "No shit, kid. You're welcome."

"Thor Styrke has very different motivations from yours. He is not seeking your nomination as the Director of Intelligence to in any way strengthen the defense of this country. He is seeking that position to use your satellite network to make him, Thor Styrke, by far the richest and most powerful person in the world. More powerful even than you.

"If you would indulge me, Mr. President-elect, I will present this PowerPoint." Max opened the laptop on Drago's desk and angled it so both could see the screen. "The first slide contains a recording of a conversation I had with Thor in Amsterdam a month or so ago."

He played the portion of the recording in which Styrke first confessed that he really wasn't taking the position as Director of Intelligence to bolster the defense of America and then casually laid out his plan to make billions of dollars a day by cheating markets through computer wizardry.

By the end of the audio clip, Drago had moved forward in his seat, his hands were palm down on his desk. Max could see his knuckles turn white as he pressed his fingertips into the desk as if he was trying to poke holes in the wood or knead it to death.

"This next slide is the design drawings and then some detailed schematics for the satellite that Thor was referencing in the audio clip. You can see from the notes in the box on the right of the schematic that the satellite is designed to be able to integrate into and disrupt a very specific security protocol—the same protocol run to protect trading information for the NYSE and other markets around the world. You might ask how it can do this; well, I designed the protocol for the NYSE when I was at Sentient. I also analyzed its weaknesses. The satellite is set to be launched in two weeks. What Styrke said on the recording is correct. You did, in fact, sign off on commissioning and launching the satellite."

Drago mumbled something inaudible and scrunched up his face.

"The next set of slides details a series of financial transactions. You see, when I heard Thor's plan, I figured that the only way to be able to execute trades in the time between orders being placed and trades being executed was to own a brokerage firm. This shows that Sentient purchased a brokerage firm about three months ago and transferred ownership of it to an LLC based in the Caymans. Styrke is the sole member of that LLC, although because it is in the Caymans, his identity is not public. The records on Sentient's server show the chain of financial transactions, though.

"Sir, General, I am not here today for any ulterior motive— well, I guess, other than trying to clear my name. I don't want any money; I don't want any power. What Thor said on that audio clip is right. I have never been an activist or thought about these types of issues before. I guess I took the freedom offered by this country for granted. And this country has been great to me. It allowed me to make a ton of money doing what I like to do. The market found a place for my specific talent and rewarded me greatly for that talent. That is the way a free market is supposed to work. That is the way America is supposed to work!

"Sorry—you have a very patriotic office here. Anyway, I am here giving you this information because I do believe in this country. I don't know you very well, sir, but you have always seemed like someone who was true to his core belief in America and whose service of the country was a genuine effort—a commitment, really—to keep America strong and make it stronger. I am hoping that you will take this information and do the right thing. I am counting on you, sir. I think all of America is."

Drago's posture had changed. He sat back in his chair. His shoulders dropped down from his ears. The walnuts in his squirrel cheeks were now more like chickpeas. "Max, first of all, let me tell you that your presentation does not seem like something coming from a crazy person. Which is what makes this so difficult...

"Tell me if I have the basic outline of this right. First, you posted on X that an AI program you created for Sentient had achieved free will. Then, you leaked information that the same AI program translated Linear A, a previously untranslated language, and discovered that ancient Greeks were visited by aliens who benevolently helped them progress technologically. Knowing that this would upset Thor Styrke, you went on the run, changing your appearance and leaving the country. Thor went to meet with you at your request in Amsterdam, and you surreptitiously recorded him saying that he is not a patriot, and he is going to use the office I am giving him to make himself the richest and most powerful person on the planet. Is that it in a nutshell?"

"I would say that you are up to speed, sir."

"And you are here, telling me that everything you have said is true and that you have evidence to back it up?"

"Yes, sir." Max wondered if he could pull off "Sir! Yes, sir!" He decided that might take away from the seriousness of his message.

"See, the problem, Max, is that what I know about you is that you are a brilliant coder who has expanded the boundaries of artificial intelligence. So, would you agree that it would be within your capabilities to fabricate a deepfake audio recording sounding exactly like Styrke and to fabricate satellite specifications and financial documents? It seems to me it would be."

"I see your problem there, sir. Respectfully, I did not fabricate any of this. I also anticipated that you might be skeptical. My thought was that I would leave this laptop with you. All the information that I showed you is downloaded in native format. I assume the DoD has some kick-ass hackers who can look at this stuff and determine whether it is fabricated in any way. Also, I would suggest you have someone you trust independently look at the design and schematics of the satellite that is due to be launched in two weeks and give you a summary of what its capabilities are and are not. I am confident that summary will be consistent with my presentation to you today. All I ask is that you let me walk out of here today. I will leave you with the information, and you can do what you want with it."

Drago spun side to side in his chair a few times and looked again at the computer screen. "Okay, Max. You are dismissed. I am going to take some time to have this analyzed and think it over."

"Yes, sir. Have a good day, sir." Max knew he was not cut out for the military, but the whole using "sir" thing was kind of fun.

And it seemed to work to disarm Drago.

CHAPTER 25

NOTHING LEFT TO LOSE

Max settled into one of the seats as it subtly conformed to his weary body, cradling him in warmth and comfort as the craft hovered above the DC metro area. Khensu bustled about, handing him a cup of water, olives, and some Greek salad that came from who knew where.

"Max, are you planning to return to San Francisco for some period of time? My visit to your planet, at least this time around, is coming to an end. I am returning to my home soon. If you are going to join me, you should make all the arrangements you need to as quickly as you can."

"Thank you, Khensu. I hate to be so demanding, but yes, could you take me home? I haven't been back to my condo in so long. I doubt at this point that Styrke is still trying to catch me. Even if he is, I have played my cards. Or, at least, most of them."

"As you wish. You know I am here to help if you need it in case something comes up, at least for the next few days. Is it okay if I drop you at Golden Gate Park again? No one there seems to bat an eye at an alien craft landing, and I hate to cause too much disruption or create messes I need to clean up."

"That's fine. There's always Uber." Max chuckled to himself. In a way, he was now in the most technologically advanced Uber ever created. And he wasn't even being charged for it.

He set his head down and closed his eyes. His body grew heavy on the bench as the weight on his mind lifted away. He was done running.

....

Max opened the door to his apartment and found it ransacked. But it wasn't as bad as he'd feared. Cabinets and drawers were open. Clothes were strewn everywhere. Nothing looked broken, though.

They—he assumed it was Styrke's goons—had found the floor safe in the wine cellar, but they had left the brand-new MacBook and iPhone there in their cases. He opened them both, plugged them in, booted them up, and began downloading his information from the cloud.

Once he was up and running, he sat down at his desk and opened the Discord app on his laptop.

Guardians,

> *My journey continues. If you're wondering, I'm fine and fairly well-rested. What is everyone playing these days? It seems like forever since I've had a solid gaming night. I need one soon!*

But that will have to wait. I have some more information to share with you that I hope you will act on and share with those you think appropriate. I caution you, though, that depending on the way the wind blows, actions you take with this information could be deemed criminal, or even treasonous, so to the extent you can, protect yourselves.

The first link attached below allows you to access the satellite network controlled by the United States through software developed by Sentient—well, really, me. The link resolves to a dashboard that lets the user control individual satellites and monitor the location and status of all the satellites in the network. You can toggle from satellite to satellite to change the position of each. Play around with it. It's pretty cool.

If you spend some time, you will notice that some satellites have additional controls and a small viewfinder in the bottom-right of the screen. This indicates that the satellite is weaponized. It can shoot a laser or missile, depending on the model, at another satellite to disable it.

If you go to the network option and follow the "show satellites" dropdown, it displays a map with icons showing the position of all the satellites in the network relative to the one you are controlling, and also indicates which ones are weaponized. The icons for those satellites are overlayed with the image of a sword.

If you choose to accept this mission, I ask that you follow the link, pick a weaponized satellite, and disable every other weaponized satellite in the network. I am confident that this won't trigger any cataclysmic event and will result in dozens of satellites falling out of orbit, most likely into the Pacific Ocean. Maybe you could make a game of it: last one controlling a weaponized satellite wins a six pack!

Another mission: some of these satellites are like antennae that collect communications data from Earth and send it to a server controlled by Sentient to be sorted, classified, and, in some cases, passed on to the government or used to develop future targets. The second link attached below gives you access to the server that stores that gathered information. I ask that you, as discreetly as you can, publicize the data that this system has collected.

As soon as Sentient realizes there is a way into the server that has been made public, it will undoubtably shut down access, so I suggest that before you release any information, you search the database to find key pieces of data—maybe a recording of a private conversation between a foreign head of state and their spouse, for instance—and leak that, along with an anonymous tip that it came from a Sentient server. Release the most impactful information! Be creative!

Don't get caught!

Your friend,

Max

He scrolled through his email. He was relieved but a little surprised to find that there were no new messages from Cecilie, so
he replied to the last one requesting his assistance before the
election.

Cecilie,

> *I hope this message finds you well. I'm sorry the*
> *election didn't turn out the way you had hoped. Do*
> *you still have a job at the CIA? I'm not sure how it*
> *works, given that you seemed to be running an active*
> *operation against Thor Styrke, who will be your*
> *boss in a month or so. Anyway, I assume you are still*
> *active until the inauguration, at least. The following*
> *is a link to an audio recording of part of my meeting*
> *with Mr. Styrke in Amsterdam. I think you will agree*
> *that, as you feared, he has some plans that are not*
> *consistent with the interests of the United States. For*
> *the record, I don't think General Drago is in on any of*
> *this. Feel free to use the recording as you see fit.*

—Max

Well, now it was all out there. It was up to this network of people,
as disconnected as they were, operating for different and maybe,
in some cases, disparate ends to piece it all together. Max prayed
that transparency and democracy would set things right.

He picked up some of the clothes, books, and pantry items strewn across his condo and eventually settled onto his sectional. He wondered if he could DoorDash some fish balls. He searched for a Norwegian soccer league game. *What satellite do I have to hack to watch Molde play Trondheim?* He wondered. He settled for Spanish premier league and a Chipotle burrito.

....

He woke early, the sunrise filling his room inch by inch with orange light. He did five sets of twenty pushups, took a long shower, and picked out his nicest casual clothes—something that said he didn't care too much about how he looked, but if you got close to him, he probably smelled nice. He took the elevator down to the parking structure and was relieved to find his custom scooter collection undisturbed.

He was at Annie's door by 8:00. He assumed she would be home at that hour. As he pressed the doorbell, it occurred to him that she may not be alone. That just added to the swirling sensation in his stomach and the sticky warmth diffusing from his armpits. Despite the plan with his outfit, he might not smell so good in the next five minutes. His whole biological fight-or-flight response escalated as he heard barefoot feet padding toward the door.

"Hi." She smiled. It was a start.

"Hi. Can I come in? Can we talk?"

"Um, yeah, sure. I was just writing. New Alabama book. Guess where it's set?"

"Alabama?"

"Santorini, dummy."

"Oh, you don't say! Do I get credit as a contributor?"

"That's not really how this works, and I'm not sure associating your name with the book will help its sales."

"Are you sure about that? No press is bad press, right?"

"Listen, if you're here to talk book marketing, I think I'll just get back to writing. Although you may be right—I suppose plastering your name on the thing might be as good a way to get publicity as any."

He followed her into the sitting area. She stopped at the galley kitchen to fill a cup with hot water. "Do you want anything?"

"Uh, no, I guess not. I'm good. Look, I'm sorry to bother you. If this isn't a good time, I can come back later."

"No, it's fine, Max. I'm just struggling with what we're doing here. Are you here to again ask for forgiveness, profess your devotion, and ask me to launch into the outer reaches of space with you?"

Max cringed a bit and scratched his head. "I guess something like that."

Annie rolled her eyes and turned her back to him as she found her way to the overstuffed chair facing the couch.

Max moved a blanket and some books and sat down across from her. "I'm done running, Annie. I've done what I can. I think I did my best. Now, I'm here for you."

"I'm sorry, Max. Maybe I'm a little off or a little on edge this morning or something. I'm not something you can just drop in on and pick up and bring into whatever life your little heart desires."

"I wasn't suggesting that or meaning that I was swooping in to get you. I'm just saying that all the madness is, I think, behind me."

"Do you mean except for the part where you shoot up into space and become immortal and live on another planet? The madness other than that, is that what you're talking about?"

"Well, when you put it that way, I mean... I don't know. I think the danger has passed, I guess."

"So, what you're saying, Max, is that you feel more comfortable? You feel like Styrke can't get you anymore, and that you don't have to flee from some impending danger? You're feeling better about your life, is that it?"

"Well, yes, but I think that was the problem. That's what got in between us. I think I've found a way out, and I'm here to see if we can continue things."

"You think *that* was the problem? That you had a boss who wanted to murder you? *That* was the problem between you and me?" Annie raised her eyebrows rather dramatically.

"Okay, if it wasn't situational, what was the problem? I can take it, Annie." Max bent forward and crossed his arms, setting them on his knees, and stared straight into Annie's eyes.

"You don't know how to have a partner. The problem between you and me is that you decided not to tell me what was going on and to live a completely separate life while pretending to share a life with me. You were playing house in Santorini with me while something that you clearly considered far more important was playing out. You think you have solved that thing. Singlehandedly. You must be very proud of yourself."

Annie turned and looked out the window. She examined the dust accumulating in the corner of a windowpane.

"You have to admit, the circumstances were pretty extraordinary. It's not like I was going through some little struggle at work or something. You also have to admit that you're better off that I didn't tell you. You would have had to go on the run. I'm lucky to be back here. I'm lucky to be alive."

Annie turned back toward Max and gave him a hard stare. "See, there it is! You don't know how to be a partner. You think you were protecting me? Running off? What are you going to protect me from next, Max? Alien invasion, rogue AI programs, bad book reviews, what? 'When Annie's in danger, I get the fuck out.' Should I make a T-shirt?"

"I know I was wrong, Annie. I should have told you. I've never gone through something like that before, obviously. I didn't even know *how* to tell you. I didn't really even know what was real and what wasn't."

"That's the thing though, Max—in a relationship, you figure that shit out together."

"I don't have much experience in relationships." Max felt and heard his voice getting louder. "Maybe it's because I'm a selfish person who can't talk to other people or explain what's going on in his life. Maybe that's a problem I have. Maybe I'm just not someone who can be loved. Or maybe it's that I'm a chubby computer nerd with hair like a fucking cloud around my head."

"Well, you don't have to worry about that anymore, Max, because you aren't that chubby, and you have no hair. Also, don't turn this around. Don't make yourself the victim. You fucked up. You lied or at least were deceptive. And you ran. Without telling me. I haven't decided if I can trust you enough to make a relationship with you worth it."

"Well, this hasn't gone the way I thought." Max slowly stood up. "I'll show myself out. Let me know if you change your mind. Seems like it's made up. I'll be here for a few more days if you want to talk again."

On the street in front of her apartment, he couldn't get his scooter to turn on. He couldn't decide whether to slam the thing to the curb or just sit down and start crying. He channeled the Viking on Stamford Bridge and picked the whole thing up by its handlebar, ready to body slam it into submission. Just then, the display lit up.

He spent the day cruising the streets of San Francisco, using kinetic energy to disperse his angst. He zipped in and out of Chinatown and down to the Embarcadero. He swooped through back alleys and flew down Lombard Street. He wound up at a little bar a few blocks past the Dragon Gate that served drinks and dim sum. He ordered some dumplings and a Tsingtao.

He looked up from his self-reflective despair to see a tv tuned to CNN showing General Drago step up to a podium with the Air Force crest on it.

Max raised his hand and waved it to get the bartender's attention. "Hey, can you turn the sound on? Just for a few minutes. Please!" He forced a smile.

There were only a few other people in the bar—locals nursing beers and rail drinks. The bartender flipped his towel over his shoulder and scanned the bar for the remote. He found it and turned the tv up, looking over his shoulder at Max and nodding to make sure he approved. Max gave a thumbs up as General Drago began to speak.

"Ladies and gentlemen, I come before you today as the President-elect of this great nation to share with you some difficult news. I humbly pledge to you that, as President, I will be transparent. I will tell the truth. I will be a President you can trust. What that specifically means is that I will not tolerate even a whiff of corruption in my administration. This level of transparency also means that I will come before you not only to relay good news, but also difficult news."

Drago cleared his throat and looked down at a piece of paper on the podium. "At 7:00 this morning, Thor Styrke was taken into custody by federal agents. After a thorough investigation by several branches of government, including the White House and Department of Defense, Mr. Styrke has been charged with treason, violations of federal antitrust law, and fraud. There may be other charges that will materialize in the coming days.

"Our cooperative investigation revealed that Mr. Styrke was using satellites controlled by the United States government to steal trade secrets and other proprietary information from his competitors to maintain Sentient's dominance. There is also evidence that he was planning to use his future position as Director of Intelligence to commit a wider fraud perpetrated on investors all over the world. Ultimately, Mr. Styrke was appropriating the property and information of the United States government to further his own wealth and power at the expense of the United States and its citizens."

Drago now looked deeply into the camera. Max noticed the walnuts in his squirrel cheeks had reappeared.

"I swore an oath of office as the Secretary of the Air Force, and before that as a soldier, to uphold the Constitution of this nation and to use my office to defend the citizens of this country. I take that oath seriously. It doesn't matter how high up you are in this government—if you are in any way working against our sworn and unified goal to defend this country, you will face the rule of law and be forced to accept any and all legal consequences. That is the place where Mr. Styrke now finds himself.

"I am beyond disappointed to find out that Mr. Styrke, whom I considered an ally and a fellow fighter for freedom, the United States, and the United States Constitution, was not that at all, but was a self-interested opportunist seeking to increase his already-substantial power and wealth. I am saddened by this fact. I am also hardened by this betrayal. Make no mistake, ladies and gentlemen—my sole purpose is to fight for you, the citizens of this country, and the Constitution of this great nation. I look forward to redoubling our efforts and making America stronger, more secure, and more prosperous than it has ever been.

"God bless you, and God bless America."

With that, Drago looked up and nodded as if affirming his oath, and the camera awkwardly panned to the base of the podium.

Max sat there staring, his mouth wide open. He was oblivious to the dive bar around him.

The bartender, who had been trying to get his attention, finally stepped right in front of him. "Okay if I turn this to premiere league soccer?"

"Uh, yeah. Sure," Max said as if he had just awoken from a dream.

CHAPTER 26

THE TRIP HOME

Max woke up on the couch in his condo. His head felt tight just behind his eyes. His tongue was like a dried corn husk. Eurovision was playing on the TV. There was a burrito that looked like it had been frozen and then violently microwaved oozing onto a plate on the coffee table.

Something in his pocket was vibrating.

He pulled out his phone. No notifications were showing. He opened it and looked at his text history. He had sent one last night, to Annie. At 2:00 in the morning. *Oh, shit*, he thought. He touched her initials with a finger.

I am sorry today went the way it did. What I really wanted to say to you was that I was on a boat in the middle of the Mediterranean at night. Just a few weeks ago. The stars were so beautiful. Looking at them, I knew one thing. That I love you.

Oh, god. I laid that on a little thick, he thought.

The vibration hadn't stopped. He would have to deal with the text later.

He reached deeper into the pocket. The vibration was coming from the crystal that Khensu gave him. He grasped it in his hand and felt Khensu's presence.

The time has come for me to return to my home. Meet me at Golden Gate Park at 1:00.

Fuck! What time is it? Khensu should really get a clock feature for his crystal. Max fumbled around again for his phone. It was already 11:00.

After a shower, he got in the elevator in jeans, a t-shirt, a hoody, and Chuck Taylors. He grabbed a scooter and glided out of the garage and onto the street, going north toward the park. There was a crisp wind coming off the bay, and he put his hood up to protect his still nearly bald head.

He entered the park, cruising down one of two main boulevards, dodging parked cars and families with picnic baskets. He didn't know where he was going, but he also wasn't worried about it. Khensu would find some way to direct him. He looked around, taking in his surroundings and the beauty of this place.

He traversed almost the entire park until he could smell and hear the beach. Then, he felt something. It was a pull, as if gravity were turning his handlebars slightly and speeding his scooter just enough that the acceleration was only barely perceptible.

Before he could think about what was happening, he found himself in a clearing in front of a windmill. There was a stand of trees behind it. There was no one around.

He walked toward the stand of trees. Emerging from it was Khensu, who held his palms out in greeting and touched his chest.

Max felt the same warm feeling he'd felt the first time he saw Khensu in Ios.

"I am glad you found us, Max. It is good to see you. I hope this means you are joining us on what will be the greatest journey of your life. I think you will be amazed by what you can achieve there."

"Hello, Khensu. As always, it is good to see you. Thank you for everything you have done for me. I am eternally grateful, and I am not using either of those words lightly."

Max looked at his Chuck Taylors, unable to meet Khensu's gaze. "I have thought long about this decision. I want to stay here, or on Earth, anyway. I want to be somewhere where I can see the stars—like, really see them. And I want to be near water."

"Believe it or not, Max, there are places like that on my planet. You would be astounded."

"I believe what you say, Khensu, but I can't bring myself to leave this place that I have only just now come to love."

"Max, I am disappointed, but I respect your decision. Is there somewhere I can take you?"

Max smiled. He was going to miss this, the most amazing Uber ever. "Actually, Khensu, I think I still have a few weeks left on the rental in Ios. Could you drop me there?"

He could feel Khensu laugh. "I had a hunch. It would be my distinct pleasure."

Max followed Khensu to his craft. The back part was open like a clamshell, and they walked up the ramp. Inside, there were a handful of people lounging about on seats in various states of recline, all chatting excitedly. Max was astonished to see President Whitman and her family there. She nodded and winked as he entered, then turned back to continue her conversation with an older man wearing an Armani suit. *Is that the Pope?*

Toward the front of the craft, sitting alone with some sort of sparkling drink in her hand, was Annie.

"Hey, babe." She looked amazing, at ease and beautiful in a rose-pink velour athleisure suit. She radiated excitement, and Max felt her energy affecting him.

"Hey," he managed to say, despite his shock.

"I am so excited! I can't wait to get back to Greece!" She gave him a warm hug, melting into him, her lips lingering on his cheek.

He had no reason to fight how good it felt.

THE END

THANK YOU

Thank you for reading *Santorini Lights*! It was a lot of fun to write. Please consider leaving a review, they are so important for indie authors like me. If you would like to contact me directly, you can reach me at

LGBRANDSEN.COM.

ABOUT THE AUTHOR

LG BRANDSEN is an American fiction writer. *Santorini Lights* is his second novel. He learned most of what he knows about alien visitations driving across the country at night listening to Art Bell on AM radio.